For Dee, who gives me time, space and an infinity of love.

THE MAGUS CONSPIRACY

Book One
of the
Tír
Saga

MICHAEL J SYNNOTT

CONTENTS

	Acknowledgments	i
1	The Journey Begins	1
2	The Boojum	12
3	Niamh	16
4	The Vanishing	21
5	The Old Lighthouse	27
6	Almha	46
7	The Cube	63
8	Kiva	82
9	The Escape Plan	87
10	The Rescue	92
11	Consequences	110
12	Mira	119
13	Keher Kuhn-Ridh	124
14	The Rowing Wheel	137
15	The Plan	142
16	Jere	157
17	The Incident at Lime Kiln Bay	190
18	Forgill & Ferrisfort	193
19	The Hunter	223
20	The Dream	233

21	The Signs	238
22	Ashtown Lane	244
23	The Crystal Grotto	248
24	Dewenisch	261
25	Abydos	276
26	The Sidh	296
27	The Other Side	304
	About The Author	308

ACKNOWLEDGMENTS

This book would not have been possible without the support and help of my wife and best friend, Dee McMahon. Dee's name should really be on the cover given her insights into the personalities of the core characters and her advice with storylines.

My dear friends Sean Solon, Michele Montijo, Karen Murphy, Michael Kenny, Annette Hiney, Gavan Cleary, Stefan Gathmann and Don Scott read the manuscript and offered advice and encouragement.

Love, respect and a lifetime of gratitude to my parents Thomas and Breda Synnott for giving me a boarding school education they could ill-afford, a love of history, literature and the arts, and for moving the family to Wicklow in the early 1970s, surrounding us with castles, towers, ruins, lighthouses, headlands, caves and all the things that fire a child's imagination.

CHAPTER ONE

THE JOURNEY BEGINS

Wicklow, Ireland.

An insert fell from the pages of Mark's comic book and landed on the bedroom floor. *Advertising*, he thought as he picked it up but something stayed his hand over the trash bin. It was a one-page story rendered in typical comic-book frames without speech bubbles or lettering except the title in the first frame: *The Journey Begins*.

The artist's style was old fashioned; hand-illustrated and monochrome. It reminded Mark of late-70s sci-fi comics, a passion he had inherited from his dad. His stomach lurched as he looked at the stacks of vintage 2000AD comics in the corner, the name *Fintan McHewell* scrawled in faded ballpoint on the masthead of each by a long-retired newsagent.

Tears stung the corners of Mark's eyes.

Don't you dare cry again, he told himself.

Mark was starting to cope with his father's disappearance but frightened inner Mark, who Mark thought of as *Spikey* - his mum's baby name for him

- manifested occasionally like a frightened poltergeist and knocked away pieces of the emotional scaffolding he was building. Teeth gritted, he wiped his eyes and forced his attention back to the page.

The first frame showed a boy sitting in his room reading a comic. In the next frame, in close-up, an insert fell from the comic to the floor. The boy picked it up and read the title: *The Journey Begins.*

Ha! That's clever, thought Mark. *I see what they're doing here. The kid even looks a bit a like me. Wow, his room looks like mine too. What are the chances of that?*

The teenager in the comic was now standing up staring at his page in shock and in the next frame was standing in his bedroom doorway looking at the paneled door opposite.

An unpleasant tingle started in the back of Mark's neck.

The boy in the comic now stood beside the paneled door, looking at a keypad set into the wall beside it.

Now Mark was on his feet staring open-mouthed at the page in his hand. In a flash of recognition, all the images on the page came together in his mind.

He opened his bedroom door. Directly opposite was the paneled door of his father's study, beside it the keypad of an electronic lock. His heart pumping, he looked at the next frame in the comic. It showed a close-up of the keypad with the number 2705 on the display. Mark's skin crawled and his stomach felt queasy. He walked on leaden feet towards the study door. *This can't be happening.*

Mark usually ignored the paneled door. The study had always been off-limits; his father's private sanctuary. Fintan kept it locked and asked that no-one went in there.

Staring at the grandiose door, Mark realized he'd never seen the inside of the study. When his father was around he would never have considered peeking in there but things were different now, or so his mother said.

He looked back at the page. In the next frame, the paneled door was open. The back of the boy's head occupied the lower-left of the frame, and over his right shoulder Mark could see a desk and office chair against the far wall, and a large bookshelf against the left. Could that really be the inside of his dad's study? Mark's curiosity overcame his unease and he typed the code shown in the comic into the keypad.

There was a loud thud from inside the door.

Mark jumped back and cried out in surprise. The electromagnetic lock sprang open and the door swung inward a fraction.

A feeling of unreality started in Mark's feet and rose tingling up his body until it felt like a cocoon. *This is impossible.* His head reeled and for a moment it felt like he was outside himself looking down at the scene. A crawling sense of misgiving tickled the small of his back. Slowly, Mark put his hand to the door and pushed.

The study door swung open and Mark found himself gazing into darkness. The study was built into the hill, beneath the roof garden, and had no windows. He felt for a light switch. A slight turn of the dimmer knob inside the door and the study was revealed in soft light. Mark went in and eased the oak door closed. The lock sprang shut.

Mark gaped. The room was exactly as depicted in the comic. The rest of the house was the epitome of ultramodern design but the study was straight out of Sherlock Holmes. It was the size of a modest living room; plush, with wooden paneling and a red carpet. It smelt cozy and safe, a combination of wood-polish and burned peat. Inside the door to the right was a large antique globe, beside it a chess table of similar vintage on which ornate pieces were poised in an unfinished game. In the middle of the right wall was an enormous fireplace, the mantelpiece level with Mark's eyes. Above the mantel, executed in burnished metal and enamel, was a huge coat-of-arms that Mark did not recognize.

A large mahogany desk stood against the far wall, before it a leather office chair. Against the wall opposite the fireplace was a monstrous Gothic bookcase, the full height and width of the wall, decorated with carved gargoyles and demons. In the low light it was hard to see the individual books but Mark guessed there were thousands. He crossed over to it and walked along it towards the desk, rubbing his hand along the spines of the books. They felt smooth and slightly dusty. When he reached the end of the bookcase he rubbed his hands on his jeans and turned to the desk. The office chair was on smooth castors and moved easily when he pulled it. On the desk were a computer monitor and laser printer, somehow absurd against the period furniture.

The last frame on the comic page showed the boy sitting at the desk and finding a keyboard and mouse in a hidden drawer. Mark searched the front of the desk and sure enough, found a shallow drawer with a wireless keyboard and mouse inside. He lifted them out onto the desktop, closed the drawer and sat down in the office chair. Six months' worth of dust came away from the screen onto his hand, and that too got wiped on his jeans. He booted the PC to the login screen and the screen displayed two names with icons beside them. The first said *Fintan;* beside it an icon of a chess knight, and beneath it, to Mark's amazement, was the name *Marco* with a picture of a sailing ship.

Why did Dad create a user account on the PC for me if I'm not supposed to come in here? Maybe this is part of what he was going to tell me about before he disappeared.

Then a more sinister thought chilled him to the core: What if his father knew he wasn't coming back and had left him a secret message knowing he would eventually find it? Spikey didn't like the idea of this at all and advised shutting down the PC and getting the hell out of there.

"Shut up, Spikey," he said to himself through clenched teeth. "There's no way I'm not checking this out."

He grabbed the mouse and clicked on his name. A dialog box appeared on the screen with the title:

Type your password

The cursor flashed like a taunt.

He searched the comic page but there were no more frames and no clue as to what the password was.

Typical! After months of heartache he had dared to believe his father had reaching out to him, and the disappointment burned like a fever in his throat. Fintan had obviously set up an account for him but hadn't gotten around to telling him the password.

Or had he?

Mark looked at the sailing ship image and an idea started to form: What if his dad had left this as a challenge for him? Fintan loved puzzles. He had taken part in a competition when he was a teenager where you had to decipher the clues in a book and figure out the location of a fabulous piece of hidden jewelry. It was one of Fintan's greatest disappointments: he'd solved the clues only to find the competition had been won years before.

Mark remembered a conversation he'd overheard, his dad's voice saying: "I want Mark to know the wonders of childhood for as long as he can." And his mother's: "You can't relive your life through Mark's."

In that instant Mark knew his father would never have put the user account on the computer had he not intended Mark to figure out the password and use it.

Excitement bubbled in Mark's stomach.

He looked at the flashing cursor then at the sailing ship icon. It was a caravel; like the ones Columbus had. His dad's voice came to him again:

"Life is an adventure, Marco; a voyage into the unknown. Each of us is his own explorer; his own Marco Polo."

A tingle crept up the back of Mark's neck, warming his ears. His hands shook as he typed:

Polo

The login screen disappeared and the hard disk chattered. He was in! He felt like he had won the lottery. The thrill of it raced around his stomach like a dance of butterflies.

A lone icon sat on the computer desktop; a folder named *My Documents*. He opened it. In the folder was a single file entitled *Three Haikus.pdf*.

Three what?

Mark shrugged and double-clicked on the icon. The file opened in Acrobat Reader:

Three Haikus

First letter of line
Implies arrangement of the
Books of all knowledge

Order seven books
Numbered by a formula
Ascending the set

Crack the hidden code
Change the natural sequence
Inspect the top shelf

It made no sense. What was a 'haiku,' anyway? He googled it.

The Haiku is one of the most important modes of Japanese poetry. Traditionally it consists of a pattern of 5, 7 and 5 phonetic units which correspond partially to the syllables of languages such as English …

OK, so they're Japanese poems. Dad loves Japanese art and poetry but why would he write these and hide them in my account on the computer?

As his head spun with the mystery of it all, his stomach grumbled. He looked at his watch. Seven o'clock! His mother would be wondering where he was. Time to go.

He couldn't risk going in and out of the study when his mother was around; best to work on it in his own room. He clicked *Print* and the document slid out onto the top of the laser printer. He grabbed the printout, shut down the PC and crept out of the study. He could hear the TV on downstairs so the coast was clear. He closed the heavy door, hid the piece of paper in his bedroom and went downstairs to the living room.

"You didn't call me for dinner!"

"Well, your bedroom door was closed, and you were so upset earlier I figured you needed some time to yourself. I knew you'd come down when you felt hungry. There's some chicken curry on the stove and some rice ready to go in the microwave; just press 'Start.' Be careful draining the rice; don't burn yourself."

"I won't."

"Bring it through to the living room when it's ready."

"OK."

She patted the sofa and smiled at him.

"You can sit beside me here while you're eating and tell me all about the first day of summer holidays."

Mark finished his dinner then watched TV with his mum for a few hours. He didn't give much away, saying he had played some video games and had read for a bit. As the food settled in his stomach he felt tired. Eventually he dozed off. He woke to find his mum shaking him gently.

"Mark, it's 10.30. Time for bed. I'm sure you don't want me to try and carry you!"

Mark rubbed his eyes then followed his mother into the kitchen to get a glass of water. As they stood at the sink looking at the darkening summer sky over Wicklow Bay, Mark said:

"Mum, will you show me how you do those cryptic crosswords tomorrow?"

Her eyebrows rose.

"Sure. Why the sudden interest?"

Mark shrugged.

"I dunno, I just want to know how they work, I suppose."

"Well, OK; I'll show you but they don't make a lot of sense at first."

You can say that again, thought Mark.

He headed out of the kitchen then stopped.

"Mum?"

"Mm-hmm?"

"Why did he leave?"

"I don't know, son. I really don't."

"It's still so strange without him. I can't get used to it."

Bree stared out the window. "Me either. I keep trying to make sense of it but I can't."

"Do you think he's still alive? I mean, maybe he was kidnapped. You hear about rich people being kidnapped all the time. It can't have been his own choice. If he was planning to leave, he'd never have done it on Christmas day."

"Oh Mark; not this again, please! There has never been a ransom request and the police told us you'd have been a more likely target for kidnappers. None of his bank accounts or credit cards has been used, he disappeared between here and his office in Wicklow, and his car – a very expensive car – has never been found. It adds up to only one thing."

"I can't believe he was carjacked and murdered on Christmas Day in Wicklow. I mean, this isn't LA, mum!"

"Mark, stop this! Stop it NOW! I can't cope!" Bree's voice took on a hysterical edge. "It's my fault. I couldn't make him listen. I mean, who goes to the office on Christmas day? Your bloody workaholic father, that's who! I should have insisted he have dinner first. If I'd put my foot down he'd still be with us but he's not, Mark. He's not waiting in the wings somewhere to make a dramatic reappearance; He's DEAD!"

Mark burst into tears. He felt in his soul it was true but to hear his mother say it like that gave it a stark reality that was shocking. Bree grabbed him and pulled him to her. He pressed his face into her shirt and cried searing salt tears into the cotton. They stayed like that for a long time, the moment a catharsis, months in the making. She held him, tears running down her own cheeks, until he stopped crying with a few shuddering breaths.

She conjured a tissue out of somewhere, as only mothers can, and handed it to him. She dabbed her own eyes with another.

They stood looking at each other for several minutes then Bree asked:

"Are you OK?"

He nodded and hugged her again.

"Goodnight, Mum."

He walked out of the kitchen, paused then turned back.

"Mum?"

"Yes, Son?"

"When you collected my comic from the newsagent's today; did anything strange happen?"

"Huh? What do you mean?"

"Well, was there anyone else there, behind the counter – other than the usual people, I mean."

Bree screwed up her eyes. "No, I don't think so. What are you getting at?"

"Ah, nothing. Goodnight Mum."

"Uh, OK. Goodnight Son."

Mark was halfway to the stairs when Bree's voice stopped him:

"Mark!"

He turned around to see Bree's head peering around the kitchen doorway.

"Mum?"

"I got you an awesome present for your birthday tomorrow."

Mark cocked his head. "Awesome?"

Bree grinned. "Isn't that what you young people say?"

"Yeah, that's what us young people say. I've no idea what you old fossils say but it isn't 'awesome'."

"Fossils! Do you want your present or not?" she said with a mock frown.

He walked back to the kitchen and put his arms around Bree. He hugged her fiercely and said "Whatever it is, I'm sure it's totally awesome. Thanks Mum."

"Yeah, careful you don't snap this old fossil in two!"

"Mum, you're more of a kid than I am, and you know it. Also, you're gorgeous. All the guys in school fancy you, which totally weirds me out but there ya go."

Bree pouted her lips and fluffed her hair up. "Really? Any of these guys good-looking?"

"Mum!"

"I'm joking, Kiddo." She flicked his nose gently. "You're so easy to wind up."

He kissed her and went upstairs.

Back in his room Mark shucked his clothes and got under the duvet. The events of the day orbited his head like stars and made him dizzy. He tried to figure out how the mysterious page got into his comic. He devised many bizarre scenarios and, as he descended into sleep, they got increasingly inventive. One thing for sure, he was going to cycle to the newsagent's the next morning and find out where the mysterious page came from, and whether it was in all current issues of 2000AD, or just his.

Sleep came eventually.

Sometime later his cell chimed, just loud enough to rouse him. Half-awake, he reached for the phone and read the text. It was from his friend Niamh.

It read: **r u awake?**

He texted back: **yes.**

After a moment his cell rang but before he could answer it, it bleeped and died. He lay there wondering where his charger was then remembered it was down in the kitchen. He groaned and debated whether to get the charger or wait until the morning. As he wrestled with his lethargy, tiredness overtook him again and he fell asleep. The phone slipped from his hand and landed on the bedroom floor.

And that seemingly innocuous act of laziness sparked a chain of events that would change their lives forever.

CHAPTER TWO

THE BOOJUM

Big Delta, Alaska, USA.

Sam Renstrom had worked on the Trans-Alaska Pipeline for years but he'd never seen anything like this.

Parked on the Richardson Highway over the Tanana River, he looked across to where the pipeline spanned the river on its narrow suspension bridge. Over the midpoint of the river, a blurry vertical disc, swirling with colors, oily and iridescent, bisected the pipeline. It was several meters in diameter - larger than the bore of the pipe - but had no depth. At least, when Sam looked at it edge-on, that's how it seemed. It reminded him of a film of soapy water in a kid's bubble maker. Whatever it was, it was mighty curious; but curiosity wasn't what had brought Sam here this morning: The weird disc, whatever it was, had stopped the flow of oil.

Sam had woken early to a call from his supervisor. His inspection shift was due to start at 8am but the call came at 6:15. The supervisor's briefing was hurried, and made no sense.

The Trans-Alaska Pipeline pipes oil thirteen-hundred kilometers from Prudhoe Bay on the north coast through twelve pumping stations to Valdez in the south. Alarms had gone off at 6:05 in Pumping Station Nine near Delta Junction, indicating a total loss of pipeline pressure. Within minutes, similar alarms went off at all downstream pumping stations right down to Station Twelve, just outside Valdez. The strange thing was that Station Eight, a hundred kilometers north, was not reporting any problems. If there were a catastrophic breach in the line large enough to cause zero flow at Station Nine, the decrease in backpressure should have set off alarms upstream. This hadn't happened, and no-one could explain it. The calls went out and all the inspectors responsible for that hundred-kilometer section were mobilized - but it was Sam's day.

He drove to the north end of the bridge and down Hansen Road to where the pipe came ashore. He parked as close as he could to the water's edge and stared though the dusty windshield at the curiosity surrounding the pipe. It sent a chill down his spine. His Pop used to tell stories about supernatural creatures that supposedly roamed the Alaskan wastes. 'Boojums' he called them. Sam had never really believed in them but he was revising his skepticism now.

"My very own Boojum," he said to himself. "What'n the hell are you?"

He rubbed his eyes and released a jaw-cracking yawn. He was bleary from the early start but he had a cure in a thermos on the passenger seat: Sam made different strengths of coffee depending on the weather and the scale of his hangover. It was a pleasant summer morning but he'd watched a hockey game and sunk too many brews up in Fairbanks the night before, so today was a High-Octane day. That meant a shot of rum in the Joe, and he savored it as he puzzled over the Boojum.

He sure didn't know what it was but it had to be what was blocking the oil. If he could figure it out and get rid of it, he'd be a hero. Hell, he might even get a raise! He had a good idea how much money was lost when the oil didn't flow, and he figured fixing it must be worth a couple thousand bucks a year extra in his pay check. Besides, this was his section of pipe. He'd maintained and inspected it for years, damn it, and he wasn't going to let some weird doohickey mess with his livelihood.

After two cups of his Calypso Joe, he was feeling a lot better - and a lot braver. Psyched up to take the responsibility – and the credit – for dealing with the Boojum, he reversed his truck under the pipeline bridge tower and stepped out. He clipped his utility belt around his waist and threw down the last of the coffee. With a grunt, he climbed onto the roof of the truck then scaled the tower until he was standing on the pipe. The company expressly forbade this but all the inspectors did it. Actually, Sam wasn't certain whether other inspectors did it or not but he sure did, and he didn't give a good goddamn what anyone else did.

Taking a deep breath, he headed out along the pipe, over the water. His years of walking the pipe illicitly served him well and he balanced easily, using the stay wires for support. After one-hundred and eighty meters, he reached his Boojum.

From three meters, the disc was humming and he felt the hairs on his arms prickling. He pulled a penny from his pocket and threw it into the shimmering face of the disc. It passed clean through and disappeared with a faint crackle, leaving a slight eddy on the disc's surface like ripples on a pond.

Sam's eyebrows rose at this and he sat down to straddle the pipe. He

14

shunted forward then lay prone to examine the pipe where the Boojum intersected it. It looked like the pipe was cut clean through but no oil was escaping. Impossible as it seemed, the oil was pouring into the disc and disappearing. He took off his grubby Alaska Aces cap – another breach of regulations but he hated hard-hats – and crawled forward for a closer look.

Once he got within a meter of the disc, he felt a strong pull on his head and shoulders, like the suck of a vacuum cleaner. He tried to scuttle backwards but it was too late. Whatever force the Boojum was exerting, he was caught in it and it pulled him forward. The cap fell from his hand and hit the water. He tried to grip the pipe with his hands and thighs but to no avail.

"Oh God! No! Help me. Somebody, please help me!"

His screams were cut off as he was sucked into the swirling disc.

The Boojum stayed in place humming contentedly but all that was left of Sam Renstrom was his hockey cap as it spun down the river.

CHAPTER THREE

NIAMH

Niamh was in secondary school when she finally admitted she needed glasses. Her first pair was small and fashionable - the blue frames suited her blue eyes and blonde hair - and they changed her perception of the world completely. The most profound effect was to distance her from other people. Folks who had looked fuzzy and friendly before now looked sharp and predatory; even her dad. Her friends told her not to be stupid but she couldn't help it.

School was worst of all. Kids with glasses always get a hard time but girls seem to get it worst from other girls. At least the taunts stopped during class and Niamh forgot about the persecution by focusing on her lessons. Her improved eyesight made a big difference to her concentration and she found a new interest in Mathematics and Geography.

She also found a new interest in Computing - but it had nothing to do with her concentration. It did, however, have rather a lot to do with Mark McHewell. He'd always been a nice guy but since he had saved her from Veronica McCabe and her cronies in the school corridor, he'd become her white knight. And now that she could see him clearly, Mark didn't look one bit predatory or sharp; she thought he looked gorgeous. He was a bit younger than her but he was tall, with dark hair and brown eyes and a lopsided smile she found irresistible.

When she found out his favorite subject was Computing she quit Home Economics and transferred over to the IT class. That was around Halloween. Soon they became good friends, and whenever students had to pair off for projects, Niamh and Mark were always lab partners. One project they had was to design a computer program to translate between Morse code and the Latin alphabet. They had a lot of fun with that and ended up calling each other Dash-Dash (for 'M') and Dash-Dot (for 'N'.) These eventually got shortened to just 'Dash' and 'Dot'. They became quite adept at Morse code and used to tap messages to each other in class by tapping their pens on the desk or on each other's hands when they were sitting together.

By the time Christmas came around, they were hanging out together. They enjoyed the same TV shows and books – sci-fi mostly – and played the same computer games. Mark - typical boy - still hadn't twigged how Niamh felt about him but as far as she was concerned, things were progressing nicely.

But then everything changed.

When Mark came back to school two weeks late after the Christmas break, everyone had heard about his father. Rumors abounded but no-one really knew what had happened to Fintan McHewell. Niamh tried to reach out to Mark, to be there for him but he was withdrawn, and all the work she had put into getting to know him seemed to have been for naught. Sure, they still talked but the ease with which they had communicated and understood each other had disappeared. She tried to recapture the warmth of their friendship but as the months rolled by she realized, with a sickening sense of loss, that the connection they'd had, the connection she'd wanted to build into something greater was gone.

As the end of year loomed, Mark wasn't always in class any more. Nasty schoolyard whispers about child psychologists and 'nut jobs' did the rounds but Niamh still attended Computing. She had a genuine aptitude for the subject and by summer break she was top of the class.

The last day of school before they broke for summer was bittersweet. As the final bell rang and the school erupted into a riot of noise and excitement, she watched Mark navigate his way through the chaos towards the door. She followed him out into the piercing sunshine and past the gymnasium towards the bike-sheds. She was about to call out to him when a stone flew across the schoolyard and cracked off Mark's head. He staggered and ducked, then fell to his knees. A voice rang out:

"Hey McTool; don't come back next year. Why don't you disappear like your stupid da, you psycho!"

Christopher McCabe; Veronica's twin brother. *That whole family are scumbags*, Niamh thought. She looked back towards Mark. He was back on his feet looking over to where McCabe and his gang stood. He was putting his hand to his head then looking at it, then repeating it as if unable to believe he wasn't bleeding. For a moment Niamh thought Mark would go over to McCabe but he just stood there staring, then turned around, picked up his rucksack and went to fetch his bike.

"Yeah, that's right; run away, Psycho. Your da must've been a nut-job and all to run away from a nice piece of totty like your ma. Maybe I'll go up and keep her company."

Niamh's anger and frustration boiled over. This poor guy - who never bothered anyone - who had such a terrible thing happen to him - who must be aching inside from grief - had the dignity to walk away while these thugs were laughing at him. It was all too much for her. Almost without realizing what she was doing she bent down. The flower beds in the schoolyard had been dug out and replaced with gravel. Amidst the gravel were many larger and sharper stones and Niamh picked up several of these.

"You bastards," she screamed, as she threw stone after stone towards McCabe and his crew. "You filthy, rotten bastards! See how you like it!" Many of the stones missed but enough made contact that McCabe was retreating out of range.

When Niamh ran out of stones and bent down to reload, he made a run towards her. She was quicker. She started another salvo and as McCabe dithered, unsure whether to continue the charge or to retreat, a stone flew through one of the gymnasium's huge windows. Niamh watched in slow-motion horror as the plate glass shattered and the glass cascaded down and smashed on the ground. The noise was horrendous and echoed around the schoolyard. The laughter and chaos evaporated as kids stopped in their tracks and looked over towards the gym. A horrible stark silence fell over the schoolyard. McCabe and his cohorts, with criminal instinct, fled towards the school gates. Niamh stood there with her mouth open and the remaining stones fell from her hands. The whole schoolyard was looking at her. As she wished the ground would open and swallow her, a shape loomed over her and Mr. Johnson, the gym teacher, said:

"Miss Kinnear, come with me."

Mr. Johnson frog marched her towards the gym. They passed by Mark and he opened his mouth to say something to the furious teacher. Niamh shook her head at him, her eyes begging him to stay out of it. Mark closed his mouth. He smiled at her and said:

"Thanks Dot. You didn't have to do that – defend me I mean, not break the window – but thanks anyway. You're a good friend."

Niamh smiled tightly.

"See you over the summer maybe?"

He nodded.

"Sure. Call me."

Her smile widened.

Mr. Johnson interjected. "Come on Miss Kinnear; you can talk to your boyfriend later. We need to call your parents and I'm not looking forward to this any more than you are. Let's get it over and done with."

She was in deep trouble she knew but somehow it didn't seem to matter so much anymore. *Call me.* Those words would get her through any trouble she was going to face in the next few days.

CHAPTER FOUR

THE VANISHING

Fate has a dark sense of humor but she must have been in particularly fickle form when she chose Christmas Day to take Fintan from his family.

Fintan knocked on Mark's door and opened it wide enough to pop his head in.

"Are you going to stay in bed all day, Lazybones?"

"Jesus, Dad; it's only seven o'clock!"

"Oh, well in that case, stay there! I thought you'd be interested in seeing your Christmas present, that's all."

Mark threw his eyes up to heaven and swung his legs out of bed. Fintan grinned. "I thought so. See you downstairs."

Mark shuffled into the living room five minutes later rubbing his eyes.

"He's down in the games room," said Bree.

Mark continued down the stairs to the room beside the garage where the snooker table, dart board, jukebox and various other diversions resided. His jaw fell open.

Standing against the far wall of the games room were three early-80s video arcade cabinets.

"Oh … my … God," said Mark, now wide awake. "Defender, Pac-Man and Battlezone. Where did you even find these?"

"Oh, I got in contact with an old guy who used to run one of the arcades in Wicklow when I was your age. He had them in his shed. Your mother and I got them restored."

Mark grasped the joysticks on the Battlezone cabinet and looked through the periscope. "I've never even seen one in real life. Does it work?"

"Oh, it most certainly does!" said Bree from the door. "He was up most of the night playing it. I'm surprised he didn't wake you."

Fintan shrugged and put on a mock sheepish look. "I just wanted to make sure it was working OK then I got hooked trying to beat my old high score."

Mark rushed over and hugged him. "Ah, thanks Dad. These are amazing!"

"You're welcome, Son. Don't forget to thank your mother too. She did most of the spade work looking for replacement circuit boards on the Internet for that Pac-Man machine."

Mark ran over and grabbed Bree in a bear-hug. "Thanks Mum. I love you."

"You're welcome, Mark. I love you too. I must do given the amount of time I've wasted on that little yellow bastard."

Mark looked shocked. "Who? Dad?"

Bree burst out laughing and back-handed him gently on the chest. "No, you ninny! Pac-Man!"

Mark turned to see Fintan leaning on the snooker table in convulsions of laughter. Mark reddened then snorted with laughter himself.

"Oh Mark," said Fintan, wiping his eyes, "that was priceless. I've been called a few things in my time but never a little yellow bastard."

"Oh God, I'm such an idiot sometimes," said Mark chuckling.

"I've called him worse," said Bree. "You'd want to hear what I called him when he arrived with those three arcade machines covered in cobwebs. Well, anyway Mark, I hope you like them."

"Aw, you guys are the best," said Mark, and the three hugged together in the door of the games room.

"Now," said Bree, "get back upstairs and get some breakfast then you can play Little Yellow Bastard or Big Green Tank to your heart's content."

*

Fintan walked into the games room later that morning and found Mark glued to the Battlezone machine.

"What's your score?"

"Ah, I've just restarted. Those missiles that come screaming down from the mountains keep killing me."

"Yeah, they're tricky. Took me a while to get the hang of dodging them."

"Um-hmm," mumbled Mark as he wrenched at the steering controls. "Ah flippin' flip! I'm dead again! Do you want a go, Dad?"

"Actually, I thought we'd get out of the house for a while."

"Yeah? Where d'you want to go?"

"How about going for a drive?"

"Sure. Whereabouts?"

"Ah, nowhere special. Let's just hit the road and see where it takes us. I'm sure your mother would be just as happy to have the house to herself for a few hours."

"Cool."

"Will we take the SUV or the Porsche?"

Mark grinned. "Oh, the Porsche. Definitely the Porsche."

Fintan headed for the door then paused, a smile playing at the edges of his lips. "'Flipping flip?' Really? Is that what you say when I'm not around?"

"Sure. What else would I say?"

"Yeah, right!" said Fintan. "Go get your jacket and say goodbye to your mother. I'll see you in the flippin' garage."

Fifteen minutes later Fintan and Mark reversed out of the garage, drove down the long avenue and out onto the coast road. They headed south then inland towards south-west Wicklow, turned off the Sat Nav, and tried to get themselves lost; a feat they often attempted but rarely achieved. After an hour they found some back roads they'd never been on, and an hour after that they came to a small town.

They drove through slowly, the low suspension of the Porsche grazing the speed-bumps. The town was almost empty but as they approached a pedestrian crossing opposite a church, a man in a black suit crossed. The Porsche glided to a halt. As the man passed the front of the car, Mark saw a flash of white at his collar: He was a priest. But he was the weirdest-looking priest Mark had ever seen: His head was shaved except for the back where the hair was plaited into a long ponytail, and a large crucifix was tattooed on the side of his neck. A gold earring in the shape of a strange symbol hung from the priest's ear. *He looks more like a Kung Fu master than a priest*, thought Mark. The priest's eyes wandered over the car then onto the people inside.

They took in Mark for a moment then flicked over to Fintan and widened. Mark sensed Fintan stiffen in his seat. The priest's step faltered for a moment then he kept walking. He gave a slight nod to Fintan which he returned almost imperceptibly. They recognized each other, no doubt about it; but Mark had no idea how. His father wasn't religious and it seemed unlikely he'd know a priest in a remote country town.

"Who was that, Dad?"

Fintan looked at him, his brow furrowed.

"I've no idea Marco; just some priest."

"Don't you know him?"

"No. How would I know him?"

"Oh, I just thought you recognized each other."

"No Marco, I've no idea who he is," said Fintan, and drove on; his face gone pale and his lips tight.

*

Later that afternoon Fintan got a phone call which he took in his study. A short while later he walked into the kitchen, cellphone in one hand, coffee cup in the other.

"Listen guys, I know it's bad timing but I have to go out for a few minutes."

"Oh Fintan!" said Bree, "Not just before Christmas dinner! You're always doing this. Can't it wait 'til after we've eaten?"

"Well, not really. I want to enjoy my Christmas dinner with you guys and have a couple of glasses of wine. I can't do that if I have to drive afterwards."

Bree glared, her head shaking slightly. Fintan raised his shoulders and held out his palms.

"Look, I need to go to the office and email some house-plans to a client. He wants to show them to his father-in-law over dinner. I'll be gone half-an-hour, max."

Bree, who knew every nuance of her husband's body-language, noticed his coffee cup hand: the pinkie was tucked up over the next finger; a sign he was nervous – or lying. She stared at him tight lipped and shaking her head then threw her eyes up to heaven. *What's the point of arguing? He's going to go anyway.*

"Go on. But remember you said 'half an hour,' OK?"

"Of course. Half an hour. Love you."

He kissed Bree then turned to Mark and grabbed him in an unusually tight hug.

"Love you too, Marco."

"Wow Dad, you're crushing me."

"Man, the height of you! I don't even have to bend down to give you a hug anymore."

Fintan looked into Mark's eyes and held the gaze for a moment; then a moment longer. Something about the look troubled Mark.

"Dad, where...?"

"Listen Marco, when I get back I've got something to tell you. I was waiting until you were old enough but I think today's the day."

"What is it, Dad?"

"I'll tell you when I get back. Gotta dash. Love you guys. Half an hour."

Then he was gone down the stairs to the garage. Mark went through to the first-floor living room. The sky was darkening over Wicklow Bay and there was rain on the hills. Moments later Fintan's Porsche appeared from the garage and Mark watched the rear lights disappear down the avenue.

And Fintan was gone.

CHAPTER FIVE

THE OLD LIGHTHOUSE

Niamh was grounded. First day of the summer holidays, glorious weather, and she was bloody grounded!

She sat on her bed and looked around her attic bedroom. It was a bright, airy room with dormer windows on the front and skylights at the back. Usually she loved spending time up there but now it was a prison cell. Other than meals and bathroom visits, she was confined to her room. No reprieve, no exceptions; her Dad and her step-mum were quite clear on that. Her summer job started in a week and she'd planned on using the free time to visit the beach, go shopping with her friends and spend some time with Mark. So much for those plans! And her first four weeks' wages would go on replacing the gym window. So much for the new shoes and hairstyle too! It was going to be a long and lonely week with only her cat Mira for company. Mira was very affectionate and quite clingy for a cat but she was, Niamh reflected, a bit short on conversation. She was also remarkably adept at disappearing inside a small three-bedroom house, when one needed her companionship most.

At least I still have my computer privileges, Niamh thought. With access to her computer, she could work on her poetry, write code, surf the Web and use Facebook and Skype. She wondered if Mark was on Facebook. Unlikely; it just wasn't his style but he was almost certainly on Skype. She had no idea what his contact details were though. It pained her how much she and Mark had lost touch since Christmas. Before, she would have known everything about him but he'd changed so much...

Thinking about Mark depressed her. Now that he had invited her back into his life, the thoughts of not being able to see him for a week tortured her. She reached for her phone and found Mark's number. Should she call him? It had been less than twenty-four hours since they'd last spoken; she didn't want to seem too needy. She tapped the phone against her teeth and considered it. Nah; best not. The cell landed back on the bed. Mira, who had been asleep near the pillow, lifted her head and peered at Niamh through sleepy, ice-blue eyes. Niamh smiled and rubbed the top of the cat's head. Mira lifted her head further and pushed it into Niamh's hand, then ran the side of her nose along Niamh's fingers, baring her teeth slightly. She emitted a low, gentle purring. Niamh tickled her under the chin for a few minutes then kissed her on the top of the head. The cat rearranged herself on the bed, curled up with a paw over her eyes and went back to sleep.

Niamh sighed and stood up. Stretching her arms above her head she walked over to the dormer window brushing her hands along the low ceiling. The window gave her a great view of the sea and of the Old Lighthouse on Long Hill. She'd been looking at this view her whole life but with her new glasses it took on a different quality. Now she could see the

Old Lighthouse properly; the six levels delineated in the exterior granite brickwork, the way it tapered slightly towards the octagonal cap with its domed roof and the quoins where each of the eight walls met its neighbors.

She liked the Old Lighthouse. She preferred it to modern lighthouses: Ugly things, in her estimation; short and squat and painted white and red. The disused Front Light was like that, except the paint had peeled off leaving it shabby. She thought it a poor cousin to its elegant, elder counterpart. She couldn't see the Front Light from her room (*no loss*, she thought) because the Old Lighthouse obscured it. Were her house a few feet to the left or right she would have been able to see one or other side of the Front Light. She realized then that the two lighthouses and her house were directly in line with each other. She smiled at that. It was the sort of thing certain people got excited about but, to her, it was just poetic.

There was a lot more activity than usual around the Old Lighthouse. Several large trucks were parked near it and there were many more vehicles driving up the narrow, rutted access road. Dozens of people milled about, unloading stuff from the trucks.

What's all that about? she wondered. *Probably a movie-shoot; they're always filming around here. Wonder what it's about.*

She leaned her forehead against the glass and watched the activity at the lighthouse, the cars going past and the occasional jogger and dog-walker. She wondered if these people fully appreciated their freedom, and decided they took it as much for granted as she did when she wasn't incarcerated.

This is wrecking my head, she thought. *There's no way I'll last a week in here. And I need to stop thinking about Mark McHewell!*

She turned on her computer and sat down at the desk. After a quick look at her emails she opened up some poetry she'd been working on. *That always passes the time.*

And it did. Sometime during the day Mira needed the litter tray and mewed at the door to be let out. Later, Niamh's step-mum called her for lunch. They didn't talk much as they ate. It wasn't that Niamh disliked Martha, or vice versa; they just didn't have much in common, and even less to talk about. Martha was the sort of person you could never have imagined being fourteen; one of those steady, boring people who seemed to have been an adult their whole life. Niamh hardly knew what to say to her and she certainly had no idea what to say to Niamh.

After lunch Niamh went back to her poetry. Sometime later Mira came back upstairs and was needy. She did her best to demand Niamh's attention by sitting by her chair and mewling piteously while looking up with big, sad blue eyes. When that didn't work she jumped up onto Niamh's lap and from there onto the desk where she proceeded to parade up and down the keyboard with her tail brushing Niamh's nose.

"Oh great, Mira. 'Mjndxctfg.' What am I going to get to rhyme with that? Shakespeare you're not. Get down."

Niamh lifted the protesting cat and put her on the floor. Mira was having none of it. A second later she was back in Niamh's lap but this time she sat there watching the screen as Niamh typed. Occasionally she made little jumps at the screen as the mouse pointer moved but a firm hand from Niamh held her in place. Eventually she lay down on Niamh's lap and went to sleep.

The girl and the cat stayed like that for several hours. Around six Niamh's dad Kenny came home and they had dinner, then it was back to her room. She watched a little TV then lay down on her bed to read. Mira snuggled in behind her knees and purred softly. Before long the book fell from Niamh's fingers and girl and cat were both asleep.

*

Niamh awoke with a start. She had no idea how long she had slept – or what had woken her - but she had the distinct feeling that something was wrong. She couldn't figure out why she felt like this until she saw Mira standing in the dormer window staring towards the Old Lighthouse. It was dark outside and she could see Mira by the dim yellow light of the street lamps. Mira's fur was standing on end and she was growling. Her tail flicked back and forwards.

"What's the matter, Puss? Why are you …?"

She gasped as a sudden blinding light lit up her bedroom. Mira shrieked and flattened herself to the floor, hissing and growling. The blue-white intensity faded and a softer light swirled on the walls of her room, multi-colored like the Aurora Borealis. Eyes wide, she watched the variegated patterns as they danced across the roof and walls. Slowly, they faded. She jumped up and looked out through the window.

The men in the trucks had been busy during the day: A security fence surrounded the Old Lighthouse and powerful spotlights stabbed upwards to illuminate it. A mobile crane was parked close by. The crane's telescopic arm stretched up to the lighthouse's cap and from the hook hung a metallic dome-shaped object, larger than the cap itself. It looked to Niamh like a large upside-down colander. Thick cables hung from the colander thing and snaked down the side of the lighthouse and across the grass to a boxy vehicle. Niamh had been on enough building sites with her dad to recognize the vehicle as a power generator. As if to confirm her hypothesis, bolts of electricity started to arc across the suspended colander thing, slowly at first then faster until it was crawling with blue-white serpents of electricity. Then, in a startling explosion of light – so intense it almost made her ears ring - the entire tower was drenched in a flowing, roiling plasma of electrical energy. She threw her arms up to shield her eyes. Mira spat and ran under the bed. The light faded and once more her room and face were illuminated with the swirling Aurora colors. It was beautiful. The colors danced around the Old Lighthouse and a shimmering effect, like the air above a hot road, surrounded it. The shimmering intensified and it looked as if ... *Surely not!* She couldn't believe her eyes: In the shimmering haze, to the right side of the Old Lighthouse, she could see the outline of the Front Light. It flickered like a badly-tuned television, then snapped into sharp focus. The image stayed solid for a moment, flickered, then the mirage, the shimmering and the swirling lights disappeared.

But that's impossible, she thought. *You just can't see the Front Light from here. What's going on?*

She sat back on her bed.

I've got to tell Mark about this. I bet he'll be able to see this from his room. Wonder if he'd go over there with me to take a look? What time is it? Wow, it's after midnight; I wonder if he's awake. He'd never be allowed out at this hour. Wonder if he'd sneak out? Where's my cell? Oh, there it is on the floor.

Niamh picked up the cellphone and texted Mark:

r u awake?

After a few moments her phone chimed.

yes.

Yes! She grinned and clapped her hands together, nearly dropping her phone. She dialed Mark's number. It rang then went to voicemail. She frowned. *Strange; he could've just ignored the text if he didn't want to talk.* Again, she dialed his number and again it went to voicemail. This time she left a message:

"Hiya Mark. Don't know what happened there. I got cut off then I got your voicemail. It's gone midnight so maybe you're too tired to talk, I dunno. Anyway; oh-my-God, I have to tell you this: There's something really weird going on at the Old Lighthouse. There's loads of men and trucks up there and bright lights and loads of machinery and everything!

They've been coming and going all day. And, oh-my-God, there was this weird light – like the Northern Lights – shining into my bedroom. It was so bright it woke me up. And the cat's going mental! She's all puffed up and hissy staring out at it. Anyway, I just wanted to know if you could see it from your room. I'd love to go out and see what's going on but Martha and Daddy have grounded me. I suppose I was hoping we'd both sneak out tonight and take a look but anyway …" Look, sure you're probably tired, and erm, well, I guess I'll call you tomorrow. Erm, see you!"

Niamh stood up and walked around her room. The bright light blasted through the window again; and again faded. A low growl came from under the bed. Niamh knelt beside the bed and pulled the reluctant cat out. She sat on the bed and put Mira on her knee. As Niamh petted her, Mira was jumpy and kept eyeing the window. Niamh held the cat gently and waited for the light to come again but after ten minutes she decided the men had finished whatever they had been doing. Mira jumped off her lap and settled on the bed. Niamh went back to the window. There was still plenty of activity by the lighthouse but a couple of the searchlights had been turned off, and as she watched, one by one, the rest went out.

The moon was full and the moonlight lay across the sea like gossamer, fluttering at the edges as the waves moved. Now that the searchlights were out, the moonlight was bright enough to throw shadows and she could pick out the men as they moved around.

Curiosity got the better of her. *I'm gonna get killed for this if I get caught, 'specially at this time of night*, she thought, *but anything's better than staying in this room for a week*. She shed her tracksuit and pulled on jeans and a tee-shirt. She paused by her shoe-rack for a moment, then grabbed her walking boots. Sitting on the bed, she pushed her feet into the boots, tied up the long laces and adjusted the tongues. As she adjusted her jean-legs over the boots, her hair fell down over her face. *I need something to tie up this hair – and a warmer top*, she thought. *Aha, I know! Two birds with one stone.* She opened her wardrobe, took out her zip-up hoody and slipped her arms into it. In the pocket was a hair elastic. She tied her blonde hair into a ponytail, stuffed her phone into the pocket of the hoody then looked up at the skylight over her computer desk.

Thank you, Moon; no need for a flashlight. OK, here we go.

She stepped up onto the chair, then onto the desk. She had to stoop while she opened the skylight but once it was open, she slid out through it and onto the gently-sloped roof. Mira watched with interest from the bed as Niamh's legs disappeared through the opening. A moment later Niamh's head popped back in.

"See you later, Mira. Don't make any noise and give me away," she whispered. The cat blinked then looked away and laid her chin on her paw.

Crouched on the roof, Niamh listened for any noise from her parents' room. After a moment, satisfied she was in the clear, she put the window-latch in the closed position and eased the skylight shut. The latch rested on the window-frame and prevented the window from closing fully.

OK, that's my way back in. I hope it doesn't rain. Fat chance in this weather, mind you.

She crept across the roof-tiles to the corner of the house, above the oil tank. She rolled onto her stomach, dropped her legs over the edge and started to lower herself down. As she did, the edge of the roof rubbed along the pocket of her hoody and her phone started to work its way out. As she dropped down to the oil tank, the phone slipped from her pocket and landed in the gutter. She never noticed, and made the short jump from the top of the oil tank to the ground. Again she paused to make sure she hadn't disturbed her parents. All was quiet. She took a few breaths, adjusted the bottom of her hoody and tiptoed around the side of the house then down the short driveway to the road.

Now that she was outside she realized she didn't really have a plan. The road south - towards Mark's house - sloped upwards and she had a vague notion of heading to the top of the hill from where she'd have a better view of the lighthouse. Somewhere deep inside there was also the impulse to walk all the way out to Mark's house and throw stones at his window. *But the gates would be closed. I'd have to climb over the wall. Maybe I could get into their property from the golf course …*

As Niamh dithered, her mind was made up for her.

Something light-colored and very fast streaked between her feet and onto the road in front of her. Niamh jumped and nearly cried out. *What the bloody hell was that?!* Standing in front of her, eyes glistening, was Mira.

"Mira! How did you get out? You shouldn't be outside. Come here."

Niamh reached down to pick up the cat but Mira, who was normally house-bound, had her first taste of freedom and had no intention of coming quietly. She ran up the road, tail bushed out and back legs kicking like a racehorse. After thirty meters or so she stopped and looked back at Niamh. Panic set in. *Oh God; Mira! She's never been outside before. If a car comes, she won't have the sense to get off the road.*

Niamh ran up the road towards the cat. She realized instantly it was the wrong thing to do. Mira recoiled then took off again, running straight up the middle of the road along the dotted white line. Tears flowed down Niamh's face as she ran after the cat. *Oh God, please don't let a car come. Oh please let me catch her and take her back home safe. I swear I'll stay in my room for the rest of the week. I'll never sneak out again, I swear. Oh please, please, please.*

But her worst fears were realized: Headlights blazed around a bend further up the road and the noise of a highly-revved engine grew louder. A car appeared and sped along the road towards them. Niamh screamed: "MIRA!" The cat stopped and looked back at her, then turned to look at the lights coming thundering down the road. She lowered her neck and crouched back as if sizing up the menace. Niamh ran up the road waving her arms, her strength sapped with fear. "NO!" she screamed, the word catching in her throat as she blubbered. Then, just as she was sure the car would hit Mira, the cat darted into the entrance to a field on the left. The car flew past Niamh, the young driver making rude signs at her.

"Idiot! It's 50 KPH along here!" she yelled at the retreating car, then turned back and ran to the field entrance. Mira was standing several meters into the field, oblivious to her near miss, sniffing at some long blades of grass. She started to chew on one of the blades, then flinched as Niamh climbed over the gate. She looked back, saw it was Niamh, and put up her tail. She ran over towards Niamh and stopped a couple of meters away. She threw herself on her side and started to pull herself around in circles with her front paws. Niamh wasn't amused.

"You stupid, stupid cat!" she cried. "I was sure you were a goner. Let me get you back home." Once more she reached down to pick up Mira and once more the cat darted away. She galloped through the grass towards the opposite ditch, the silver in her fur glinting in the moonlight.

"Aughhhhhh! MIRA!" Niamh shouted through gritted teeth but she had no choice. She ran after the cat again. Mira led her through the next ditch and into the next field. As she ran, Niamh was filled with a strange combination of concern and annoyance. It occurred to her this might be how her parents felt when she came home late or didn't check in when she was supposed to. She hoped not; it was a horrible feeling. *God, I meant what I said; please let me catch her and I'll never sneak out again, I promise.*

Mira had other ideas. She was investigating discarded hay bales, cow-pats, bits of machinery left in the field; anything she came across. But as soon as Niamh came within range she was off again. Niamh had no idea how long the chase lasted – it felt like hours - but she eventually caught up with Mira at the wall near the Old Lighthouse. She saw Mira go around the corner and under the pedestrian gate into the lighthouse grounds. When Niamh got through the gate Mira was preoccupied with some small creature at the bottom of the wall and didn't seem to hear her approaching. Niamh scooped her up and said 'Gotcha!'

At that moment a hand grabbed Niamh's shoulder and a deep voice said "What have we here, then?"

Niamh screamed and dropped Mira. The cat hit the ground running and disappeared back out through the gate. Niamh tried to turn around but it was difficult with the man gripping her shoulder.

"How long have you been here? How much did you see?"

"I, I …"

The man spun her around. She looked up at his face but he was wearing a hat with a low brim and she couldn't make out his features. There seemed to be something unusual about one of his eyes but she couldn't be sure. None of it really registered, though: She was petrified. Her heart thudding, she tried to stammer out the story of the runaway cat. The man spoke across her:

"My God, you're only a kid! Still, we can't take any chances. You're coming with me."

He walked towards the Old Lighthouse, dragging Niamh behind him. She was crying uncontrollably.

"Please Mister, don't hurt me. I didn't see anything; I only wanted to get my cat."

The man ignored her and strode on. Around them, men were breaking down the equipment and pieces of the security fence were being loaded onto a trailer. One of the men stopped what he was doing and his mouth fell open in disbelief.

"What the hell are you doing? Who's the kid?"

"Shut your mouth and get that trailer loaded," growled The Man In The

Hat, wrenching Niamh's arm. She pulled against his grip, dug in her heels and kicked at his legs but his grip stayed strong and he didn't react. This lack of reaction scared her more than any expression of anger would have.

Moments later they arrived at the open door of the lighthouse and he pulled her inside. There was just enough moonlight to see by. Still gripping her wrist he reached down and pulled open a trapdoor. He dragged her down some wooden steps and into a circular cellar. At the bottom he pushed her hard and she flew towards the curved wall and fell over. The man strode back up the steps and out of the cellar.

He was going to lock her in!

Niamh scrambled to her feet and raced up the steps. He bolted the trapdoor just as she reached it. The moonlight was cut off leaving the cellar in total darkness.

"NO!" she screamed. "Don't leave me down here. Please don't leave me down here. My cat's out and she'll get killed on the road. And my dad will kill me. He'll be worried sick. Please! PLEASE!"

But the man didn't answer. Niamh heard the front door of the lighthouse close then a metallic clank and the grate of a key turning in a lock.

She banged on the trapdoor and screamed until her knuckles and throat were raw but no-one came back. Shortly she heard engines starting and the vehicles moved out. Soon, even the sound of those faded and it was silent.

For a few moments she stood in the dark, not quite believing where she was and what had happened to her. As the reality of the situation descended on her, panic threatened to engulf her. A low moaning noise escaped her lips. She felt her way back up the steps and reached the trapdoor again. She felt around the inside of the trapdoor but couldn't open it: it was bolted from the outside. Sitting on the steps she put her head in her hands and sobbed. The tears racked her, and she cried until the lump in her throat felt like a burning coal.

Then she remembered her cellphone. She felt in the pocket of her hoody then frantically went through her other pockets but the phone wasn't there. This was too much. It hurt to cry now but she couldn't stop. She cried until a coughing fit punctuated her sobs. In between coughs and taking huge gulps of air, she thought she heard a noise beneath her. Her breath caught and she stiffened. Trying not to make a sound she turned her head this way and that, ears straining.

From somewhere inside the cellar she heard a low groan. She shrieked then clapped her hands to her mouth. Her pulse hammering in her ears, she pressed herself back up against the trapdoor. The groan came again; then a man's voice – very low – said:

"Help me."

Niamh's eyes widened and the moaning noise started again in her throat. Terror paralyzed her but something about the voice made Niamh realize the man was in a bad way. She crept back down the steps and whispered:

"Where are you?"

Again the voice said: "Help me."

The voice was coming from under the steps. Niamh moved around behind the steps, feeling her way. Her arm brushed against something and she realized it was the man's leg. She knelt down and shuffled over to where the thought the man's head was. Her knee knocked against something small and hard on the floor. As it rolled away from her, a light erupted from it, scaring the hell out of her. She covered her eyes until they adjusted then realized the object was a small flashlight. She picked it up and looked at the man. Her heart skipped a beat.

"The Kung-Fu priest," she whispered. Mark had told her about the weird priest with the neck tattoo and the ponytail he'd seen in the village, now here he was trapped in the same cellar as Niamh - and seemingly very ill. She put the flashlight on the wooden steps and bent down to him again.

"Are you OK?"

The man's breathing was labored. His skin looked grey and there were beads of sweat on his forehead. He struggled to speak and failed. Niamh put her ear down to his mouth. He drew in a ragged breath, wet his lips and tried again:

"It's Magus ... he's trying to get ... free again. His minions have come back ... to this *tír*. "

He had a foreign accent. It sounded German to Niamh.

"Who? Who's come back?"

The priest raised his hand and brushed her cheek. The touch felt brittle, like the crumbling rasp of a dead leaf.

"Ah, *Mädchen*; there was a time the ... mention of his name would have str ... uurrgh ... struck fear in your heart. The good tír folk taught rhymes to their children lest they forget."

The priest took a gurgling breath, as deep as he dared, and started to chant:

> *Spiteful, sinful Simon Magus,*
> *Brought his armies to enslave us.*
> *Opened gates from tír to tír*
> *Rent and robbed and razed for years.*

He rolled his head around in pain, hissed air in through his teeth and spoke again:

"We thought we knew better; thought we had banished him forever. We wanted folk to ... forget who Magus was and ... what he had done – forbade them to speak of him - forbade the rhymes and stories; and when that did not work we rewrote history. We were ... too successful, too arrogant. And now that the danger has returned … no one remembers … no one understands the threat. *Ach du lieber Gott*, if he gets loose …"

Niamh started to talk but the priest shook his head and touched her mouth with his hand.

"Listen, Mädchen: He must be stopped. The Sentinelium has been infiltrated and destroyed. I was the last Proctor in this tír. They killed e… everyone… except… The Mason. He got away through … The *Saiph* … to join … the Felkynd Allegiance. He needs help. Find the new Mason; The Apprentice… find Oisín. He has to follow… has to go through. He needs the four Tetroi – the four parts of The Index to open the gate. Find Oisín and tell… tell him to collect all four Tetroi – *The Mason, The Templar, The Nobleman* and *The Cleric*."

"What? Who's Oisín? And who are these people he has to gather? You said they were all dead except the Mason."

"Not people. Not people any more. The Tetroi are pieces of a key called The Index. Each Tetros has a guardian – a Proctor – and the location of each Tetros is known only to its Proctor. We were supposed to keep them separate so the gate could never be opened again but now The Apprentice must gather the Tetroi and reconstruct the Index to open the gate and go through."

"But, what gate?"

The priest shook his head violently from side to side.

"No Mädchen, there isn't time. I cannot tell you where to find the other Tetroi but mine is hidden in plain sight. It's …"

The priests eyes started to become unfocused. He coughed then, to Niamh's horror, he started to laugh hysterically.

"Hah hah hah! They've been staring at it for years, not even knowing it was there. Hah hah!"

"Who have?"

"The... the penitents... it's been right there under their noses. Hah hah hah!"

"Where?"

"Oh, you'll see it. If you're truly penitent you'll see it. Ah hah hah hah! Oh, but you'll need the key. You can't just take it ... that would be crazy ... ah hah hah hah!"

"What key?"

"The priest stopped laughing and a choking sound came from his throat. His eyed widened and a look of fear crossed his face. He clutched Niamh's arm."

"I don't want to die."

Niamh stifled a little shriek. She began to stammer something in response but the priest started to roll his head from side to side.

"I don't want to die. I don't want to die. I don't want ..."

Niamh took the priest's head in her hands and looked into his eyes. She had no idea what he was talking about but she felt in her gut that it was important.

"Father," said Niamh, "Where's the key?"

He looked at her transfixed then raised his hand to her face again. His eyelids blinked several times and his eyes rolled upwards.

"The falls. The falls are the key. The falls along the way."

The priest's head fell to the side. He was dead.

Niamh screamed and scuttled back until she hit the wall. Her skin crawled as the priest's dead eyes stared across at her. She thought she should probably close them - *isn't that what you were supposed to do?* - but she couldn't bring herself to touch him. After several moments of indecision, she crept forward, snatched the flashlight off the steps and darted back to the wall. She turned off the flashlight but the darkness was worse than the priest's eyes. She turned the flashlight back on and took off her glasses.

That was better. Now she could see enough to move around but not the detail of the man's face.

She took stock of her situation. Being trapped in here had been bad enough but in the back of her mind, she had believed The Man in the Hat would come back and let her out. Now somebody was dead. That changed everything and strangely, it gave her more resolve. She thought it entirely possible that the man wouldn't come back; that he had left her there to die; or worse again, that he *would* come back and kill her. She knew then that she had to get out of the cellar.

Now that she had a flashlight she could search for her phone. She put her glasses on and avoiding the priest's face, looked all around the body where she had been kneeling. Nothing. She checked the entire cellar – even places she hadn't been – but the phone wasn't there. *Oh, well; it was a long shot anyway*, she thought. It was far more likely she'd dropped it while running after Mira – or when she'd slid down the roof of her house.

Not quite sure what she was looking for, she shone the flashlight around the walls of the cellar. Apart from a couple of loose stones on the floor, the walls were solid. *Anyway*, she reasoned, *even if I could break through the walls, I'm still underground.* She checked the roof too. It was a stone roof and the only way out was through the trapdoor. Taking a deep breath she went to the top of the steps. With the flashlight illuminating the trapdoor she could see the wood was old. She put her shoulder against the underside of the trapdoor and pushed up with her legs. The trapdoor creaked against the bolt but it stayed firm. She pushed a little harder. To her alarm, the step under her feet creaked and emitted a very slight snapping sound. *Ooh, I'm not doing that again*, she thought.

She put her glasses on and shone the flashlight around the edges of the trapdoor. There was a narrow gap between the trapdoor and the edge of the cellar ceiling, and she could see the metal bolt through it. She put her finger up through the gap and managed to touch the bolt. She put sideward pressure on the bolt with her finger but it wouldn't move. She realized the weight of the trapdoor was creating too much friction between the bolt and the hole it was secured in. Standing on the top step she bent over and put her back against the trapdoor. Flexing her legs she lifted the trapdoor slightly and tried the bolt with her finger again.

It moved!

It was almost imperceptible but the bolt definitely slid back. She tried again. Again it moved.

It was a fiddly process, and it took half an hour but by rocking the trapdoor up and down and pushing the bolt with her finger, she eventually slid it all the way back. She gave the trapdoor a good push and it swung upwards and fell back against the wall. Niamh climbed up the last step and out into the lighthouse. She was out of the cellar! *YES!* She punched the air in delight.

Eager to get out, she opened the lighthouse door. Her heart sank as she stumbled into the security gate. *No!* She grabbed the bars and rattled the gate hard but it stayed fast. It was agony: she was so close to freedom, yet no better off than she had been in the cellar. She could see the outside world, feel the summer night air whisper across her skin but there was no way past the gate. She pushed her face up against it and closed her eyes as if willing herself to pass though like a phantom.

"No! Not again!" she shouted. She felt the tears welling but they were overtaken by an overwhelming anger. How dare that man lock her in! How dare he terrify her to the point of insanity! She kicked the gate then turned around and slammed the trapdoor shut. She stomped around the ground floor of the lighthouse screaming in rage and pulling at her hair.

Eventually the anger cooled to a steely resolve. She'd gotten out of the cellar, and by God, she'd get out of the lighthouse too! She looked around for other possible exits. There were no windows and no way past the locked gate. Her only option was to go up the spiral staircase to the floors above. She shone the flashlight up the steps but nothing she could see gave her any clue as to what was up there.

She put her foot on the first step. Hoping there were no more surprises, she held her breath and started up the stairs.

CHAPTER SIX

ALMHA

Mark woke up early on the second day of his summer holidays. He felt depressed but forced himself to get up and get ready to cycle to the newsagent's in Wicklow. Thoughts of the locked study and 2000AD comic brought inexorable memories of his dad. The awful, gut-churning sense of loss had lessened but today would be particularly difficult.

In the days beforehand, he had convinced himself that turning fourteen would make it easier to cope with his loss. It hadn't. Hitting this milestone without his dad around was unbearable.

What made it so bad was that Fintan had always taken the first week of Mark's summer holidays off work; and they made the most of it: They got up at dawn and went hiking or cycling. Sometimes they played soccer.

46

When the weather was good, they took Fintan's yacht out.

They would come back from one activity, tear through the house getting clothing and equipment together and head out again, leaving a trail of devastation behind them. One day, Bree said they were like a pair of Tasmanian Devils, and the name stuck.

Some years, Fintan's friend Hugh McMurnagh and his son Ferdia would join them for Taz Week. Hugh had been an engineer in the army and had been injured on peace-keeping duty in Africa. He wore a patch over his right eye. Fintan called him 'Golly' and teased him over it. Mark just thought it was cool.

Ferdia was two years older than Mark and had an insanely high IQ. There was talk of him having some type of mild autism. Mark thought he was overly particular and a bit fidgety but he got on fine with him for all that. Hugh often said Ferdia understood more about engineering, mathematics and the sciences than he did but Ferdia, for all his smarts didn't seem to mind hanging out with the younger Mark. In any case, during Taz Week, age and intellect were set aside. It was an excuse for the men and the teenagers to do what men like doing best; behave like kids.

But that was other years. Before school had broken up, Hugh had called Mark's mum and offered to take the week off but Mark wasn't interested. Doing Taz Week without his Dad would be plain wrong.

Mark bolted down some cereal, fetched his bike from the garage and headed down the avenue.

Ireland was in the throes of a heat wave. It was a glorious summer's day; the kind you remember for years, where the shadows are sharp and everything else seems hazy. It was a day of rich summer smells; of melting asphalt and freshly mown grass and barbecues; a day where white contrails carved across the sky by silent jets kindle visceral yearnings to travel to faraway places. It was a day for laughter.

But there was no laughter in Mark. The heat of the sun and the distant shouts of children on the beach stirred nothing in him. There was a splinter in his soul.

He cycled down the avenue from the house, the sun beating down on the hat his father had brought him from Australia. He paused when he reached the road. A few kids on holidays with their families were playing soccer in the caravan park opposite. One of them saw him looking over the gate and beckoned him over. He considered it for a moment then shook his head and moved away.

It was four kilometers north along the winding coast road into Wicklow. Mark bumbled along in the heat, savoring the occasional breeze off the sea. He passed the caravan park entrance, then up a long gentle hill with wild hedges on both sides. At the top he passed the entrance to Silver Strand, a misnamed golden beach, and the road leveled. The hedge to his right was lower here and he had a spectacular view of the ocean. The vibrant green of the fields sloped away from him then gave way to the jeweled blue-green of the sea. Myriad sailing boats appeared as colored dots offshore. Further out, hazy cargo ships plied the horizon.

Mark cycled on. The heat and the rhythm of cycling had a hypnotic effect, and his mind wandered.

Ahead, an imposing 18th century octagonal lighthouse dominated the gorse-covered headland. The gently tapering walls of the tower rose to meet an elegant dome-shaped cap that had been added in the 1800s after lightning destroyed the original lenses and lanterns. A newer but equally defunct lighthouse known as the Front Light stood shabby and squat to its right, closer to the sea cliffs.

Mark recalled previous years when his dad had taken him out to Wicklow Head with its cluster of derelict buildings. Fintan loved the aesthetics of the Old Lighthouse, and had designed the logo of his architecture practice around it. Mark found it kind-of creepy. The windswept headland was desolate and eerie, and the abandoned buildings were somehow sinister. He always felt a frisson of fear and excitement as he got close to the Old Lighthouse. When he looked up, the height of the tower and the clouds scudding by gave the impression it was toppling onto him. If he lay at the foot of the tower the effect was amplified, and the urge to get up and run away was overwhelming. He wondered if there was a word for the enjoyment of fear. He hoped so; boys of his age could make good use of such a word. Wicklow Head scared the daylights out of him, no doubt about it but on some primal level, it called to him too.

"Towers have a subtle energy," Fintan had said. "You can feel it as you get close to them. Your science teacher would disagree but it's there nonetheless – at least in this tír."

"In this *what*, Dad?"

But Fintan didn't explain. He just shook his head like he'd said something he shouldn't.

"Never mind, Marco. I'm just rambling."

All this puzzled Mark. He knew towers were motifs of his father's design style but he also knew this fascination and talk of mysterious energies came from somewhere within his father that was nothing to do with his being an architect. Still, strange as all this was, Mark thought he could feel this energy. He felt a peculiar compulsion to go out to the bleak headland on his own after dark sometime – if only to challenge himself. The thoughts of it sent delicious thrills of horror down his spine.

When they drove back down the access road, the Old Lighthouse swaying in the rear window from potholes, Mark felt a mix of relief and melancholy. Scary as it was, Mark felt for the grand old tower stuck out on the hill. He often had empathic feelings for inanimate objects but never voiced them. Some thoughts were better kept to oneself.

The blare of a car-horn wrenched Mark back to reality and he found himself in the middle of the road. He swerved to the side and a car sped by barely missing him. He'd travelled quite a distance during his amble through his memories and the Old Lighthouse was now far over to his right. Shocked to alertness by the near miss, he focused on the job in hand. Harnessing the adrenaline, he worked the pedals harder. He was halfway along an undulating narrow straight, cottages and bigger houses now more frequent on both sides.

The hedge heightened once again to obscure the lighthouses and the headland. Soon the road widened and he came to the outskirts of the town. On he went, past the gates at the end of the lighthouse access road and along by the golf course.

The breeze whipped his hair. Now that he was on the flat, the pedals seemed to pump themselves in an effortless perpetual motion. Despite his cares, Mark was enjoying himself.

Ahead, the angular clubhouse on Wicklow golf course stood on a hill, surveying its demesne. Far in the distance, the soft curves of the Wicklow Mountains, blue in the summer haze, lay like discarded pillows on the horizon. In the middle distance was Wicklow Bay. The salt-water lagoon known as the Murrough glinted in the sunlight and the long curved beach along the Murrough peninsula bit like a sickle into the Irish Sea.

Now it was downhill all the way.

Click! The derailleur rattled into top gear.

He sped along the die-straight Dunbur Road with its honor-guard of detached houses, over the zebra crossing, then down the steep white-knuckle ride of Summerhill. Hard on the brakes at the bottom, he skidded to a halt outside the newsagent's.

Head spinning and heart racing from the exhilaration of the hill, Mark dismounted onto wobbly legs. He steadied himself against the bike for a moment then chained it to the railing outside the store. Eyes adjusting to the dim interior, he went inside.

The store was an oasis of cool after the sun-drenched expedition from home. He got a bottle of water from the fridge and approached the counter. With practiced indifference, the girl took his money without looking at him or speaking once. He sipped the water and headed over to the magazine rack. He flicked through every issue of 2000AD on the shelf but none of them had the mysterious insert.

Maybe it was only put into mine. But by who?

Mark approached the girl again. She was reading a hardback novel that looked like it weighed more than she did.

"Excuse me."

She looked up, seemingly aghast at such politeness. Now that he could see her face, she was quite pretty; late-teens, with the air of someone that wished they were anywhere but behind the counter in a newsagent's.

"What?"

"Was there someone new working here yesterday?"

She looked at him like he was a particularly annoying wasp.

"No. Just me. So what?"

"Uh, no reason. Was there anyone weird or suspicious hanging around yesterday?"

"No, but there is today. You're cute and all but I'm too old for you kid; buzz off."

Mark blushed until his ears burned. "No, no – I'm not trying to ask you to go with me, I was just wondering if …"

"Seriously, get lost Dude, I'm busy." She went back to her book.

In the shade of the store's awning, Mark took a long drink of the chilled water, adjusted his hat then braved the sunshine. He unchained the bike and pointed it back up the hill. Standing in the pedals, he started his journey home. His body occupied with the effort of climbing the hill, his thoughts took flight and turned, as they so often did, to the day his father left.

None of it made sense. How could he have just driven away and abandoned them? There were no problems at home; he was sure of that. His parents loved each other and they never really argued. When they did disagree, it was calm and rational – and it usually concerned Mark; like the day Fintan bought Mark his mountain bike:

"Finn, you're going to spoil that boy!"

"Oh come on, every boy needs to be spoiled by his dad, once in a while; isn't that right Marco?"

"It's 'Mark,' for heaven's sake! Don't call him 'Marco'; it makes him sound like some thug in a gangster movie."

"Or a great adventurer; like Marco Polo. You're going to be an explorer, aren't you, Marco. Your life is going to be one great journey into the unknown and you're going to explore every nook and cranny of it, aren't you, son?"

Mark didn't really follow what his dad was saying but he grinned and nodded. Bree rolled her eyes and went out to the kitchen.

Later, Mark heard his parents talking again:

"Look, I don't want to keep banging on about it, but don't spoil him, Finn. He needs to understand the value of things and if you keep buying him everything he wants he'll have no idea what it's like to have to work for a living."

"And would that be so bad? Look Bree, my dad was never there. He worked himself to death to look after us and we only ever had just enough to get by. He had that damned stupid old Irish work ethic where every penny had to come through hardship. He worked hard – too hard -- and even as a child I knew it was killing him. I also knew – on some level – things didn't need to be that difficult. I never want Mark to go through the hardship I did; I want him to be happy. I want him to know the wonders of childhood and the thrill of discovery for as long as he can."

"Finn, you can't rewrite your father's life through your own actions or relive your childhood through Mark's. Your father was a good man. You're a good man - and a smart man - and you've made us very wealthy but you're going to have to let Mark grow up and work for a living someday."

"Of course he will. He'll join the firm and work alongside me. It's all for him; you know that, Bree.

"But he might not want to study architecture; might not want to join your firm. Have you thought about that? As he gets older he'll get more independent and we're not always going to be there for him. He's going to need common sense and be as streetwise as possible; and if you keep mollycoddling him he's not going to be prepared for life out there."

"Oh, come on! He's only a child. You're talking like he's about to head off to university or something."

"Well, that day will come around quicker than you think and you're going to need to be as prepared for it as he is."

Fintan sighed.

"I know you right. I know it but I can't bear the thought of him wanting for anything."

"You're a good father Finn, and a great husband; just don't spoil the boy." She rapped him on the chest with a wooden spoon and kissed him. *"And stop calling him 'Marco'."*

Mark stopped the bike and burst into tears. It was so unfair. Summer holidays were what every kid looked forward to most but what good were they when they just gave you more time to think about the bad stuff? He walked the bike to the car park overlooking the golf course and the Glen Strand and sat at a picnic table. He cried his heart out until the whole knot of anger and frustration made its way to his throat.

"Why?" he screamed into the air. "Bastard! Why did you leave? Why?"

A pair of golfers on the tee looked over and one of them gestured at him to be quiet but Mark didn't care. He kicked his bicycle and it fell over. He kicked it again. Then he kicked the leg of the picnic table. The wood hurt his toe through his training shoe but he kicked it again. This time he caught his shin on the edge of the wooden seat and pain exploded in his leg. He fell on the ground screaming in pain and anger and cried until his soul felt desiccated. He had no idea how long he stayed there but when he stopped crying, his leg and his heart were numb. He picked himself up and forced the rest of the water past the lump in his throat. After a few minutes, the worst of the grief had passed, and he thought about going back home. He had no idea what he would do when he got there but he needed the solace of his own room. His heart like lead, he got back on his bicycle and headed south.

No memory fugues this time, no appreciation of the views; he trudged on in the heat, counting the turns of the pedals. A while later he arrived at the avenue entrance. Stone walls flanked a pair of tall wooden gates. Polished stone plaques set into either wall read *Almha*. Straddling the crossbar, he tapped his access number into the keypad on the wall and the gates swung open. He cycled up the avenue; tree-filtered sunlight speckling the asphalt. After a minute he rounded a corner, and the house his father was so proud of came into view.

Fintan had designed his dream home before Mark was born. He had built it on a steep incline overlooking the coast, with the back of the house built right into the hill. The front was three floors of gleaming angular glass, uninterrupted by steel or concrete, which caught the morning sun like a glacier. The avenue ran three hundred meters up from the public road, then widened and ended at a curved stainless steel railing five meters from the house. Behind the railing was a semi-circular fish pond continuing right back to the glass front and extending the full width of the house. The glass frontage swept down and disappeared below the pool's surface to basement level. From inside the glass-fronted basement, the view of the pool, illuminated by underwater lights, was that of a quiet tropical aquarium. The grounds were planted with exotic trees and vines which overhung the avenue, giving the impression of approaching a waterfall in a lush jungle grotto.

Mark stopped at the railing and dismounted. He pressed a button on his key-ring and a metal causeway, wide enough for two cars, rose out of the water. The causeway locked into place with a solid mechanical clunk and as the last of the water ran off the top, the glass-fronted garage door swung upwards. The railing before the causeway retracted into the ground.

Mark walked his bike over the rubberized surface of the causeway and into the garage. He maneuvered the pedals between his mother's Volvo SUV and the wall, avoiding the empty space on the other side where his father's Porsche should have been. He couldn't bring himself to walk through the space it used to occupy.

Once his bike was stowed, he walked back across the causeway and pressed the button again. The garage door closed, the railing rose and the causeway sank back below the water. He walked across a footbridge to the front door, entered his personal entry code on the keypad and went inside. In the hallway a door on the right led into the garage area and a stairway led up to the first floor. He went upstairs into the main part of the house and put his hat in the closet.

"Mum!" he called.

No answer. He walked into the large open plan living area with its panoramic view of Wicklow bay and looked around. The bay looked beautiful in the sunshine and the distant curve of the coastline to the north, with the mountains behind it, was straight off a postcard. But there was no sign of his mum. He walked through to the kitchen and utility room area;

still nothing. He pressed a button on the wall intercom.

"Mum? Are you home?"

After a moment the intercom crackled and his mum's voice came back:

"Hi Mark. I'm up in the garden. Come on up, and bring some water, will you."

Mark got a glass jug from the cupboard and filled it from the water dispenser on the fridge. He grabbed a glass and headed out of the kitchen towards the stairs to the second floor. On the second floor, in the front left-hand side of the house, was a spiral staircase hidden by a semi-circular wall of glass bricks. The staircase wound upwards into a cylindrical room which Mark's dad had called The Watch. The room was eight meters across, with a circular leather bench seat around the inner wall. Mounted in the center of the room was a large telescope angled up towards a Perspex domed roof. A ladder led up from the floor to a metal walkway which ran around the inside of the room, three meters above the circular leather seat. On the floor of The Watch, a break in the seat gave access to a door which led out into the roof garden.

The Watch protruded from the top of the house where the glass and metal roof over the second floor bedrooms sloped back and joined seamlessly with the brow of the hill. Where the steel merged with the earth, the garden swept back from the edge, bounded by a railing at the front and brick walls at the sides that met in a semi-circle at the back. The garden had a clipped lawn surrounded by pebbled paths. At the back of the garden, in the semi-circle, was a rockery with a water feature from where neat flowerbeds ran to the front of the garden on either side. The door from The Watch opened into the front left side of the garden.

Mark walked out into the garden and saw his mum kneeling at one of the flower beds with a trowel. He brought the jug of water over to her and poured a glass for her.

"Oh thanks Mark; I was parched, and I was too lazy to go all the way down to the kitchen. Whoo, it's hot!"

She took off her sun hat and fanned herself with it. Mark wished he'd brought his.

"Where did you go?" she asked, standing up and sipping her water.

"Into Wicklow; just for a cycle," he said.

"I hope you were careful on the road. You know they drive like lunatics along there. Want some?" She proffered the glass. Mark shook his head and looked at his feet.

"No thanks. I'm going back inside in a minute."

She cocked her head and considered him for a moment. He looked back at her and she could see the hurt in him. Tears sprang to her eyes and she pulled him to her.

"Oh Mark. You can't stay inside for the whole summer."

"But I've just been out."

"I know, I know, but before you'd have been out all day."

She cradled his head and stroked his hair. He leaned into her shoulder for a moment then pulled away.

"I'm OK, Mum."

She held him at arms' length and regarded him. "Are you sure?"

He nodded.

"OK then. I'll be done in an hour and I'll make us some lunch."

"Cool. I'll be in my room."

*

Well, that was a fat lot of help!

Mark was in his room poring over the haikus. His mother's lunchtime explanation of cryptic clues, anagrams, common abbreviations and keywords had been fascinating, and a lot of it went over his head but he was starting to see the attraction of such puzzles. And that was all very well but none of it seemed applicable to the haikus.

"When all else fails," his mother had said, "break the clues into smaller parts and solve those. It doesn't always work but sometimes it gives you a fresh perspective."

Mark tried that but those fresh perspectives were being elusive. He had a notepad covered with words and parts of words but he hadn't found any anagrams, hidden words or abbreviations. He was about to read the haikus again when his cell rang. The screen said "Ferdia." Mark groaned. He wasn't sure he wanted to speak to Ferdia. The last thing he wanted was to burst into tears on the phone, and given that his dad had still been around the last time he and Ferdia had spoken, there was a real danger of that. The phone continued to buzz in his hand. Almost without realizing it, he pressed the *Answer* button and said "Hi Ferd."

"Hi Mark. How are you doing?"

"Uh, I'm fine!" he said, his voice just a little too chirpy to be believable.

"Listen, I got your text, and I want to help, whatever the problem is."

"What text?"

"The text you sent me earlier."

"I never sent you a text, Ferd."

"Yes, you did. I've got a text here from you that says: *'Hi Ferd. Need ur help. Can u call me?'*"

Ferdia emphasized the *ur* and *u* to show his disdain for text-speak.

"You sent it at half-ten this morning."

"But I never sent you a text this morning."

"Really? Ok, I must have gotten it mixed up. Anyway, what are you up to?"

"Nothing much. Well, I'm trying to figure out a puzzle. Well, I think it's a puzzle; it might not be."

There was a moment of hesitation as Ferdia digested this.

"How can you not know if a puzzle is a puzzle or not? I mean... OK, Mark; that doesn't make sense."

"Well, there's this poem my dad left for me in his computer..."

Mark told Ferdia the story of finding the haikus but left out the freaky comic book page.

Ferdia whistled. His voice carried admiration and a growing excitement.

"Wow! Good work, Mark. What do the haikus say?"

Mark read the three verses down the phone.

"Well, it certainly sounds like a puzzle; I mean with all that stuff about cracking the hidden codes. Do you want me to help you solve it?"

"Um, yeah sure. I mean, I've been looking at it for ages and I haven't a clue. I was going to show it to my mum."

"No! Don't do that. Your dad wanted *you* to figure this out. If it's something he wanted your mum to know he'd have just told her."

"I suppose..."

"And what if it was something he didn't want your mum to know? I mean, he hid it in the computer in an account under your name. I'm sure he wanted only you to know about it."

"Well..."

"Mark, can you email those haikus to me? I'll read them and see if I can come up with anything."

"Uh, yeah, Ok. I'll go back to my dad's computer and send them from there."

"Good. This is exciting. A hidden message from your dad! Have you heard from him?"

"Uh, no. Nothing. But we still..." Mark's voice trailed off.

Ferdia realized he had been insensitive.

"Mark, I'm sorry. That was a stupid thing to say. I don't know how to talk about things like this."

"It's OK. It's the same in school." Mark's voice started to crack. "People just stopped talking to me. Even my friends don't call any more."

"I'm so sorry Mark. It's a really horrible thing to happen."

Mark could tell this was just something Ferdia had learned to say in such situations. He couldn't genuinely empathize with Mark. There were a few moments of heavy silence.

"Any... anyway, listen; after I got that text from ... well, from whoever, I asked my mum if we could drive down and see you. My dad's already down in Wicklow working on some engineering job. So my mum was wondering if your mum was interested in playing golf tomorrow. She was going to call my dad and find out which hotel he's staying in and we were going to stay there. Even if you didn't text me it sounds like you could use my help with those haikus anyway. What do you think?"

"Um, yeah sure. I'll ask my mum."

Mark brought the phone down to Bree. Her eyes brightened when she heard the McMurnaghs were coming down. She asked Ferdia to put his mum on the phone.

It was arranged in minutes. Bree wouldn't hear of them staying in a hotel: Kiva and Ferdia would stay in *Almha* for a few days. There was loads of room; besides, Mark could use the company, and having Ferdia around would give her a break from worrying about him.

Bree handed the cellphone back to him. As she did she noticed a message icon on the screen.

"Hey, you have an answer-phone message."

Mark looked askance at her.

"Mum; 21st century! They call it voicemail these days."

"Oh well pardon me! You have a *voicemail*. Maybe it's one of your friends

60

wanting you to go to the beach or something." *I hope.*

Mark remembered the missed call from Niamh the night before. He took the phone and went up to the roof garden. Sitting on a shaded bench he called his voicemail service. Niamh's excited voice spilled from the phone. She told of men and trucks and strange lights up at the Old Lighthouse, and the cat being spooked, and her wanting to go up there and take a look.

Mark stared at the phone. Weird lights at the Old Lighthouse? Freaked-out cats? Was everyone's life going bonkers? He walked to the front of the roof garden and looked over towards the Old Lighthouse. There were no trucks or anything else over there. The area was abandoned.

He pulled his phone from his pocket and dialed Niamh's number. Her cell rang a few times then went to voicemail. He left her a quick apology for not calling her back the previous night and rang off.

He watched the lighthouse for a few more minutes then shrugged and looked around the garden. He wondered how to kill time until Ferdia arrived. He knew he wasn't going to get any further with the haikus and there wasn't any point in hanging around the house. Maybe the beach wasn't such a bad idea. He was bound to meet somebody he knew down there. OK, the beach it was! He went down to his room and grabbed his rucksack. He shoved his swimming shorts, sun-block and a large beach towel into it. Before he went downstairs, he let himself into the study and emailed the haikus to Ferdia. With his rucksack over his shoulder, he went down to the garage and unlocked his bike. He called his mum on the garage intercom, told her where he was going, and off he went. Bree was delighted he seemed happier today.

She was even more delighted when he cycled back up the avenue at tea time with a smile, a tanned face and the McMurnagh's car behind him.

*

After dinner, Bree and Kiva settled down in the living room and got deep in conversation. Mark and Ferdia took the opportunity to sneak into the study and examine the haikus. A couple of fruitless hours later they gave up and joined the women downstairs. After hot chocolate, Mark felt exhausted and said he was going to bed. Ferdia excused himself too and followed Mark upstairs. He took the haiku printout from Mark's room and retired to one of the guest bedrooms. Mark got under the covers and was asleep in minutes.

CHAPTER SEVEN

THE CUBE

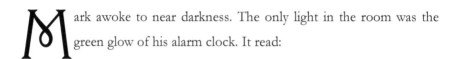ark awoke to near darkness. The only light in the room was the green glow of his alarm clock. It read:

3:02ᴬᴹ

Someone was shaking him.

"Mark. Mark; wake up."

Mark sat bolt upright.

"Wh … wha…?"

He could just make out Ferdia standing beside his bed, his finger to his lips."

"Shh. Keep your voice down."

"What are you doing up at three am?"

"Just a moment; mind your eyes."

Mark shielded his eyes and Ferdia flicked on the lamp beside the bed. When Mark's eyes adjusted, Ferdia was crouching on the floor with a huge grin on his face.

"What are you so happy about?"

"I've cracked it."

Mark was still a little woolly.

"What have you cracked? Is it broken?"

"I've cracked the haiku puzzle. What else could it be?"

Now Mark was fully awake. Eyes wide, he swung his legs from under the covers and sat facing Ferdia.

"You've cracked it! Wow! So what does it mean?"

"Not here. Let's go into the study and talk there."

The boys crept out of Mark's room and into the study. Once inside, Ferdia flicked on the light and motioned Mark over to the desk. He unfolded the printout of the haikus and flattened it with the palm of his hand.

"OK, when I first saw this puzzle, I started breaking the haikus down into lines.

"The first line says '*First letter of line*'. I thought it might be a riddle. Well, the first letter of 'line' is 'L,' but what does that mean? I thought it might be 50 because L is the Roman numeral for 50 but that didn't work."

"Ferd, did you get any sleep tonight at all?"

"Shush! Then I realized your dad might have meant the actual lines of the haikus themselves and that's when I cracked it. The first letter of each line of the haikus spells out *Fibonacci*."

Ferdia slapped his hand on the desk and looked at Mark expectantly. Mark looked back at him, his face a picture of incomprehension.

"Don't you see? Fibonacci? No?"

"Um, no … What should I see? What does *fibbernadgy* mean?"

"Fibonacci. It's the name of an Italian mathematician. Look."

Ferdia grabbed a pen and started scribbling on the haiku printout.

"The Fibonacci sequence is a series of numbers where each number is the sum of the two previous numbers in the set. You start the sequence with the numbers 0 and 1, and then you just keep adding the last two numbers in the set to give the next one:"

Ferdia wrote:

$0 + 1 = 1$

$1 + 1 = 2$

$1 + 2 = 3$

$2 + 3 = 5$

$3 + 5 = 8$

$5 + 8 = 13$

$8 + 13 = 21$

$13 + 21 = 34$

$21 + 34 = 55$

etc.

"So if you read the first number on each line, you get the Fibonacci sequence; 0, 1, 1, 2, 3, 5, 8, 13, 21, 34, 55, and so on. See?"

"Yeah, I can see what you're doing but I still don't know why you're doing it."

"Look, the Fibonacci sequence is one of the most important number sequences in mathematics. It occurs in nature, it's closely related to the Golden Mean, and it's used in architecture - just the sort of thing your dad would have used in a puzzle."

"But what are we supposed to do with it?"

"Well, if I'm right about this, we have to use the Fibonacci sequence to organize the 'books of all knowledge,' whatever they are. Now, books are mentioned twice in the haikus. The second haiku says:

"'*Order seven books numbered by a formula ascending the set.*'

"So the *books of all knowledge* are books that are numbered and can be arranged in sequence. You know what that sounds like to me?"

"What?"

"An encyclopedia."

"Ferd..." Mark started to speak but Ferdia was on a roll.

"So your dad was telling you to organize a collection of encyclopedia volumes according to the Fibonacci sequence ... "

"Ferd ..."

"Hang on a sec; so somewhere in the house there must be a set of encyclopedias and ... "

"FERD!"

"*What?*"

Mark pointed. Ferdia's eyes followed the line of Mark's outstretched finger to the top shelf of the Gothic bookcase. There, arranged in numerical order, was a leather-bound encyclopedia in thirty volumes.

"'*Inspect the top shelf*,'" said Mark.

Ferdia stood frozen for a second then turned to Mark.

"Yes, that's it. All we have to do is put them in the right order and ... "

"And what?"

"Well, I don't know. Let's do it and find out. Look, there are seven Fibonacci numbers less than thirty: 1, 2, 3, 5, 8, 13 and 21, so you must have to put those volumes next to each other."

"Yeah, that must be right, 'cause the first line of the second haiku says '*Order seven books*,'" said Mark.

"Yes, exactly. Grab that chair and I'll hold it for you. It's your puzzle; you should do it."

Mark pulled the chair over to the bookshelf and stood on it. Ferdia held it steady as Mark pulled out the relevant volumes and put them in order. As he pushed volume twenty-one into place next to volume thirteen, the boys heard a loud click and a creak from behind them.

Startled, Ferdia let go of the chair and turned around to where the noise came from. At the same time Mark swung around to look. The office chair rotated with him throwing him off balance. He flailed in the air trying to grab the bookshelf to steady himself but the chair shot away from beneath him like a skateboard. Ferdia turned just in time and caught him but their foreheads cracked together and they fell on the floor groaning. They sat clutching their heads for a moment and as the pain subsided they both looked up in the direction the click had come from.

Their eyes took in the wood paneled wall to the left of the fireplace.

They widened.

A large section of the paneling had swung open, revealing a dark space behind.

"Jesus, Mark; what was your dad up to in here?" said Ferdia, his mouth open.

"I don't know," whispered Mark, "but it's cool!"

The boys got to their feet and approached the door. His heart hammering, Mark reached out to the secret door and pushed it open. As the door creaked aside, the light from the study revealed a dusty concrete floor and little else. A bare light bulb could be seen in the ceiling. Mark reached around the door-frame and found a switch.

Harsh light flooded a room half the size of the study. The walls were as bare as the floor and the only furniture was a small table against the rear wall. A perceptible drop in temperature made the boys shiver as they stepped into the concrete cell. In the severe light, Mark could see the table bore a small lacquered chest, reminiscent of his mum's jewelry box. The chest was cherry wood, buffed to a high polish, the lid decorated with an intricate inlay of lighter materials. It was secured with a gold clasp which Mark flicked open. He raised the heavy lid and rested it against the concrete wall.

Then he saw it for the first time.

Nestled inside the lacquered case on a bed of red velvet was a beautiful wooden device.

It was a perfect cube; just the right size to fit in Mark's hand. He couldn't identify all the woods used in its construction but they were smooth and oily and spoke of exotic forests. Despite the cube's beauty, it seemed grave and somehow sinister in contrast to the extravagance of the lacquered chest. This was a device with a purpose.

The top of the cube was decorated with alternating pieces of polished black marble and cream marble; sixteen of them in rows and columns like one quarter of a chessboard. The individual pieces of marble seemed to penetrate down into the cube but they were so flush against each other that it was impossible to see down into the cube itself. Mark ran his thumb over the top of the pieces and noticed a small depression in the top of each square. When he tilted the cube, the depressions glinted in the harsh bulb light like small circular lenses of clear crystal. As he poked at them he felt the pieces depress very slightly as if spring-loaded but he couldn't depress them more than a millimeter or so.

As Mark examined the cube, he got a strong feeling it was part of a bigger object, composed of four cubes in total. There was a raised border, the width of a finger, around two of the top edges of the cube, forming an 'L' shape. This border was about a finger-width higher than where the marble pieces disappeared into the interior of the cube, and the tops of the marble pieces were level with the top of it. Inlaid into the wooden border, was a seam of some translucent green mineral. Etched into the mineral was gold writing in a strange script. The writing flowed all the way along one top edge, turned through 90 degrees at the corner and continued along the other edge. The writing at the edges of the green marble seemed cut off, as if it were supposed to continue on an adjacent cube. The sides of the cube below the inlaid borders were of well-polished and finished wood, but on the opposite sides the wood was unpolished and drab. It seemed to Mark the polished sides were meant to be seen but the unfinished sides were not. On the two unfinished sides of the cube, several wooden dowels of different shapes were inlaid, flush with the unfinished faces. When he touched them, they moved in and out slightly as if spring-loaded. If there were more cubes, they would interlock by the inward and outward movement of these dowels. Above the dowels were two small holes, side by side - each the diameter of a pencil.

Mark was so engrossed in the cube that he had almost forgotten Ferdia was standing behind him. He turned to him holding out the cube and said:

"Ferdia, look! What do you think this is?"

Ferdia's eyes widened. He moved a little closer and took the cube from Mark. He turned it around and around in his hands, looking at all the faces.

Mark pointed out the dowels and the holes.

"See the way two of the sides are different; the wood is plainer and not as shiny; and see the holes and the pieces of wood there? I bet this box is meant to connect to another three boxes and make some kind of a chessboard. There must be three more of these somewhere. And see the way that weird writing seems to cut off at both edges?"

Ferdia examined the writing around the edge of the cube.

"It's Runic," said Ferdia.

"What?"

"The writing; it's Runic. An old Norse alphabet."

"Can you read it, Ferd?"

"Not right now, but I'll be able to look the individual letters up and translate it back to the Latin alphabet."

As Ferdia looked at the cube, a strange look came to his eye. He cocked his head to one side, pursed his lips then looked away into the distance.

"You know ... I've seen this thing before."

Jealousy bubbled in Mark.

"What? Has my dad shown you around in here before?"

"No! Of course not. I don't recognize it from here. It's from my granddad Vincent's place; when I used to go there as a kid, before he fell out with my parents."

"Which granddad?"

"My mum's dad. There was some kind of a family argument and they don't speak any more."

"So ... your granddad has one of these boxes?"

"I think so. It was only seven when I saw it but it looks the same."

"But that's great! Maybe we can talk to your granddad and find out what it is. See if they're part of a bigger ... thing. Did he ever tell you what it was?"

"No. He was annoyed with me. Granddad used to work in a lab at one of the big pharmaceutical companies and always had cool stuff lying about. I was mooching around and I found it in his wardrobe. He caught me and told me to put it back and forget about it. I guess I did – until now. You're right, though; we could ask him. He lives up in Bray."

"Cool! That's only half an hour away. We could go up there tomorrow and take this to show him."

"We'd have to lie about where we're going. My mum won't let me see him. She says he has strange ideas and knows the wrong people and he'd be a bad influence on me."

"Well, we could say we're going to the amusements on the seafront in Bray, and then it's only a half-lie."

"Yeah, OK; but how are we going to get there?"

"We'll go on the bus. There's one at ten o'clock. My mum will let me go as long as you're with me, and I'm sure she'll drive us into Wicklow to catch it."

"OK, well we'd better get some sleep then; that's only a few hours away."

"Yeah; good idea. I won't be able to sleep though."

"Me either, but I'm gonna try."

The boys closed up the secret room and padded out of the study. Mark watched until Ferdia snuck back to the guest room then closed up the study and crept back to his own room, the strange cube in his hand. He got into bed, hid the cube under the covers then rolled over and tried to get some sleep.

The next day the mystery deepened.

It was another glorious day and the mothers were going golfing. When the boys announced over breakfast that they wanted to go to the amusements in Bray, Bree and Kiva looked at each other, shrugged, and then agreed. They issued the usual dire warnings about care and safety, handed over money and Kiva dropped the boys into Wicklow to catch the ten o'clock bus.

As they waited, Ferdia told Mark about Granddad Vincent, of the times he used to visit there as a small child and how he had found the strange cube hidden in the bottom of his granddad's wardrobe. Mark asked about Ferdia's grandmother and Ferdia told him she had died before he was born. He didn't know the details.

Soon the bus arrived and the boys boarded. They bought their tickets and Ferdia led Mark to the empty seats at the back of the bus.

"Why are we sitting back here?"

"For privacy. We are going to have a look at that cube and do some translating."

Ferdia reached into his rucksack and pulled out his iPad.

"I downloaded a Rune translation app onto my tablet this morning. You hold the cube up so I can see the runes and I'll tap them in. We should have this cracked in no time."

Mark got the cube out of his rucksack and held it up so Ferdia could see the characters. He leaned over to watch the screen on the tablet.

"Right, what's that first symbol? OK, I'll just select it... Right, that's an "A". Next one …"

He wrote in the next character.

"That's a *g* then … *a*, then *i* …*n* …*s* … *t* - against! It's in English! Let's keep going and see what we get."

After much work, and just as the bus pulled into Bray, Ferdia had a cramp in his writing hand and Mark had a strained neck, but for their pains, they had a translation of the runes:

Against the sable backdrop of the night,
The starry actors glide across the stage.
In jeweled costumes sewn with threads of light,
They read their parts, then turn tomorrow's page.

The earthly audience watches from the dust,
As cosmic players tread Forever's boards.
Our bearing on our travels we entrust,
To these bejeweled heroes of the Gods.

Mark looked at Ferdia.

"What does it mean?"

Ferdia shook his head. "I have no idea. I guess we'll just have to wait and see what my granddad says – assuming he knows."

Ten minutes later, they were walking up Cuala Road towards Vincent's house. Cuala Road climbed gently upwards from the busy Putland Road towards the foot of Bray Head. Neat but unremarkable semi-detached homes with walled front gardens lined both sides. Vincent's house was three-quarters of the way up on the left-hand side and the boys soon arrived at the front gate.

It was immediately obvious to Ferdia that something was wrong.

The grass in the front garden was overgrown and the hedge was overhanging the sidewalk.

"I guess your granddad doesn't spend much time in the garden," said Mark.

Ferdia was visibly upset.

"No, this is wrong. He's a neat freak. My mum told me he drove her mad when she was a kid. She and her brothers couldn't leave anything lying around for a moment or he was on to them like a flash. He'd never leave his garden like this."

Ferdia opened the gate and they walked down to the front door. Through the frosted glass they could see a pile of mail on the floor inside the door.

"This place is empty," said Ferdia. "No-one's been here for ages."

He rang the doorbell. They waited but no-one answered.

Mark had a horrible thought and turned to Ferdia with a sick look on his face.

"You don't think he's in there ... like ... dead, do you?"

Ferdia swallowed and licked his lips. He looked absolutely terrified.

"I ... I don't know. But I've got to find out."

"Maybe you should call your mum."

"I guess. She's going to kill me for being here, though. And for lying to her. Listen, before I call her I want to find out what's going on here. If he's not in there maybe he's gone away and she already knows about it. I mean, she wouldn't have told me. Anyway, he used to keep a house-key hidden under a rock behind the garage. I'll see if it's still there."

Ferdia started towards the garage but Mark grabbed his arm.

"Ferd, I'm scared. I've never seen somebody dead. I don't want to go inside."

Ferdia looked at Mark for a moment then smiled and put his hand on his shoulder.

"Ok, you wait out here. He's my granddad, my responsibility. You don't have to go in if you don't want to."

Ferdia continued to the garage and looked through the glass windows on the wooden garage doors.

"Hey, his car's not here. Maybe he *has* gone away."

Relieved by the absent car, Ferdia walked down the passageway between the house and the garage and found the rock. The key was still there. He took it and returned to the front of the house. Mark sat on the wall and watched him. He put the key in the lock and opened the front door. The door brushed the pile of mail aside.

"Granddad?" he called. "Granddad, it's Ferdia. Are you here?"

No answer came. Ferdia looked back at Mark, grimaced, and then stepped into the house. He stooped and gathered up the mail and placed it in several neat stacks on the telephone table inside the door. Leaving the front door open, he walked down the hallway and into the living room. It was exactly as he remembered it; comfortable and neat. It was clear his

74

granddad hadn't been there for some time though: A thick layer of dust lay on every surface and several Christmas cards stood in a neat line on the mantelpiece. He walked back to the hallway and down to the kitchen. There was no sign of his grandfather in there either.

Heart hammering, he climbed the stairs and searched the rooms upstairs. To his relief his grandfather wasn't there. He went to the wardrobe in Vincent's room and rummaged around in the bottom of it until he found the mysterious cube in its presentation box. He brought the box downstairs, called Mark in and walked down to the living room. Mark crept in to the living room like he was walking on eggshells. He looked around like a frightened bird.

"It's OK, he's not here," said Ferdia, "and look what I've found."

He opened the presentation box and took out the cube. He placed it on the coffee table.

"Wow!" said Mark, "it's exactly the same!"

He opened his rucksack, took out his own cube and put it on the table beside Ferdia's. They spent some minutes examining them and turning them around on the table.

"Well, they're not identical," said Ferdia, "but I think you're right about them connecting. Look, the rods on the side of this one and the side of that one match up. And the two small holes are in the same place."

He placed the cubes side by side and pushed them together.

"Hey, look," said Mark, "the runes on the top edge continue on the other cube. These are definitely meant to go together."

"Yeah," said Ferdia, "but something must make the rods push in and out so they click on to each other."

He looked distant for a moment, then said:

"I have an idea. Have you got a pen in your rucksack?"

"Uh, yeah."

Mark rummaged in his rucksack and produced a ballpoint pen.

"Here."

Ferdia took the Biro and pushed it into one of the small holes on his cube. Nothing happened, but when he pushed it into the second hole, something clicked deep inside and a wooden rod sprang about two centimeters out of the first hole. They both jumped.

"Jeez!" said Mark. "That frightened the crap out of me!"

Ferdia was nodding.

"I thought so. I knew there must be a way to get the mechanism started. Let's see what happens when we put these together now."

He moved the two cubes together again, guiding the protruding rod into the matching hole on the other cube. When he pushed them fully together a loud *thunk* sounded from inside the cubes and he felt them lock firmly together. At the same time, two more rods sprang out, one from each of the remaining exposed rough faces on the cubes.

"Well, I guess that clinches it," said Ferdia. "There are definitely two more cubes somewhere that connect on to these."

"Yeah, but where are they?" asked Mark.

"I have no idea," said Ferdia, "and I have no idea how we go about finding them, either."

"What do you reckon the runes on this one mean?"

"Well, let's find out. I wonder if we can get these apart."

He pushed one of the rods back in and it retracted with a snap. He pushed the other and this too retracted but then a deep spring-loaded *clunk* sounded inside the cubes and they jumped apart slightly. Now both cubes were back to their original states with their various rods and dowels fully retracted. Ferdia took out his iPhone and put it on the table.

At that moment, to Mark and Ferdia's horror, an elderly woman appeared in the door of the living room and shouted:

"What the hell are you two young thugs doing in here? Who are you?"

Ferdia stood up and started to speak. The woman took a step back and shrieked:

"Don't come near me! I'll call the police."

Ferdia put up his hands in a placatory gesture.

"It's all right Mrs. O'Brien, it's me: Ferdia; Vincent's grandson."

The old woman looked very relieved indeed.

"Ferdia! Well holy God, look at the size of you! I haven't seen you in years. You were only this big the last time I saw you. You gave me an awful turn. I saw the front door sitting wide open and I thought your granddad was back. And who's this young fella?"

"This is my friend Mark from Wicklow. Mark, this is Mrs O'Brien from next door."

Mark nodded and mumbled "Pleased to meet you."

"Well I'm pleased to meet you too, Mark. Now, this is a surprise and no mistake."

She sat down in an armchair.

"Now, have you any word of your grandfather? How's he getting on on his travels?"

Ferdia squinted.

"Travels?"

"Travels, yes. He headed off out of here months ago and we've not heard a word from him since. I met him as he was getting into his car and he said he was going away from a while. I thought he must have been going to visit family, it being Christmas day and all."

Mark felt the hair on the back of his neck standing up. He and Ferdia looked at each other.

"Christmas day," they said in unison.

"That's right. I thought it was a bit strange. Have you not seen him?"

Not knowing quite what to say, Ferdia decided a few white lies would be the best option.

"Well, you probably know that he and my mum don't talk anymore, so I don't get to see him much. He went away to visit some friends in England at Christmas and stayed on a bit longer to travel around. He rang me a few days ago to tell me about a couple of antiques he wanted me to pick up."

Ferdia gestured at the cubes on the table.

"I said I'd drop in and collect them and check out the house when I was here."

Mrs. O'Brien looked as if she had been slapped.

"Well, he's never called me and Pat in six months and we used to be great friends. And he has our number! Himself and Pat used to go for a drink the odd time too. Ah well, I suppose he has his reasons. And he doesn't talk to your mother anymore? I never knew that. Sure, that's terrible. But sure, I suppose you never know what goes on in families and it's probably none of my business either but he was probably lonely here on his own and when you're old …"

Mrs. O'Brien was on a roll and didn't look like stopping for a long while. Ferdia was uncomfortable about lying to her, particularly since she was so put out that Vincent hadn't been in touch with her, and now he just wanted to get away.

He interrupted her.

"Mrs. O'Brien, I'm really sorry but we have to meet my mum down at the seafront in a few minutes. I'm sorry if we gave you a fright. I'll ask my granddad to give you call when I'm speaking to him. I'm sure he didn't mean to ignore you."

"Oh, yes. Well, of course you have to go. Give my regards to your mother and don't worry about your granddad. Sure, I suppose he'll call when he's good and ready. It was nice to see you again, Ferdia."

She got up and walked out to the front door. The boys followed her.

"Bye bye Ferdia. Bye bye to you too Mark."

"Bye bye Mrs. O'Brien," they both said.

Ferdia closed the front door behind her and the boys went back in to the living room. They stood staring at each other for a long time. Eventually Mark spoke.

"Christmas day, Ferdia. He disappeared on Christmas day, just like my dad."

"I know. And they both had these cubes. There's definitely some connection between my granddad and your dad."

"Ferdia, we need to find the other two cubes. If we find them maybe we'll find out what the whole thing does and maybe we'll find out what's happened to my dad and your granddad."

"Yeah, but how do we find them?"

"I don't know Ferd. I don't think we can tell our parents about this though."

"They'd hardly believe us anyway." He sat down and rubbed his eyes. When he looked up at Mark, he looked like he hadn't slept for a week. "This is the weirdest thing that's ever happened to me."

Mark decided to lay all his cards on the table.

"Actually, there's more."

"More! How can there be more than this?"

"Well, I never told you about what made me go into Dad's study in the first place, or how I found out the entry code for the lock on the study door."

With disbelief growing on Ferdia's face, Mark told him about the mysterious page in his comic.

Ferdia's face went red. He stood up and waved his arms.

"No way! Just… no way, Mark. That's crap! Don't be so stupid! Why are you making up baby stories?"

"I'm not! Look."

Mark reached into his rucksack and pulled out the comic-book page. He handed it to Ferdia. Ferdia looked through it slowly and his mouth fell open. He sank back into the armchair. He read through it again, then again. Eventually he dropped the page on the floor and without a word, got up, walked out of the room and sat on the stairs. After a few moments Mark followed him out. Ferdia looked up and the look on his face scared Mark more than anything he had ever seen. Ferdia's voice quaked as he spoke:

"We're in over our heads. What you've just shown me is impossible. I … I … I just don't know what to think. I can't figure out what's going on."

Mark's stomach felt ill, and it did a little handspring as something else occurred to him. He was almost afraid to mention it in case it tipped Ferdia over the edge. He decided full disclosure was best:

"Remember that text you said you got from me? I never sent you that. I swear I never sent it."

Strangely, this seemed to make Ferdia happier. He stood up and wiped his hands together.

"Well, that's it then. Somebody's behind all of this. I don't know how they're doing it but they can have pages added to your comic and they can make texts appear as if they've come from your phone."

Yeah, but who?"

"Well, it's got to be your dad. No-one else knew the code to the study. Maybe he needs your help and can't contact you directly. Maybe he's involved in something top secret and he's being watched so the only way he can get through to you is like this."

"So you think my dad's still alive?"

"I don't know. Maybe."

"That's a lot of maybes, Ferdia, and if he needs my help why doesn't he just ask for it? And where does your granddad fit into all of this?"

"I don't know, Mark. This whole thing has melted my brain, but that's the only explanation I can think of."

Through the frosted glass of the front door, the boys noticed Mrs. O'Brien hanging around near the front gate.

"We need to get out of here," said Ferdia. "I don't think we're going to figure anything else out and I don't want Mrs. O'Brien to get suspicious and call my mum. Look, you look after the cubes. I'll take a photo of the runes and translate them later."

The boys returned to the living room. Ferdia picked up his iPhone and took several photographs of both cubes then handed them and the presentation box to Mark. Mark tucked them in his rucksack and the boys left the house. Ferdia locked up and put the key in his pocket.

"I'm hanging on to this," he whispered. "We might need to get back in and I don't want to risk putting it back under the rock."

Mark nodded and hefted the heavy rucksack on to his shoulder. The boys walked up the path, waved goodbye to Mrs. O'Brien and headed back down Cuala Road.

CHAPTER EIGHT

KIVA

The boys arrived back in Wicklow to a frosty reception.

They were surprised to see Bree's SUV parked near the bus stop, the two mums inside. Mark smiled as he crossed the road to the car but realized the smile wasn't returned. Bree and Kiva looked furious.

Uh-oh, he thought. As they got into the car, Mark hissed out of the corner of his mouth: "I think we've been rumbled."

During the drive back to *Almha*, Kiva turned around in the passenger seat to look at Ferdia.

"How did you get on in Bray?"

There was an edge to her voice that both boys picked up on.

"Uh ..." Ferdia glanced at Mark. Mark held his breath and waited for what Ferdia would say. Ferdia knew the game was up. He sighed.

"How did you find out?"

"Never mind how I found out, what the hell did you think you were doing?"

"Mother, if I'd told you where we were going, you'd never have let us go."

"You're damn right I wouldn't! I told you to stay away from my father. Damn it, Ferdia you lied to me. You lied right to my face. And I would have expected more of you, Mark."

Mark stammered. "But we ... I ..."

Bree glared at him in the rear-view mirror. "Don't even go there, Mark! You're just as much to blame. And you're in just as much trouble."

"Ferdia," said Kiva, "as soon as we get back to Bree's, pack your stuff. I'm taking you home. Your father's back from his business trip too. I wouldn't want to be in your shoes when he finds out about this."

"Ah, Mother!"

Kiva's jaw jutted.

"DON'T answer me back. DO NOT try my patience."

Ferdia snorted.

"Oh, come on, Mother! All we did was go to see Grandfather. You are just pissed off because we almost got one over on you!"

Mark's jaw dropped. He stared at Ferdia. He'd never heard him speak like this.

A look like thunder came over Kiva's face.

"How dare ..."

"Did you know he's disappeared?"

"Ferdia, you shut up this minute ..."

"No! YOU listen for a minute. Grandfather has disappeared. Did you know about that? Do you even care?"

Bree started to speak: "Ferdia, I really think you should show your

83

mother a bit more ..."

Kiva bared her teeth and swung her left hand at Ferdia. There wasn't much room for her to maneuver between the head-rests but the crack of her hand hitting his face made them all jump. Bree swerved in surprise.

"Jesus, Kiva; what are you doing?"

"Shut up and stay out of this, Bree."

Bree didn't retort; she was too shocked. She glanced at Mark in the mirror. He was looking at Ferdia, his hand to his mouth. Ferdia had the strangest look on his face: He grinned like a satisfied maniac.

"Well, Mother; I always knew you were touchy about Grandfather but I never knew *how* touchy!"

"Ferdia, shut your mouth. You don't know the half of it."

"Oh, I think I know enough. I know he was involved in something dodgy. And I know it was something to do with Fintan."

"Ferdia, I'm warning you ..."

Bree interrupted: "Oh Ferdia, don't be ridiculous. Fintan didn't know your grandfather. Your mum and he fell out long before we all got to know each other."

"Really? Did you know he disappeared last Christmas Day?"

Bree stood on the brake and the big Volvo ground to a halt. She turned around in her seat to face the boys. Her face was white.

"What?!"

"He disappeared on Christmas Day; the same day as Fintan."

Bree looked at Kiva.

"Did you know about this?"

"No! God, Bree; of course not! I don't see my father any more, you know that."

Ferdia jumped back in:

"Maybe not, but there's something else: Grandfather and Fintan both

84

had *owwwww!*"

Ferdia stared at Mark, a hurt look on his face. Mark had grabbed the flesh on Ferdia's thigh and pinched it hard.

"What the ..."

Mark stared at Ferdia, his brows knotted. The look shut Ferdia up immediately.

"Mum," said Mark, "Mrs. McMurnagh, I'm really sorry we lied to you. It's all my fault. We were talking about Ferd's granddad last night and I thought it would be cool to go and see him. But he wasn't there, and we thought we saw Christmas cards up on the mantelpiece in the house. We just started talking about how weird it would be if he'd disappeared the same day as my dad, that's all. We didn't mean any harm."

Kiva looked at him and Mark knew she knew he was lying. To his relief and great surprise she didn't expose him.

"Ok, well I suppose there's no harm done." She wagged her finger at Ferdia. "But you're still in deep trouble, Buster!"

Bree looked from Ferdia to Kiva and back again. She had her '*I'm going to get to the bottom of this*' look on her face.

"What were you going to say, Ferdia?" she asked.

"Ignore him, Bree," Kiva interjected. "He gets like this when he's been caught out."

Bree persisted: "Ferdia, what were you going to say?"

Ferdia looked out the window. "Nothing; I was just angry with Mother." He looked back to Bree. "I'm sorry, Bree. It was wrong to bring up Fintan. I didn't mean anything by it."

Bree was far from satisfied. She looked at Ferdia for a long moment then turned around, jammed the transmission into *Drive* and continued towards *Almha*.

As they pulled away, Mark realized they'd been stopped outside Niamh's house. There was a police car parked in the driveway.

What's that all about?

He looked up at her window. Niamh's cat was sitting there looking out towards the Old Lighthouse but there was no sign of Niamh.

I wonder how she's getting on, he thought.

CHAPTER NINE

THE ESCAPE PLAN

Niamh was discovering that boredom was worse than fear.

She'd been trapped in the lighthouse for two days and she just wanted out. The dreadful occurrences in the basement felt distant now and it seemed unlikely the Man in the Hat would come back at this stage.

Besides, now she had a plan.

*

When she'd started up the spiral staircase from the ground floor she'd been terrified. It was difficult to see up the stairs because of the curvature, and the flashlight wasn't very powerful. She crept up the metal steps, her ears pricked for the slightest sound.

Soon she arrived at the next floor. The tower was deathly silent and she was jumpy as she shone the flashlight around the room. It was octagonal, matching the exterior shape of the tower, and was furnished as a comfortable living area. The narrow beam of her flashlight picked out expensive leather furniture, sumptuous cushions and antiques. There was a dark red patterned rug covering most of the varnished wooden floor. She'd often wondered what was inside the Old Lighthouse but had never dreamed it would be like this.

As she stepped up into the room hugging the wall, her shoulder snagged on a light-switch. She flicked it, expecting it not to work but to her surprise, the octagonal room was lit up by a chandelier hanging from the timber roof. She held her breath, waiting to see if the light roused anybody in the lighthouse. Still the tower was silent

She put the flashlight on a mahogany coffee table and looked around the room. There were tall windows that started at floor level in four of the eight walls. She knew this already from looking at the lighthouse for so many years but it was weird to be seeing them from the inside. In one of the windows facing the sea was a large telescope on a tripod. She went over and looked through it. Early dawn light was starting to creep into the sky over the horizon but it was still too dim to see any detail.

There wasn't much else of interest. What she really needed was a phone or cell and the living room offered neither. She decided to keep exploring, and the only way was up.

On the next floor she had an exciting find. At the top of the stairs was a fire-door that separated the upper and lower halves of the tower. Next to the fire-door was a bathroom and mounted on the wall of the bathroom was a small metal safe. The safe door was slightly ajar and when she opened it, she discovered several keys with plastic tags hanging in neat rows on hooks. One of the tags read: 'Front Security Gate'. Her heart leaped. She grabbed the key and scampered down the stairway.

Oh, please; oh, please; oh, please!

She reached the security gate and realized there was no keyhole on the inside; the gate could only be unlocked from the other side. With disappointment and fear gnawing at her, she studied the back of the lock. The area around the lock was solid metal and there was no way to tell where the keyhole was on the other side. An idea occurred to her and she ran back up to the bathroom. Near the sink she found what she was looking for and ran back down to the security gate. She pushed her arm out through the bars and held the newly discovered shaving mirror at arm's length. By now, a fair amount of dawn light had filtered into the sky and she could see the outside of the lock well enough. She spotted the keyhole and memorized its location. Swapping the mirror for the key she pushed her arm out through the bars again.

But she couldn't reach the keyhole.

There was so much solid metal around the lock that no matter what angle she tried from, her forearm just wasn't long enough to reach the keyhole. She had no idea how long she persevered but by the time she gave up, the sun was fully up and her arm was bruised and grazed from the bars and the edge of the lock. She put down the mirror, sat on the floor of the lighthouse and cried again. It just wasn't fair. Eventually she reasoned that, even in this remote place, someone would come along. She just hoped it wouldn't be The Man in the Hat. She also hoped it wouldn't be too long. People walked their dogs up here all the time, didn't they? In the meantime, she was stuck in the tower and all she could do was wait.

*

Now, a day and a half later, she knew every inch of the tower, and had established that she was indeed alone. She'd discovered bedrooms, storage closets, and on the top floor a fully stocked kitchen. She'd also found a better flashlight - one of those big yellow ones that shine for miles.

But there was no phone and so far, no-one had come along.

She'd tried various escape routes but found herself well and truly incarcerated. There were tall windows - taller than her - in some of the rooms but they were too high off the ground. Even if she had broken one, there were security bars on the outside.

The boredom was the worst thing. There was no TV and no computer. There were books in various rooms but she really didn't feel like reading. She spent a lot of time in the kitchen. The fridge was full of food and eating took her mind off things. The kitchen had tiny porthole windows and on one visit, as she wolfed through a packet of cooked ham, she noticed the sun glinting off a bright surface in the distance. It was the glass front of Mark's house. She tried to see her own house through one of the other portholes but it was in the wrong place. That got to her. Over the two days she'd cried a lot and despaired – particularly when she thought of the body in the cellar. She tried not to think of her parents and how worried they'd be. She tried particularly hard not to think about Mira and the possibility that she might never see her again, and that really upset her.

Late on the first day, she'd locked herself into the upper-half of the tower and felt safe enough to sleep. Stretched out on the bed in the master bedroom, her dreams were dark and gothic, and did their best to ruin her sleep but when she finally surfaced from them, to her surprise, she brought with her a fully-formed escape plan. The strange thing was, she'd dreamt that Mira had appeared in the room and whispered the plan in her ear.

Now she was sitting in the kitchen surrounded by her escape kit: She'd fetched the telescope from the first floor and set it up in the porthole window pointing towards Mark's house. She positioned the big flashlight on top of the microwave and pointed it out the same window. On the table beside her was a large serving tray. Now all she needed was nightfall and the good fortune that Mark would be in his room when darkness fell.

CHAPTER TEN

THE RESCUE

Mark was on his own again.

Ferdia and Kiva had left a few hours earlier, and his mum wasn't speaking to him. That didn't bother him too much, though - his mum's wobblers never lasted long. Also, he sensed that Bree was more upset by how Kiva had spoken to her in the car than she was with Mark lying to her. Still, he felt bad about deceiving her over the trip to Bray. He had tried to apologize but she just kept her face in the book she was reading and said "Not now, Mark. I'm not ready to talk to you yet. Just go to your room and stay there."

And he had.

Now, alone in his room, he had the opportunity to take stock of all that had happened over the previous few days. Between the comic-book page, the puzzle-boxes and the connection between his dad and Ferdia's granddad, it was all a bit much to take. *How did my life get this complicated?* he wondered. Little did he know how much more complicated it was about to get.

At that moment, the door of his bedroom opened and Bree stood there wearing an expression he'd never seen before. *Wow, she must be really pissed off; she usually knocks,* he thought. Before he had a chance to ask her what was wrong she said:

"The police are on their way up the avenue and they want to talk to you. What have you been up to?"

The color drained from Mark's face. The police? Why did they want to speak to him? He mentally flicked through all that had happened over the previous few days: Sure, it was weird but there was nothing that should involve the police, was there? Then a horrible thought occurred to him.

"You don't think it's about Dad, do you?"

Bree shook her head. He could tell she'd already considered this.

"If it was about your father they'd have asked for me."

She wagged her finger at him.

"If you've been up to something, you need to tell me right now."

Thoughts of telling Bree about the events of recent days made Mark's stomach churn. He had no idea where he would start or how she would react. And he still had no idea why the police were involved. Then he remembered seeing the police car at Niamh's house.

Oh man, I bet it's just something to do with the gym window. I was there when it happened. They just want a statement or something.

Now that he had a plausible explanation for the police calling he felt a lot better. Had he considered the time of night, he might have realized the police would never call that late over something so trivial but, in his anxious state of mind, his subconscious overlooked this.

"Mum, I've not been up to anything dodgy. If it's not about Dad, I don't know why the police are here."

"Hmm. Okay, wash your face and brush your hair and come down to the living room. I'll let them in."

*

People in uniform always look out of place inside a house - this was the first thing that struck Mark as he walked into the living room. Detective Fiona Kelly and Officer Pat Ryan were youngish and neither was tall or well built but their presence made the room seem smaller. Despite his own rationale about their visit, he started to feel nervous.

Bree invited them to sit down. She sat beside Mark and put her arm around him. The arm felt strange to Mark; not motherly and soft but stiff and awkward, like a metal bar draped around his shoulders.

"This is my son Mark. What's this all about?"

Detective Kelly smiled at Mark.

"Hi Mark, we're investigating a report of a missing girl – Niamh Kinnear. Do you know her?"

A rushing sound filled Mark's ears and his head grew light. He felt Bree's arm relax and she pulled him protectively towards her. Her other hand went to her mouth. Mark's head spun. *Niamh? Missing?* Detective Kelly pressed him:

"Mark? Niamh Kinnear; do you know her?"

He nodded. "She's a friend from school."

"Did she call you two nights ago?"

He nodded again. Detective Kelly looked at her companion. His face was unreadable.

"What did you talk about?"

"Well, we didn't get a chance to talk. My battery died before I could answer and I then I fell asleep."

"Did she leave a message?"

Mark's mind raced. He didn't want to hand over the mystery he was involved in to the adults but the police were here and Niamh seemed to be missing. It was time to fess up.

He opened his mouth with every intention of telling them about Niamh's message about the lighthouse but what came out was:

"No. She didn't leave any message."

He startled himself. It was almost as if one half of his brain was misleading the other. He had no idea on a conscious level why he had lied to the police and his mother but now the lie was out there.

"Are you sure?" asked Detective Kelly. "You're not covering for her, are you?"

Mark shook his head. Detective Kelly peered at him with an expression only teachers and police officers can muster.

"You see Mark, in the majority of these cases, particularly with young women, the alleged victim has actually run away. Has she run away, Mark? Did she tell you where she was going?"

"No; look, I told you, I didn't speak to her and she didn't leave a message. She texted me to see if I was awake and I texted her back, then the phone rang and my battery died. That's it"

"Does she often call you at that hour of the night?"

"Well, no - I guess that is pretty weird."

"And did you try to call her back?"

"Uh, yeah I did, but not 'til the next day. Her phone rang out and went to voicemail."

"What time would that have been?"

"Um, after lunch sometime – half-two, or something."

The two police officers looked at each other for a moment. Officer Ryan stood up and took something out of his pocket. It was a sealed plastic evidence bag. In it was a small pink cellphone with a Japanese cartoon cat on it.

"We found this in the gutter of the Kinnears' house," he said. "It seems she dropped it when she climbed out the skylight. Now that you know we have her phone, do you want to change your story, at all?"

Mark shook his head.

"OK, fair enough. I had to check; you're the last person she spoke to before she disappeared. Well, your story tallies with the call and text logs on Miss Kinnear's phone," said Officer Ryan, "so I suppose that'll be all for now. If you think of anything else, or if you hear from her, give Wicklow police station a call and report it. Will you do that?"

Mark nodded. His voice came out dry and raspy:

"Yes. Yes I will."

"Good lad. OK, sorry to have bothered you so late, Mrs McMurnagh. We'll leave you to it."

Bree saw the police officers out and came back upstairs. She walked straight over to Mark and threw her arms around him.

"I'm so sorry I suspected you. It's just you hear of so many teenagers getting into trouble. My imagination got the better of me."

Normally Mark hated lying and now the lies were mounting. He hugged her back for a moment then pulled away. He felt wretched and couldn't look her in the eye.

"Ah Mum, it's all right. I did lie to you about where Ferd and I were going, so I suppose I deserved it."

He stared at the floor as he said this. Bree took this to mean he was annoyed with her or disappointed that she'd suspected him of something. She burst into tears.

"Mark, I'm so, so sorry. I should have known you'd never do anything to get into trouble with the police. And poor Niamh; I hope she's all right - and her poor parents."

Mark wanted to be sick. He'd never felt as low or as shameful in his life. Oh God, this was terrible. He could hardly bear it. He forced himself to look her in the eye and dredged up a watery smile.

"It's OK, Mum. I'm sure Niamh will be all right. Knowing her, she just threw a strop and went off to stay with a friend. And I'm really sorry about the Bray thing. I lied to you and I'd never do that normally so I'm not surprised you thought I was in trouble when the police arrived. Mum, I'm really, really sorry."

Bree hugged him tightly then held him by both shoulders at arm's length. She looked him up and down for a moment then kissed him on the cheek.

"You're growing up to be just like your dad – the good bits of your dad, I mean." She smiled tightly at this then gestured towards the kitchen with a tilt of her head. "Go and make us both some hot chocolate. I'm going to call Martha and Kenny and see if I can do anything to help."

Mark made the drinks then went up to his room. He sat on the edge of his bed with the steaming drink cupped in his hands. He was exhausted and felt like a lying rat. Jesus, the look on his mother's face after the police left, and the way she kept apologizing to him…

He put the hot chocolate on his bedside locker – he couldn't stomach it. Things were getting out of control and he had some serious decisions to make. He couldn't keep lying to everyone - well, he *could but* he didn't feel good about it. Still, he had to get to the bottom of the mystery that was unfolding around him. On an instinctive level, he knew that if he told his mum about it, other adults – maybe even the police - would get involved and he would be side-lined. And that wasn't how it was supposed to play out; his gut told him that too.

And then there was Niamh. What had happened to her? He didn't believe she'd run away to stay with a friend – it wasn't her style. He tried to remember her message – the message he'd lied so blatantly about. She'd said there was something going on at the lighthouse and she wanted to sneak out and take a look. What if she'd gone up there and something had happened to her? Should he go up there and check? He shied away from the thought – it terrified him. It was creepy enough up there during the day; at night … ughh! He shuddered. The hair on the back of his neck stood up just thinking about it. Then a far worse thought surfaced: Niamh could be injured or trapped up there on her own. His stomach lurched. Why did he torture himself with these thoughts? Oh God; what to do? He should probably wait until morning but the thoughts of Niamh in danger were too much to bear. There was no avoiding it, he had to check it out. He'd wait until his mum went to bed then head up there and take a look. With the decision made, a strange sense of inevitability came over him; as if he'd always known he'd have to do it.

He knew his mum wouldn't go to bed for a while so he kicked off his trainers and lay down. He set his alarm for 1am in case he fell asleep, then switched off his bedside lamp and waited.

*

Niamh hunched over the telescope. She could see Mark sitting on the edge of his bed. She whispered a mantra to herself:

"Turn off the light; turn off the light; turn off the light."

After a moment he leaned back and disappeared from sight. A moment after that his light went out.

Yes!

Niamh switched on the big yellow flashlight and pointed it towards Mark's room.

*

Mark lay in the dark staring at the ceiling. There was no chance of falling asleep – he was terrified.

A sudden light from outside illuminated the opposite wall of his bedroom. It moved around, then went off and on and moved around some more. This repeated a few more times and then the light settled and stayed on.

What the hell was that?

He stood up and looked out his window. A light was shining from the top of the old lighthouse right into his room. *What the…?*

The light started to flash. The flashing continued for quite some time then stopped. After a moment it started again. He realized there was a pattern to the flashes. It was Morse code!

… AMH – SOS – NIAMH – SOS – NIAMH - SOS

Niamh! She *was* in the old lighthouse!

He reached for his LED flashlight and signaled in response:

NIAMH – YOU – OK?

There was a pause from the lighthouse then:

YES – BUT – TRAPPED – 2 – DAYS. GET – ME – OUT. HAVE – KEY – BUT – CANT – REACH – LOCK.

Mark thought for a moment then signaled:

ANYONE – ELSE – THERE?

NO. HURRY – PLEASE.

ON – MY – WAY.

*

Ten minutes later Mark was cycling down the avenue of Almha in bright moonlight. In his rucksack he had a flashlight and a sharp knife he'd taken from the kitchen. He had no idea what he might do with the knife but the thoughts of going up to Wicklow Head unarmed in the dead of night didn't appeal to him. In fact, the idea of going up at all was scaring the heck out of him but Niamh was in trouble and that overrode all other concerns.

When he got to the end of the avenue, he dropped his bike over the wall then clambered over and lowered himself down to the road. Opening the gates would have set off an alarm in the house and he didn't want to annoy his mother any further. She'd really blow a gasket if she knew he was sneaking around at night.

Back on his bike, he turned towards Wicklow and pedaled hard. To reach the Old Lighthouse he had to ride three kilometers to the entrance, then another two kilometers over the hilly, pitted surface of the access road. It was going to take quite some time and he didn't want Niamh to be trapped any longer than necessary. With his moon-shadow stretching out in front of him, he pumped the pedals, not even noticing the long uphill stretches. Soon he barreled around a sharp corner and onto the straight that would take him past Niamh's house. The moonlight picked out something in the road ahead. At first he thought it was a paper bag, then a rabbit, then he realized:

It's a cat! Move out of the way, cat!

The cat was sitting in the middle of the road looking at him. It made no attempt to move.

Stupid death-wish cat!

Without slowing, he moved to the other side of the road. As he did, the cat ran in front of him. He gasped and swerved, his hands clenching the brake levers. The bike went out of control and shimmied left and right then careened into a field entrance that was barred by a gate. The front wheel caught in a tire track and Mark flew off the bike into the overgrown hedge lining the road. The hedge was deep and it cushioned his landing but was full of brambles. As he came to a stop, his hands and face scratched by the thorns, the bike flipped over and landed against the gate.

He lay in the hedge groaning for a few moments then began the slow process of freeing himself from the brambles. Once back on his feet he went to examine the bike for damage. It seemed OK and he was just about to remount when he heard a loud *meow* from the other side of the gate. The cat was in the field, eyeing him intently.

"You dumb cat, you're lucky I wasn't a car. You're lucky I don't wring your neck too – you nearly killed me!"

The cat just stared with ice-blue eyes.

"Hey, I recognize you – you're Niamh's cat. Are you out looking for her too?"

As if to answer his question, Mira meowed loudly, ran a short distance into the field then stopped. She looked back at him then meowed again.

"Stupid animal! I don't have time to play, I have to go. Ah, these scratches sting. Oww! Stupid cat."

He picked up the bike and stepped astride it. He was about to continue on his way when Mira ran back towards the entrance, climbed up the bars of the gate, until she was level with his face and meowed several times. She then jumped back down, ran a good distance into the field and stopped. He shook his head in amazement then realized she was running directly towards the Old Lighthouse.

"Is that what you're trying to tell me – it's shorter this way?"

Mira put her tail up and ran back towards the gate. She meowed once more then walked around in circles purring loudly.

"I don't believe this. I'm getting directions from a cat."

It does look shorter though. I guess I'll follow her. Jeez, I must be going mental.

Mark lifted the bike over the gate and hid it in the hedge. Mira purred around his feet and rubbed her face on his jeans then took off across the field like a greyhound. Shaking his head, Mark adjusted his rucksack then ran after her.

*

Niamh had no idea how long she'd been waiting on the bottom step of the lighthouse stairs but she was starting to get uneasy.

Is he coming? How long does it take to get from his house to here? Oh, why isn't he here yet?

The questions weighed on her mind but evaporated when Mira suddenly ran through the bars of the gate and up onto her lap.

"Oh my God! Oh Mira, it's so good to see you! I was so afraid you were dead."

She picked up the cat and cuddled her against her neck. Mira struggled to escape but Niamh held her tight, tears streaming down her cheeks. The cat gave up the struggle and relaxed into Niamh's shoulder, purring.

"Oh puss, I've been so scared. I hope Mark gets here soon."

"I already am."

Mark stood outside the gate grinning. Niamh gasped and jumped up, letting Mira drop to the floor. The cat ran back through the gate and into the night. Niamh put her arms out through the gate and pulled Mark to her. His head banged against the bars.

"Whoa! Ouch! Hey, easy there – I've only got one head!"

"Oh Mark; I'm so glad … I'm, I'm …"

But the tears had come again and she couldn't talk through them.

"Hey, hey – it's OK. I can get you out now. Where's the key?"

She sniffled and pulled the key from her pocket. Mark took it and found the keyhole. For a moment, Niamh was terrified the key wouldn't work but it slipped into the lock and turned easily.

Mark swung the gate open and Niamh was free.

She ran out of the lighthouse and threw her arms around him again. She hugged him tightly and held him for what seemed to Mark like several minutes.

"Thank you. Thank you so, so much for coming to get me. You're a hero."

She kissed his cheek then kissed it again. After a moment she slid her check across his and kissed him softly on the lips.

I think I love you, she thought. She knew what Martha would say: *Don't be so stupid; you're only a kid.* A tear ran down her cheek. Mark held the kiss for a moment then pulled away. It wasn't that he didn't like it – he did; it made his head spin and he thought his heart was going to leap out of his chest but he'd never really thought of Niamh in that way and he felt strangely out of his depth. Unfamiliar feelings welled up inside him and he didn't know quite how to deal with them.

"Um, how… how did you get locked in there?" asked Mark.

Niamh told him the story from where she saw the bright lights from her room, right up to where she signaled to him with the flashlight."

"Wow!" said Mark with some admiration. "Fair play to you with the Morse code trick. I'm not sure I'd have come up with that."

"Of course you would! You're a genius – just like me!"

"I guess. You know I was coming up here tonight to look for you anyway?"

"No way!"

"Yeah, I was waiting for my mum to go to bed when I saw your signal."

"Well, if you'd figured it out, why did you leave me in there so long, you git?"

"I only found out you were missing tonight when the police told us! I lied to them about you leaving me a message and then figured you must have come up here and gotten into trouble. Well, I was right, wasn't I?"

She laughed and kissed him again. Mark was still uneasy with the closeness and he was eager to leave.

"Right, this place gives me the creeps; let's get the heck out of here," he said.

Niamh grabbed his arm.

"No, before we go there's something you need to see."

"What? You're nuts! You've been stuck in there for days and now you want to hang around?"

"Seriously, Mark; there's something in the cellar you really need to see."

"What is it?"

"I'm not telling you. If I did, you wouldn't go down there but you really, really need to see it."

If she told him, he wouldn't want to go? This didn't sound like a good idea to Mark, at all. Niamh handed him the big yellow flashlight and lifted the cellar trapdoor. She gestured at the steps and fixed him with her eyes. *Oh, what the heck.* Mark shrugged and started down the steps. Then Niamh remembered the dodgy second step and started to say: "Don't stand on the second step ..." when there was an almighty cracking sound, a shout of surprise from Mark, then the sounds of him tumbling down the steps and landing on the cellar floor.

"Mark!" she shrieked, and tore down the steps forgetting her fear. Mark was already on his feet and brushing himself down when she got to him.

"Are you OK?"

"Yeah – just grazed my elbow and shin a bit."

"Ooh; does it hurt?"

"Nah, it's grand. Look, let's just get out of here, OK?"

He started back up the steps but Niamh said "No!" and grabbed his arm. She looked around for the flashlight and saw it lying near the cellar wall, still on. Pulling Mark after her, she picked it up and shone the beam under the steps.

Her breath caught in her chest and her nails sank into Mark's arm.

"Owwwwww! Niamh! What...?"

"He's gone."

"What? Who's gone?"

"The... the Kung-Fu Priest! He was here. I saw him. I spoke to him then he died."

"*What?*"

Niamh was crying now, her voice rising.

"The Kung-Fu Priest. The first night I was here, he was trapped in here same as me, then he died and now he's gone!"

"The Kung-Fu Priest?" You mean that priest I told you about with the ponytail?"

She sniffled and nodded.

"He was here? And he *died*? Are you sure? I mean, you had a bad fright when that guy in the hat locked you in here, and you told me you had really bad dreams. You could have ..."

"I didn't bloody dream it, Mark," she shouted. "I saw the priest in here and he bloody-well spoke to me. "

"Well, he's not here now. Are you *sure* he died? Maybe he was only unconscious and he woke up."

Niamh looked around uneasily and shone the flashlight around the cellar. There was no-one else there. She aimed it back under the stairs again as if to double-check the body really wasn't there. Mark noticed something glinting in the dirt of the cellar floor. He walked forward and picked it up. It was a large gold earring.

"He was wearing that!" exclaimed Niamh. "I *knew* I hadn't dreamt it."

Mark was nodding. "Yeah, when I saw him last year he was wearing this – or something very like it. But where is he now? He must've woken up and let himself out."

Niamh said nothing. She knew what she'd seen but she couldn't explain why the body was no longer there. At least they'd found the earring so Mark knew she wasn't making it up. Mark was still studying the earring. Almost absentmindedly, he asked:

"What did he say to you – before he died ... or whatever?"

"He flipping did die!"

"OK, OK; he died. What did he say before he died?"

"He was kind of rambling but he kept saying something about a guild, and everyone except a builder being killed, and something about pieces of a key, and a third something and a ninth something else, and a church."

"Well, that makes no sense at all. Can you remember any more?"

"No. It was hard to hear him, and with the shock of him dying right in front of me, it went out of my head."

"Well, I guess that's no surprise. Maybe it'll come back to you later. Anyway, he's not here now so let's get out of here."

Mark ushered Niamh up the cellar steps. Just as they were about to go out the lighthouse door, they heard the noise of a vehicle coming up the access road and saw the twin beams of the headlights. Niamh drew a breath and gripped Mark's arm. Mark grabbed her hand and started to lead her out the door.

"C'mon, we can hide in those bushes and leg it out the gate when they go inside."

But Niamh was paralyzed with fear and by the time Mark got through to her, the vehicle – a BMW SUV – was coming through the gate. Gritting his teeth, he measured the distance to the bushes versus the speed of the approaching vehicle. They'd never make it.

There was nothing for it: Mark pulled the outside gate shut and closed the inner door. He bolted the cellar trapdoor and lead Niamh up the spiral steps to the next floor. He positioned himself on the steps so that he could just see the ground floor.

Then they waited.

After several agonizing minutes, he heard two men approaching. Their voices were indistinct but became clearer as they neared the lighthouse. A key rattled in the metal security gate then the hinges creaked as it swung open. One of the men said:

"Hey, this gate was open."

"What! Mac said he'd locked it. Damn it! They better still be here. Give me those keys."

A key slid into the lock on the inner door then that too opened. Mark saw a flashlight play around the floor of the lighthouse and the men entered. From his vantage point, he could only see their legs. One of the men came to the bottom of the steps then stopped.

"Look, the trapdoor's still bolted. They're still in there. I'll grab the girl; you get the priest. No messing; Mac wants this done clean."

As he stepped towards the trapdoor, the man stepped on the shaving mirror Niamh had left of the floor. It crunched and shattered under his feet."

"What the hell … Who left that there?"

"That's seven years' bad luck, Mate," said the other man.

"Yeah, right. Get that trapdoor open and let's get this sorted."

The men's feet disappeared as they moved towards the trapdoor. The bolt slid back with a loud thud and the trapdoor banged against the wall.

The first man shouted out:

"OK girly, we're going to let you out. No funny stuff."

The first step creaked, and then the man cried out as his foot flailed in mid-air trying to find a step that wasn't there. There was a loud thud then a sickening crack as the man landed hard on the bottom of the cellar. He screamed in agony:

"My leg! Ahh, Jesus!"

The other man shouted "Jim!" then jumped down after his companion. In that instant Mark knew what he had to do. He scampered down the steps and slammed the trapdoor. A shout of surprise came from the cellar and Mark threw his weight on the trapdoor just as the man started to push on it from below. Lying on the trapdoor, he managed to get it bolted as the man heaved against it. The man hammered on the trapdoor.

"Let us out! I'll kill you," he bellowed.

There were several more thumps against the trapdoor then a muffled crack as another step gave way. Mark didn't wait to see what happened next. He ran back up the steps, grabbed Niamh's hand and led her down and out the lighthouse door. He closed the inner door, slammed the security gate shut, locked it and snapped off the key in the lock. He threw the head of the key into the undergrowth.

"That'll hold them until we can call the police. We'd better call them soon too – I think that first guy broke his leg when he fell."

"Good enough for him," said Niamh in a very shaky voice. "See how he likes it down there."

"OK, let's go Dot. Your parents are frantic. Time to face the music."

Niamh looked up at him, her face pale and teary-eyed.

"What are we going to tell them?"

"Exactly what happened. Tell them you went up on your roof to see what was going on at the lighthouse. Tell them Mira got out and you had to go after her. Tell them everything. Just leave out the bit about the Kung-Fu Priest dying and disappearing. They'll never believe you."

"You believe me though, don't you?"

"Yeah, I do. With what's been going on in my life recently, I'd believe anything."

"Why, what's been going on in your life?"

And as Mark led Niamh back across the fields, Mira watching from the shadows, he told her everything.

CHAPTER ELEVEN

CONSEQUENCES

"Ok Niamh, let me get this straight," said Detective Fiona Kelly consulting her notebook, "you snuck out of your room because you saw some strange lights up at the old lighthouse. Then, somehow, your cat got out of a locked house. You chased her, and she led you right to where these lights were coming from. There, you were captured by a mysterious man in a hat who locked you in the cellar of the lighthouse. You managed to escape from the cellar but couldn't escape from the lighthouse itself, despite having found a key for the door. After two days of imprisonment, you managed to signal Mark McHewell with a flashlight and he came up to rescue you. Is that correct, so far?"

Niamh looked around the living room of her parent's house. Crammed into the small room, were Detective Kelly and Officer Ryan, Niamh's parents, and Mark and Bree. Her heart quailed as she looked at the skeptical adults. Martha, in particular, wore an expression of disbelief and disdain. Even to Niamh's own ears, hearing her experiences recounted in this fashion made them seem outlandish, and she could understand why the adults found it all so hard to believe. She glanced at Mark who caught her look and smiled at her, giving a little nod of his head as if to say *Go on, you're doing great.*

She looked back at Detective Kelly and said "Yes. That's right."

Detective Kelly made a noise that may have been a snort and shook her head slightly. She flipped a page in her notebook, read for a moment, and with an expression that spoke volumes about wasting police time, turned to Mark.

"Now Mark, according to you; after you received this ... signal from Niamh, you cycled to the lighthouse and released her using the key she'd found. Before you could leave, two men arrived in a car and you both hid in an upstairs floor of the lighthouse. When the men entered, they broke a mirror then one of them fell into the cellar and broke his leg. The other man followed him down and you locked them in there. Is that correct?"

For obvious reasons, Mark hadn't told them about Mira intercepting him on his way to the access road and leading him across the fields.

"Yes. I bolted the trapdoor, locked the security gate and snapped off the key in the lock so that they couldn't escape, and no-one could let them out until we could call you."

"Hmm. Then you brought Niamh back here, woke Mr and Mrs Kinnear and went home."

"Yes."

"What did you do then?"

"I woke my mum and told her what had happened. I was worried about the guy in the basement with the broken leg, and I wanted her to call the police station right away."

Detective Kelly looked at Bree.

"Which you did?"

Bree nodded. Detective Kelly regarded Bree for a moment.

"And you believe this story, Mrs. McHewell?"

Bree looked offended.

"Well, I've always brought my son up to…"

Mark had had enough. He stood up and shouted at Detective Kelly.

"Look, I don't know why you don't want to believe us but all you have to do is go up and check the flipping basement. There are two guys trapped in there and their car is parked right outside."

He stood there, red in the face with tears in his eyes, and his bottom lip quivering.

Detective Kelly stared at him coolly.

"Sit down and stop shouting, Mark. There's been a patrol car up there for the past hour. We spoke to them just before we came in. And they told us some interesting things."

She counted off on her fingers:

"There is no BMW SUV parked outside, there are no men in the cellar, there is no key broken off in the lock and here is no broken mirror on the floor. The man who lives in the lighthouse, Mr …" She consulted her notes. "… Rogan – a retired barrister - says he's been there for the past week and has seen nothing strange. How do you explain that, Mark?"

Mark looked at Niamh, his eyes like saucers. Niamh looked just as shocked. He looked at his mum, then at Niamh's parents and finally back to Detective Kelly. Bree and the Kinnears looked confused and angry. The detective looked furious.

Mark felt trapped. The adults were looking at him, waiting for an answer. He stammered, not knowing what to say; then his sense of justice came to his rescue. An indignant anger rose in him. Sure, he and Niamh had broken a few rules but Niamh was the real victim in all this, and she was being doubted and treated like a criminal. Both he and Niamh knew what had really happened and he wasn't going to let whoever was behind it get away with it. He tried to keep his composure but his voice was angry and shaky:

"Well. the old guy who lives there is lying. He must be mixed up in whatever's going on. The man that locked Niamh in the basement must have come back after we left and got the men out, then cleaned up, then … then changed the lock on the gate, and taken the car away. It's the only explanation."

"It is NOT the only explanation, Mark," shouted Detective Kelly. "Do you really expect us to believe that a retired barrister – a *barrister*, Mark – would lie to the police about something like this? And that someone would be able to erase all trace of themselves and change locks in" – she looked at her watch – "five hours? When are you going to start telling the truth, Mark?"

"That *is* the truth, I swear!"

Detective Kelly made an exasperated sound, raised her hands and slapped them down on her knees.

"Ok Mark, have it your way. But no-one in this room believes you. We *know* what really happened: Niamh ran away to give her parents a fright because she was angry about being grounded. She got you to hide her in your house. You probably put her up to it, God knows! After a couple of days, you both got scared of the consequences and concocted this fantasy about kidnappers."

Mark exploded.

"That's bullshit!" he screamed at Detective Kelly. "If you were doing your job right, you'd find evidence we were up there and that Niamh was kidnapped. You're just ignoring us 'cause we're kids."

"Mark!" shouted Bree, her palm on her chest in disbelief. "You will not speak to the officer like that!"

Detective Kelly stood up and gestured to Officer Ryan to follow her.

"We're done here. You're lucky I don't do all of you for wasting our time."

Mark was still shouting.

"You're a disgrace. I'm going to take proof to the station and you'll be in serious trouble for not doing your job."

Bree ran around the sofa and grabbed his arm but he shook her off.

"It's just like my dad. You never really looked for him. You just thought he ran off with another woman, or something and didn't bother your arses. I mean, he was in his car! How many red Porsche 911 GT3s are there in Ireland? Don't tell me you couldn't find that! You're crap!"

Detective Kelly looked at Bree with a threatening expression, and Bree grabbed Mark's arm again to calm him down. She didn't have to try hard: He was spent. He sank into an armchair and bawled.

He was only barely aware of his mum and the Kinnears walking out of the room with the police officers, apologizing profusely, and Detective Kelly advising them to get control of their children. Niamh came over and put her arm around him.

"Forget it, Mark," she said. "They'll never believe us."

"They bloody *will* believe us," he said through his sobs. "I'll make sure they do. I'm going back up there and I'm going to find proof. I'll talk to the old git they were going on about and find out why he's lying."

"Please, Mark. Please don't. Let's just forget all about it."

"No way, Dot. I've had enough of being ignored. I've had enough of being treated like crap."

Niamh started to respond but the front door slammed, and the three adults came back into the room with faces like thunder.

*

Twenty minutes later, Niamh was confined to her room again and Mark was in the passenger seat of Bree's SUV as they headed home. Mark tried to plead his case but Bree was tight-lipped.

"Mum, I wasn't lying. I swear to God, everything we told you was true."

Silence.

"Mum, I've never lied to you."

Bree's eyebrows went up and she impaled him with a stare.

"Ok, Ok, I lied to you about the trip to Bray but I'm not lying about this."

She held the stare for a long uncomfortable moment then turned back to the road.

"Mum, please!"

Silence.

"Oh God! This is so unfair."

Silence.

"I'm going back up there tonight."

That worked. Bree's head whipped round.

"No you bloody are not! You'll be lucky to get out of the house for the rest of the summer. I can't believe you lied to me about Niamh. And did you really hide her in my house?"

"No! Aughhhhhhhhh! How many times do I have to tell you; she was trapped in the lighthouse. It's true!"

Bree stared at the road for long moments. Mark thought he could see the glisten of tears in the corner of her eye. She shook her head and rubbed her eye with the back of her hand.

"I don't know what's going on with you Mark, I really don't but it scares me. I'm taking you back to the psychologist as soon as I can get an appointment."

"Mum, you don't need to do that."

"Oh, I do. I can't cope with this. I need someone to help me figure it out."

"There's nothing to figure out. I'm telling the truth!"

Bree thought for a moment, a muscle ticking in her jaw.

"Did all this really happen, or did you imagine it all; or are you lying to my face again?"

"It really happened."

"I wish I could believe that, Mark."

Mark stared out the window at the passing countryside. They were nearly home. Suddenly he turned to Bree:

"What if I could prove it to you?"

"Prove what to me?"

"What if I could prove I was telling the truth about one little bit of the story? Would you believe the rest of it?"

Bree pulled into the entrance to *Almha* and stopped at the gates. She turned in her seat and looked at Mark.

"I want to believe, more than *anything*, that you're telling the truth. But it's outlandish, Mark! Spooky lights, kidnappers, Morse code signals."

"I know, Mum. But that's the point. If we were going to make up a story, we'd have come up with something better."

"Well, I suppose …"

"Mum, please take me up to the lighthouse. I think I can find something that'll prove I'm not lying."

"Absolutely not, Mark. I don't know what your fascination with that place is but we're not going up there and that's final."

"Well I'll go up myself later."

"Mark, you're grounded, and if you leave the house without my permission anytime during the next week, you'll be grounded for the whole summer."

"Well, I've got nothing to lose then, do I? I'm doing this whether you like it or not, Mum."

"Mark! You will do as you're told!"

"I'm sorry, Mum. I love you. but you're being totally unfair to me so I don't think I have to obey you anymore."

Bree was speechless.

"Look, we can sort this out straight away," said Mark. "Just take me up to the lighthouse and I can prove to you we were there."

Bree clicked her tongue and spun the SUV around in the entrance. She pointed the car back the way they'd come then stopped and put on the parking brake. Again, she turned to Mark."

"If this is a trick, or if you're lying to me again, there will be hell to pay, Mister."

"It's not a trick, Mum; you'll see."

"Ok, then. Let's go."

They drove back towards Wicklow and turned onto the lighthouse access road. On the way up the narrow road, they had to pull in to let an oncoming police patrol car get past. Minutes later, Bree pulled the Volvo up to the door of the lighthouse and Mark jumped out. He ran over to a patch of deep grass and rummaged through it. He found what he was looking for and ran back to the car. As he jumped in, Bree asked:

"What have you got there?"

Mark grinned and held out his hand. Sitting on his palm was the top of a broken key. Attached to the key was a tag that read 'Front Security Gate.'

"This is the key I broke off in the lock."

Bree's hand flew to her mouth.

"Oh, my God! Oh, my *GOD*! Oh, Mark, I am so sorry."

CHAPTER TWELVE

MIRA

Niamh was dreaming. Lying on her side, facing the wall, she whimpered as the death of the priest haunted her again. In her dreams, he suffered a variety of deaths, each more hideous than the last. She tried to call out, to bring an end to the phantasm but could not.

The door of her bedroom brushed open and Mira slipped inside. She stood near the bed watching Niamh's travails for a few moments then jumped up onto the covers. She wormed her way into the narrow gap between Niamh and the wall and rubbed her whiskers against Niamh's face. Niamh wrinkled her nose and rolled onto her back. Her eyes fluttered for a moment but she stayed asleep. Mira climbed onto Niamh's chest and padded forward until her nose was level with Niamh's chin. There she lay down like a sphinx, and stretched her paws out until they were on either side of Niamh's jaw-line. The cat then pressed her nose into Niamh's throat and closed her eyes. She started a strange rhythmic purring, almost like a mantra, flexing her front paws very slightly to the cadence of the chant. To anyone looking on, it would have seemed as if the cat was meditating.

It had an immediate and profound effect on Niamh: The muscles in her jaw relaxed and her breathing slowed. The monstrous visions strobing through her head slowed until she was left with a single image; the priest just before he died. He opened his mouth to speak.

In that instant Niamh gasped and sat bolt upright, knocking the cat to the floor. The priest's words were ringing in her head as clearly as the night she'd heard them. She flicked on the lamp beside her bed and grabbed the poetry notepad she kept on her bedside locker. Freeing the pencil from the loops of the notepad, she started writing.

After several minutes of frantic scribbling, she put down the pencil and read back over the page. Her brow furrowed. She'd remembered what the priest had said but it still made no sense. She read it again, wondering at the strange mix of English, Irish and German. She'd only been studying German for a year, and didn't even know some of the words she'd written. How was that even possible?

She shivered.

A sudden yawn coursed through her, catching her by surprise, and she realized how little rest she'd gotten from her disturbed sleep. She put the notepad back on her locker and flicked out the light.

I'll show it to Mark tomorrow and see if he can make head or tail of it.

She yawned again, rolled over on her side and soon fell asleep. This time her sleep was deep and undisturbed. A slight smile flickered at the edge of her lips as she slept.

From beneath the bed, Mira listened as Niamh's breathing slowed. Once it settled into a steady rhythm, she jumped back onto the bed near Niamh's face. She watched Niamh sleep for a moment then closed her eyes and rubbed her nose on the girl's temple.

She didn't lie down; she didn't purr. She couldn't. She was too upset by what she had to do.

Since the night she and Niamh had seen the lights around the Old Lighthouse, Mira's life had changed. Her life as a domestic cat was over. The activity at the lighthouse signaled the beginning of a terrible chain of events; a day that Mira and generations of felkynd before her had hoped would never come.

But come it had.

Mira jumped down from the bed and padded towards the window. Lights were on in the Old Lighthouse and Mira stared at them for a few moments. Hating the thoughts of leaving, and fearing the hardships ahead, she looked over her shoulder at the sleeping girl. A human-like look of sadness flickered in her eyes.

I'm so sorry, thought the cat. *You have been good to me and you deserve better than to be abandoned in the middle of the night. But I have to do this; there's too much at stake.*

Mira slipped back out through the door and down the stairs. She padded down the hall, through the kitchen and into the utility room where one of the window locks was loose. After a few moments of worrying the lock with her paw and teeth the window was open and Mira was out. She padded around to the front of the house and down the driveway to the road. She looked up at Niamh's bedroom window.

This is going to be hard but one day you will understand. I'll miss you, Niamh Goldenhair.

With a last look over her shoulder, the little cat headed down the moonlit road and disappeared around the bend.

*

Mr. McElhinney was too old for this nonsense. He'd had a tiring day with visiting grandchildren and he just wanted his bed but his cats weren't cooperating. He had called them several times to no avail. Even the old trick of banging their food dishes together had failed to effect an appearance and he was starting to worry.

He stepped down from the porch and down the front lawn towards the road, his slippers scuffing in the short grass.

"Hugo? Jessie?" he called as he looked around the garden. He was about to head back to the front door when he caught a movement out of the corner of his eye. Something was moving along the hedge bordering the field next to his property.

"Puss? Pssh pssh pssh! Is that you, puss?"

He saw the movement again and the creature at the foot of the hedge turned its head towards him. Two pure white marbles of light reflected the porch light and the animal's fur glinted in the moonlight. It was a cat.

"Well, hello Puss! You're a pretty one but you're not one of mine. Have you seen my Hugo or Jessie anywhere?"

The cat turned away and burrowed through the hedge into the adjacent field. Mr. McElhinney walked over to where he'd seen the animal disappear and looked over the hedge.

His jaw dropped.

In the field were numerous cats arranged in three overlapping circles.

"Hugo! Jessie!"

His own cats turned towards him and held his gaze for a moment then turned away. On some cue imperceptible to Mr. McElhinney's senses, the cats began to walk in perfect unison along the path of the interlinking circles, moving from one circle to the next in a complex interweaving pattern, rubbing noses as they met at the intersections. A rhythmic resonance filled the air as the cats began purring.

The air around the cats started to shimmer.

Mr. McElhinney gasped and took a step back. His own breathing rasped in his ears but the low susurrate cadence of the cats' purring was growing in intensity and burrowing into his head. The shimmering around the cats intensified and they started to snap in and out of focus. Mr. McElhinney gripped his head in both hands. *This isn't happening. I'm having hallucinations; a stroke, or a heart attack* ...

The purring continued to increase in volume and frequency until his eyeballs started to itch in their sockets. Just when he thought his head would explode, the shimmering knotted bubble that enveloped the interlinked circles folded in on itself taking the cats with it.

The sudden silence hit Mr. McElhinney like a hammer blow and he collapsed unconscious on the lawn.

CHAPTER THIRTEEN

KEHER KUHN-RIDH

Sam Renstrom woke up. He was lying face down in the dirt but, beyond that, he had no idea where he was. He felt battered and bruised, and his head hurt like hell. For a moment, he thought he'd drunk too much and passed out somewhere; then he remembered the Boojum. Afraid to lift his head, he looked from side-to-side, his beard rubbing the ground.

Patchy grass and heather surrounded the bare patch of dirt he lay in. The ground was dry and pitted with stones but the air smelt moist and earthy. Another smell pervaded the air. Sam knew it well: It was the smell of crude oil.

Seeing no obvious danger, he struggled to his feet, wincing at the pain in his ribs. He put his hand to his side and gasped as a sharp pain shot through him. Ay! A few of those suckers are cracked, he thought. He dusted himself down as best he could and looked at his surroundings.

We're not in Alaska anymore, Toto, he thought.

He was standing on the top of a small mountain, at the mainland end of a long peninsula. The peninsula stretched many kilometers out to sea, the mountain range zigzagging along its spine. On each side of the mountain, the steep rocky escarpments gave way to broad green plains. Beyond the plains lay white beaches and the sea. In the distance, on both sides, other peninsulas jutted out to sea.

Wherever I am, I'm on a real jagged coastline, he thought.

The breeze blew, ruffling Sam's beard, and the smell of crude oil got stronger. He turned around and jumped in shock.

"Jesus!" he shouted. There was a huge shape with many arms towering over him. He staggered back a few steps and fell on his backside. He was in such shock it took him several seconds to realize the monster was a huge metal riser, many meters in diameter and at least three times his height. The 'arms' were myriad pipes, protruding at right angles and at various heights from its surface.

Sam, you fool; it's only a riser!

With great relief, he stood up and walked around the construct. Stopcocks adorned the pipes where they joined the riser. Then Sam noticed the other ends of the horizontal pipes: They all disappeared into holes in the air. It was really hard to look at. His eyes almost refused to process it.

The holes were disturbingly familiar. Edge-on, they had no depth and disappeared from view. They looked like thin discs of obsidian on both faces but reflected no light. Yesterday he would have thought them totally weird but after his earlier experiences he knew what they were.

Now, Sam didn't know diddly-squat about physics but he'd heard about worm-holes and stuff, and he was pretty sure one of these was the 'other-side' of his Boojum. He reckoned he'd slipped through and fallen off the pipe on this side, breaking his ribs and knocking himself out. Then another thought struck him. If this was the other side of the Boojum, there was a chance he could slip back through to where he belonged. But which one had he come through?

Sam stared at the pipes and scratched his head. There were metal rungs leading to the top of the riser. Sam had no idea how he would figure out which pipe was his but thought he might get a better idea if he looked from above. Favoring his ribs, he climbed up the riser. Standing on the flat top of the riser, he peered down at the horizontal pipes. They were all pretty much the same, and the holes they disappeared into all looked identical. Then something caught his eye: Lying on one of the pipes was a penny; the same penny he'd flipped through the Boojum. That had to be his pipe!

Gritting his teeth, he climbed down the riser and straddled the horizontal pipe. He picked up the lucky penny then scooted along the pipe to the black disc. Groaning from the pain in his ribs, he lay on the pipe and crawled forward. He laid his palm against the black disc and pushed.

It was the weirdest thing he'd ever felt.

As he pushed against the disc, it felt as if his hand was pushing forward through it but his eyes told him his hand was sliding sideways along the surface of the disc. He shook his head, as if to clear his eyes, and pulled his hand back. He tried again. Again, he experienced the weird discrepancy between sight and touch. No matter where he pushed on the disc, the same thing happened. Panic started to rise in his gut. Ignoring his ribs, he stood on the pipe and pushed his shoulder against the disc. He slid sideways and nearly fell. He just managed to get his balance and straddle the pipe again. One thing was sure: He wasn't getting back though this hole.

He laid his head on the pipe and cried. He hadn't cried in years and it felt alien and familiar all at once. He could hear his Pop's voice in his head:

Whatcha cryin' fer, ya girl? That just made it worse. He'd never felt as alone and scared in his life. He bawled on the pipe until a loud shout interrupted him:

"Kei hei tōsa? Kad a jein tu er on viepe? Tar anūis!"

Sam's head snapped up from the pipe. Two men in bizarre clothing stood beneath him. They were tall and blond with close-cropped blond beards. They wore light armor made from coarse black cloth and leather, leather boots, and metal helmets atop heads of long blond hair. One had his hair loose and had his hand at the hilt of a sheathed sword. The other had his locks in braids and held a black spear. He was doing the shouting and seemed to be in charge. Sam had no idea what Braids was saying but the 'come down' gesture he was making was universal. Unsure what to do, Sam stared at the men. The men stared back. Braids repeated the gesture and brandished the spear.

"Tar anūis, a kara - no skwielvie mei hu!"

No mistaking that gesture either. Sam was a sitting duck on the pipe, and preferred his chances on the ground. He brushed away tears with the backs of his hands and wiped his nose in the sleeve of his jacket. He scooted back along the pipe to the riser and climbed down the rungs. The men met him at the bottom and Loose-Hair pinned his hands behind his back. Braids stood in front of him and regarded him critically.

The blond men were incredibly tall. Sam was a meter eighty-five but these guys dwarfed him. Braids grabbed Sam's face in one hand and turned his head left and right. He released him, brought his face close to Sam's and spoke in a quiet voice:

"Kad is anem det? Kad ata tu eg jenew len on viepe?"

Loose-Hair nudged him hard, as if persuading him to answer a question. Sam's voice tumbled out of him:

"Look guys; I don't know what you're sayin' and I don't know why I'm here. Hell, I don't even know where here is! I'm just tryin' to get home, and I don't mind tellin' ya – I'm scared as hell."

Loose-Hair's grip loosened for a second and Braids's eyes widened. Sam knew he had surprised them but didn't know why. Braids stared at Loose-Hair and they said in unison:

"Kuiewchek!"

Braids turned on his heel and started walking away downhill. He looked over his shoulder and shouted:

"Ber ei!"

Loose-Hair frog-marched Sam after Braids and soon they came to a crest. The ground dropped away revealing the most beautiful valley Sam had ever seen. A few hundred meters away, a tarn lay nestled in the embrace of the hills. A river ran downhill from the tarn and meandered down the valley as far as the eye could see. Near the bottom of the valley, the bare stone and scree gave way to verdant flood-plain. The water in the tarn was steel-blue, almost indigo, and spoke of ice-crystal purity and unfathomable depths. Sam shivered just looking at it. There was an elemental sense of ancient cold about it that even an Alaskan winter couldn't match.

Loose-Hair walked him down the hill towards the tarn. As they approached the edge, what Sam had taken to be a huge bowl-shaped boulder, turned out to be a boat. At least, it looked like a boat: It reminded Sam of a circular coracle; wooden, with several rows of molded bench-seats inside, and what looked like a steering console at the front. He couldn't see any outboard means of propulsion though. Braids jumped into the vehicle and sat at the console. He gestured to Loose-Hair who lifted all ninety-five kilos of Sam off his feet and deposited him into the boat. He jumped in beside him and barked:

"Sie schiess!"

Sam stammered: "I don't ..."

Loose-Hair pointed at the seat and pushed down hard on Sam's shoulder. Sam got the idea and sat down. The molded wooden seats were covered in some kind of padded leather and were surprisingly comfortable. Loose-Hair sat in the bench behind Sam with a grunt that Sam took to mean "I'm watching you!"

For several moments, nothing happened. Sam expected one or both of the blond men to push the boat into the water but as he waited, Braids moved his hand in a peculiar gesture over the console and a low-frequency vibration began in the hull. It wasn't unpleasant but it was unfamiliar, and made Sam edgy.

He soon realized the craft wasn't a boat. Not in the traditional sense.

Seconds after the humming started the craft make a crackling noise and floated a few centimeters off the ground. Sam grabbed the edges of the seat and looked around wildly. Loose-Hair snorted in ridicule behind him. As Sam clung on, the vehicle spun on its axis and glided away over the surface of the tarn. When they were over the midpoint of the tarn, Braids turned the craft so they were facing the way they had come. The craft descended until it almost touched the water. An electrical popping noise emanated from the hull and the water around them started to bubble. The air became charged and Sam's beard and hair started to itch. A smell of ozone reached his nostrils. Suddenly the craft shot into the air and headed towards the peak they had come from. Sam hyperventilated as if on a rollercoaster, and clung on for dear life.

Braids steered the craft towards a mountain adjacent to the one where Sam had woken up. As they approached the peak, a huge edifice came into view. From Sam's aerial perspective, it was made up of five concentric rings of sandstone, each taller than its outer counterpart. The walls must have been five or six meters thick, he adjudged. An octagonal stone tower, as tall as an office building, stood at the center and five circular towers reminiscent of chess rooks were spaced evenly on the outer ring. Two smaller towers of similar design flanked a wide lancet-arched recess in the outer wall. The craft banked over the structure, and Braids set them down on a large flat area nearby. The outer ring of the fortress was featureless but for the large arched recess. The recess penetrated several meters into the outer ring and ended in blunt stone.

Braids stepped out of the vehicle and gestured at Loose-Hair to bring Sam along. As they approached the recess, guards with strange weapons watched from the towers. Braids removed a small flat stone from a pouch on his belt. He pointed the object at the fortress and muttered under his breath. A seismic grinding noise came from deep within, and the rear wall of the recess slid sideways. An opening that matched the shape of the arch slid into view and lined up with it. Sam could now see through to the circular open area between the two outer rings. Braids gestured then headed in through the huge entrance. Loose-Hair pushed Sam in the small of the back. He stumbled then got his footing and followed Braids into the entrance.

Under the eyes of the guards in the towers, the men led Sam through the outer ring area to another door in the second wall. They followed a circuitous path through doors and corridors in the various rings until they emerged into the expansive circular courtyard where the octagonal tower stood. The courtyard was cobbled in black with white stones picking out geometric patterns between the central tower and the positions of the five outer watchtowers. The courtyard was busy and there was a market in progress. The variety of colors and smells was incredible, and the noise was deafening. People haggled at volume over foodstuffs and pottery, and near one of the huge inner walls were several fenced-off rings in which a livestock mart was underway. No one paid any attention as the men led

Sam to a door in the base of the octagonal tower. They brought him inside and closed the door, cutting off the noise from the courtyard. The inside of the tower was cold and dimly-lit, and the men led Sam down a spiral staircase to a large basement area.

Sam didn't like the look of the basement one bit. Eight barred cells were set into the walls of the basement. Braids opened one of the cell doors and Loose-Hair manhandled Sam towards it. Sam was no stranger to the drunk-tank but he certainly didn't want to be imprisoned in a strange place where no-one spoke his language, and with no knowledge of when he might get out. He struggled against Loose-Hair's grip.

"Oh no, you're not putting me in there. There's no way I'm …"

Loose-Hair cracked him on the back of the head and Sam slumped to the floor.

He woke up on the wooden bunk in the cell with a humdinger of a headache. He groaned as he sat up and felt the egg-sized bump on the back of his head. As he got his bearings, he realized his boots and utility belt were gone. He looked around the cell but all he found was a filthy bucket under the bunk. He was so preoccupied with searching that he never noticed the little man sitting on the stool outside his cell.

The man cleared his throat and rapped on the bars of Sam's cell. Sam head whipped around at the noise and he noticed the man for the first time. His beard and hair were reddish, going to grey, and he wore a long green robe. On his knee was an ornate briefcase, which he now placed on the ground as he stood up. He gestured Sam towards the bars and said:

"On dikken tu mei?"

Sam looked at the man blankly. After a moment, apparently satisfied, the man nodded and picked up the briefcase. He placed it on the stool, unsnapped the locks and opened it so that Sam could see the contents. It was divided into numerous small compartments with a small plaque on the lid of each. The man removed the first plaque and held it through the bars. He gestured at Sam to take it. Sam stood as far as he could from the bars, reached forward and snatched it from the man's hand.

It was the size and shape of a business card but felt like a thin piece of ivory. It was embossed with black markings. Sam looked at the man and made a "what do I do with this?" gesture. The man pointed at the card with one hard and pointed at his eyes with the other.

He wants me to read it.

The markings may or may not have been writing but they meant nothing to Sam. He shook his head and handed the card back. The man put it back in the case and gave Sam the next card. Sam looked at it, shook his head and handed it back. They repeated this many times over the next fifteen minutes and Sam was getting weary when the man handed him a plaque that read:

ENGLISH

Sam held the card out to the man and tapped on it with the forefinger of the other hand.

"English," he said. "I speak English."

The man took the card with a faintly surprised look muttering "*Ber-lè*" to himself as he replaced it in the case. He opened the relevant compartment and removed a small velvet bag from which he dropped a tear-shaped stone into the palm of his hand. From another compartment he removed a similar stone on a leather thong.

He held the stones together and muttered something. There was a slight pop from the stones like a static discharge and a vague smell of ozone. He handed the stone on the thong to Sam and gestured for him to place it around his neck. With some trepidation, Sam did so. The man mimed pulling his collar forward and dropping the amulet inside his robe. He mimed it again and pointed at Sam. When Sam dropped the amulet inside his shirt against his skin, he felt a weird jolt pass through him. It wasn't painful but it felt like a mild electric shock that passed from the stone, back to his spine and up into his brain. His ears buzzed and his eyes went hazy for a moment. Sam gasped and staggered slightly.

The man smiled, as if he knew something Sam did not, and said:

"*On dikken tu mei anisch?*"

Sam gasped again. He knew the man had spoken his own language but what Sam's brain registered was:

"Do you understand me now?"

Sam nodded.

"Say it, my friend," said the man. "Tell me out loud you understand me."

"I... I understand you."

The man smiled. He closed up his briefcase and put it on the floor.

"Excellent! What I've just given you is called a *mejrok*. Everyone here wears one. A mejrok can do many things depending on the patterns imprinted on it but for now I've imprinted yours to enable you to converse with us and read our language. Do you understand?"

Sam nodded again.

"Capital! Well, now that we understand each other, perhaps you could tell me your name."

"Er, Sam ... Sam Renstrom."

"And where are you from, Sam Renstrom?"

"Alaska."

"Alaska? Never heard of that place. Which tír is it in?" There was no direct English translation for tír but the mejrok delivered a concept that was a blend of land, country and parallel reality.

"Er, I don't know. It's in the States."

"The states? Which states?"

"The United States of America."

"United States of America? I have never heard of those, either."

Sam began to comprehend just how far away from home he was.

"So, where'n the hell am I?" he asked.

"We shall get to that in due course. Now, perhaps you would tell me how you got in to a restricted area with patrols around the perimeter."

"I don't know."

"Oh come, come, Sam Renstrom; the guards found you sitting on an inflow pipe interfering with a tuned sidh." Sam's brain registered sidh as portal//corridor.

"I … I wasn't interferin'. I was tryin' to get back."

"Whatever do you mean?"

"I was tryin' to get back through the disc; back where I came from."

"Back where you …" The man's brow rumpled. "Do you mean you arrived here through a sidh?"

"If you mean a weird swirlin' disc around an oil pipe then, yeah, I think so. I was checkin' out a problem with an oil pipe back in Alaska and I got pulled into one of those suckers. Next thing, I wake up beside one on an oil pipe here. When your boys caught me I was tryin' to get back through. Didn't work though."

Sam lowered his gaze. The man turned around and picked up his briefcase. He looked distressed.

"Thank you, Sam Renstrom. I'll be back," he said and disappeared up the spiral stairway.

"Wait! Hey Mister, wait! When do I get out of here?"

But the man was gone.

"Hey! Come back! Hey! God damn it!"

"Keep it down over there."

The quiet voice came from one of the other cells. Sam crouched instinctively and peered around the cells to see where the voice's owner was.

"Where are you, Mister?"

A man appeared at the bars of the cell opposite. Sam noted he was dressed in 'regular' clothes - jeans and a sweater.

"So, 'Sam' is it? From Alaska. You're a long way from home, Sam from Alaska."

Sam realized the guy was speaking English.

"Where am I?"

They call this place Keher Kuhn-Ridh. In English, that means the City of Kuhn-Ridh. Kuhn-Ridh is the chieftain that runs this place and the province around us."

"I mean, what country is this?"

"Well, it's Ireland ... in a manner of speaking."

"Whaddya mean?"

Well, if you looked at an atlas of this planet, you'd think it was Earth, and I suppose it is, to an extent. It's just not our Earth. I guess you'd call it an alternate reality."

"You're kiddin'!"

"Nope. There are a few similarities between this reality and ours but it's mostly differences. In our reality, this place would be in the Slieve Mish Mountains in Kerry. They don't call it that, though."

"So how long have you been here?"

"I've lost track. A few months, I suppose. They have a use for me, so they keep me alive."

"You mean, if they don't have a use for me, they'll kill me."

"Probably. Right now they're trying to figure out who you are and where you came from. Your story about coming through a portal has old Mug-Ruit rattled."

"Who?"

"Mug-Ruit, Kuhn-Ridh's head of security; the little old fart you've just been talking to. The tuned portals are supposed to be secure. You came through on his watch. Kuhn-Ridh won't like that."

"So they'll kill me?"

"That depends. What was your job back in Alaska?"

"I was a maintenance man on the Trans-Alaska oil pipeline."

The guy in the jeans threw his head back and laughed.

"Oh man! I don't know if it's your lucky day or theirs. I'll tell you this, though: You tell them you know about pumping oil and they'll welcome you with open arms."

"Mister, all I wanna do is go home."

"So do I but until we figure out a way to do that, we're stuck here. Hey, if they put you to work on the pipeline, maybe you can put in a good word for me – might get out of this cell more often."

Sam snorted a cynical laugh.

"I'll see what I can do. Say, what's your name? I can't keep calling you 'Mister'."

"I'm Fintan. Fintan McHewell."

CHAPTER FOURTEEN

THE ROWING WHEEL

GPS Ground Control Station, Diego Garcia, Indian Ocean.

"Master Sergeant, there goes another one!" shouted Airman Taylor.

In the dim control room, the glow of the computer screen threw deep shadows across his face. The Master Sergeant's head jerked up from his console.

"Report."

Taylor looked frightened.

"Another satellite has gone offline Sir."

The Master Sergeant crossed to Taylor's station and peered over his shoulder. Taking in the information on the display, he picked up the phone handset beside Taylor's keyboard and punched in a number.

"This is Steinmetz at Diego Garcia. We've lost signal from three GPS birds in the past fifteen minutes. We're running … hold on."

Taylor was gesturing to the screen and holding up four fingers. Steinmetz raised his eyebrows and Taylor nodded.

"Make that four; all four satellites in orbit-plane C have gone dark. We're running diagnostics now but the degradation of accuracy and intel from other ground stations is consistent with shutdown of four birds."

The voice on the other end spoke briefly.

"No sir, we have no idea. Terrorist action is not presumed at this time."

Again, Steinmetz listened.

"No sir, they could not be shut down by a foreign power. We encrypt all the tasking commands. It would have to be done from within our own control systems."

The voice barked down the phone again then rang off.

Over the next two hours, ground-control stations around the world monitored the failure of every satellite in the GPS system. The world felt the effect immediately. Airline pilots and ships' steersmen reported failures in navigation systems. Cellular networks that relied on timing signals from the GPS system collapsed. NATO countries went on high alert and the United States went to DEFCON Three.

The assumption was that the satellites had shut down. It did not occur to anyone they were physically gone. They presumed such a thing was impossible.

They presumed wrong.

*

Goddard Space Flight Centre, Greenbelt, Maryland, USA.

The ground controllers of the Hubble Space Telescope were the first to see the strange craft. When the first GPS satellites had gone offline, the US Air Force had requested the telescope be re-tasked to look in the direction of the failed birds.

Dr. James King and a few colleagues were huddled around a cluster of computer monitors, examining the area of space where they expected the GPS satellites to be. A US Air Force Major stood behind them.

"Wait a minute," said someone. "What's that?"

There was an object near one of the GPS satellites. It might have been an optical glitch until it shifted slightly and glinted in reflected earthlight. King zoomed the telescope in for a closer look.

It was a spacecraft.

From a distance, it looked like a dark metal disc with gold strips traversing it. They zoomed closer until the craft filled the screen. At first, the image was blurred, then the computers finished their sharpening algorithms and revealed the craft in exquisite detail.

"No freaking way!" said one of the observers.

The Major pushed between two civilian scientists and leaned into the screen. As finer images of the craft arrived, the particulars of its construction became clear. None of them could believe what they were seeing.

"Is that ... wood?" asked the Major.

The craft was constructed of huge planks of timber, treated until pitch black, and overlapping like a clinker-built rowboat. The planks must have come from trees that were in excess of five-hundred meters tall, and the designers had curved and shaped the planks to make a perfect wheel-shaped craft. Along the fascia of every third plank was a strip of bronze embossed with geometric patterns.

"This is incredible! Look at those symbols," said Dr. King. "They're all

Celtic. That's a triskelion, and that's a triquetra.

"I don't know what we're seeing here," said one of King's associates, "but I doubt the Irish are sending up flying saucers made of wood – or any other spacecraft for that matter."

A snicker went round the group. The Major cleared his throat and looked pointedly at Dr. King. King's eyes flicked back and forth, his mind racing.

"Well, this is a trick," said King. "It has to be. Someone's playing an elaborate practical joke on us."

The Major bristled.

"Our GPS systems are offline, and we have a bogey parked in the same orbit as our satellites – I don't see any joke here, Doctor."

"With respect Major, that's not what I'm saying. This can't be real. A wooden spacecraft is not viable, so it's more likely someone is interlacing these images into the video feed from Hubble."

"Yeah? And how do you explain the GPS failures?"

They were arguing amongst themselves when the Major got his answer.

"What the hell is that?" said King, pointing at the screen.

A bubble of energy appeared at the edge of the craft, at first indistinct and almost hidden by King's finger on the screen. The Major slapped his hand out of the way. In seconds, the bubble elongated and flattened out into a shimmering vertical disc. It looked like a thin film of soapy water in a child's bubble-blowing loop. The disc moved away from the craft towards the nearest GPS satellite, growing all the time. It intercepted the satellite and scrubbed across it like a cosmic eraser. The satellite and the shimmering disc winked out of existence.

The Major strode away and reached for a telephone.

"Did anyone else just see that?" asked King.

Everyone had but no one could believe it.

And then things got stranger.

Many apertures opened in the edge of the craft, and out from each slid a long pole with a flattened blade on the end, energy fields arcing and dancing around the blades. Another bubble formed at the edge of the vehicle and snapped open to form another larger portal. In perfect synchronization, the poles started an elliptical rowing motion and after a brief pause, the craft rowed smoothly into the shimmering disc and disappeared.

CHAPTER FIFTEEN

THE PLAN

Ferdia was in his element. Behind him on the bedroom floor were stacks of books; poetry, encyclopedias, dictionaries. A large computer desk accommodated more books in perfect piles, and neatly arranged sheaves of written notes and color printouts. He was finishing the translation of the runes on his grandfather's cube when the call came in. Skype appeared on the computer screen, with the message:

Mark Calling

Ferdia put on his headset and answered. Mark's face appeared on Ferdia's monitor.

"Hey Ferd! You're there."

"Well, you did say you would call at exactly 10 am."

"Yeah, I did – dunno why I'm surprised; you're so OCD!"

"I'm not OCD! I hate it when people call me that."

"Oh yeah," Mark laughed, "what are you doing with that stack of paper then?"

Ferdia was unconsciously lining up a stack of paper with the thumbs and forefingers of both hands. He snatched his hands away. Mark grinned at him.

"See?"

"There's nothing wrong with being neat. Anyway, is Niamh online?"

"Yeah, she is. Hang on, I'll invite her in."

Through the webcam, Ferdia could see Mark working away at his PC. After a moment, Niamh's face appeared beside Mark's on Ferdia's screen. Her eyes looked puffy and red. Ferdia started to say, "OK, let's get started …" but Mark interjected:

"Hey Niamh, are you OK? You look like you've been crying."

"Oh, it's Mira. I know she's been gone over a week but I just can't get used to it. I keep thinking I hear a cat's meow and I run to the windows – or downstairs – but she's not there. I can't figure out how she kept getting out. My dad's searched every ditch along the road but there's no sign of … of her … body."

Niamh burst into tears again. She buried her face in her hands and wept bitterly. All the boys could see was the top of her head as she sobbed. Her voice came through their headsets:

"Oh God, I miss her so much."

Ferdia wasn't a cat person but he could see how much Mira had meant to Niamh, and he felt for her. He supposed she might even miss Mira as much as Mark missed his dad. He shifted in his chair and cleared his throat. He didn't know Niamh very well and crying made him uncomfortable. He cleared his throat again, and said:

"Look Niamh, err … maybe you want to do this later, or something."

She grabbed a tissue and wiped her eyes, then blew her nose. Eventually, she looked up and said:

"No, no; let's do this. I need something to take my mind off her."

"Are you sure? We can do this any time."

"No, I'm grand. Really. C'mon, let's get on with it."

"OK, well … yes, let's do that. OK …"

He cleared his throat again.

"Right, well some strange stuff has been going on and it is time we pooled our information and got to the bottom of it. I've created a shared folder online on Google Drive to keep all our notes together. Just before you called I finished transliterating the runes on my grandfather's cube and put the translation up. Here's the link."

As the link appeared on Skype, they clicked on it and the Google Drive folder opened in their respective browsers.

"Can you see the file? It's called *Cubes*."

Mark and Niamh both nodded.

"OK, go ahead and open it. We'll read through and see if we can make sense of it. I've got some ideas but I want to see if you come to the same conclusions."

Mark and Niamh opened the file.

Cubes

Fintan's Cube

Against the sable backdrop of the night,

The starry actors glide across the stage.
In jeweled costumes sewn with threads of light,
They read their parts, then turn tomorrow's page.

The earthly audience watches from the dust,
As cosmic players tread Forever's boards.
Our bearing on our travels we entrust,
To these bejeweled heroes of the Gods.

Vincent's Cube

The Hunter leads the lambent stellar ranks;
His faithful Dogs attending his foray.
His hunting grounds are Danu's fertile banks;
The Unicorn and Hare, his timeless prey.

The Hunter tempers Man's conceited traits,
And teaches him the limit of his worth.
And Man in turn has sought to emulate,
The august Hunter's works on austere Earth.

There were several minutes of silence as all three read the verses. Niamh's brow was furrowed. Mark was shaking his head slightly and mouthing the words as he read them. Niamh took a breath and started to speak, then stopped. She looked at her screen again then said:

"Stars. It's talking about the stars."

Ferdia grinned and nodded his head.

"Yes, or more precisely constellations given that it talks about travelers getting their bearings from 'bejeweled heroes of the Gods.' I'm even more convinced now, having read the verses on Granddad's cube."

"But what's 'The Hunter?'"

Mark cleared his throat and said, "It's the constellation Orion."

Ferdia nodded again. He knew Mark would get this. Fintan had been teaching Mark about astronomy since he was old enough to look through the telescope.

"Why Orion?" asked Niamh.

"Well, Orion was known as The Hunter by the Greeks. The 'faithful dogs' must be the dog constellations *Canis Major* and *Canis Minor*, which are very close to Orion. The Unicorn and Hare are *Monoceros* and *Lepus*, which are right next to Orion. He's often shown hunting them in old drawings. I'm not sure what 'Danu's fertile banks' are, though."

Ferdia's grin widened.

"That's the constellation *Eridanus*, the river," he said. "It was identified with the Celtic goddess Danu."

Mark slapped his forehead.

"Of course. How could I miss that? Eridanus ends right by Orion's left foot at the star Rigel."

Niamh was still looking puzzled.

"What does the last verse mean, then?"

Mark shrugged. "I haven't a clue. Ferd?"

Ferdia wrinkled his nose.

"I'm not sure. It talks about mankind being humbled by Orion, for some reason, and trying to copy him or represent him on Earth in some way. I don't know what it means, though. I think we're going to need the rest of the cubes to get to the bottom of it."

"So there's not much more we can do with this for now?"

"I don't think so. Let's look at everything else that's happened and see how it all links up. I'll create a new document."

Mark and Niamh saw the document appear on their screens and start to fill with text. Ferdia typed as he talked, documenting the events that wove their lives together in an uncanny web.

"OK, Fintan disappeared on Christmas Day. He had one of these mysterious cubes. Granddad Vincent *also* disappeared on Christmas Day. He *also* had a cube. Far too unlikely to be coincidence; agreed?"

"Agreed," said Niamh and Mark in unison.

"OK, good. Now we come to the priest. Another connection. Niamh saw him die in the lighthouse cellar, and Mark has told us his father recognized him. Niamh, Mark also tells me you've remembered what the priest said to you before he died."

Niamh moved closer to her camera.

"Yes, I've typed it up on my PC. I'll paste it into the Google document now. It doesn't make a lot of sense, though."

The priest's final words, as transcribed by Niamh, appeared on Ferdia's screen. He read through it looking puzzled.

"Well, you weren't exaggerating when you said it didn't make sense. It rambles all over the place."

"Yeah, it's pretty weird. The priest said someone called Magus was trying to get free from somewhere. When I asked him who he meant, he recited that nursery rhyme to me. He told me they – whoever 'they' are – had banished Magus, and forbidden people to talk about him. Now he's coming back, and no-one remembers the danger.

"He said the *Sentinelium* – whatever that is - had been infiltrated and destroyed, and that he was the last *Proctor* in this tír. Magus's people killed everyone except *The Mason*. He got away through the *Saiph* – whatever THAT is - to join the *Felkynd Allegiance*.

"He then said I had to find *The Mason's Apprentice*, someone called

Oisin."

At the mention of Oisin, a strange look came over Mark's face. He went pale and moved back from his camera slightly. Neither Niamh nor Ferdia noticed. Niamh continued:

"This Oisin person has to follow The Mason – through the Saiph, I guess. He needs a thing called The Index to do that, and the Index is in four pieces, called Tetroi. I thought he meant people at first, but he said they're not people; not anymore."

She wrinkled her nose.

"None of this makes any sense. Anyway, the Tetroi are called *The Mason, The Templar, The Nobleman* and *The Cleric.* The priest said that last one belonged to him.

"He tried to tell me where his Tetros was, but he was …"

Here Niamh swallowed a few times, and made several attempts to continue. Eventually she found her voice:

"He was … dying; and it came out really garbled. He said if I was truly penitent it would be right under my nose, and that I'd need a key. He said the 'the falls are the key. The falls along the way.'"

Ferdia knitted his brow and his eyes glazed over. Mark recognized the expression and knew what was happening: Disconnected scraps of information were spinning through Ferdia's head and organizing themselves into a coherent whole. Mark could almost follow the process by the expression changes on Ferdia's face, and he knew the exact moment it all crystallized. Ferdia's face relaxed and his eyes regained their focus. He looked directly into his camera and said:

"I know where The Cleric Tetros is."

"Really? Wow! How did you figure it out?"

"Well, if a priest is going on about someone being truly penitent, he's talking about confession. I believe the Tetros is hidden in or around the confessional in his church.

"But what's that bit about the key?" asked Niamh.

"Hmmm … I don't know. I need more context. If we were there, it would probably be obvious. It's also obvious that the Tetroi he's talking about are the cubes Fintan and my granddad had."

Mark still looked a bit green when he spoke:

"I think you're right. And I think my dad is The Mason."

"What makes you say that?" asked Niamh.

"Because I'm the Mason's Apprentice. I'm Oisin."

Niamh's mouth fell open.

"But your name's Mark."

"Mark's my middle name. My real name is Oisin. My mum wanted to call me Mark, but Dad put Oisin on my birth cert. Some family tradition, or something. My mum went mental. She hates the name, and she always called me Mark. It kind of stuck."

Ferdia nodded.

"This makes perfect sense. My granddad Vincent is a member of a society called the Knights of Leinster. He must be The Templar. Which means… Oh God …"

Ferdia looked extremely upset.

"What is it?" asked Niamh.

"The priest said that Magus's people had killed all the members of the society except The Mason. That means my granddad is dead."

"Oh, Ferdia; you're right. Oh, I'm so sorry."

Ferdia turned away from the camera for a moment. The others could see him fighting tears. Mark felt worried. This was all becoming too real and immediate.

"According to the priest, I have to get the four Tetroi, put them together to make a device that will let me follow my dad through one of these portals. But why?"

Niamh looked sympathetic.

"We don't know why, Mark. The priest didn't say. But if this apprentice really is you, you won't have to do this on your own. We'll go with you, won't we Ferdia?"

Ferdia found his voice.

"Y … yes. Of course, we shall. I have to find out what happened to my granddad too. In the meantime, as I see it, we have three things to focus on."

Ferdia typed a bulleted list into Skype:

- Who is The Nobleman?
- Where is the priest's church?
- What is the significance of the character Simon Magus?

"So, The Nobleman - who is he? We know who all the other Sentinels are - or were – but we have no clues to his identity; and no way of finding the fourth Tetros. So let's leave that for now.

"Item two: Where is the priest's church?"

"I have an idea about that," said Mark. "When dad and I saw him, he was crossing the road towards the village church. It's got to be the church he meant."

"Yes, that would be most likely. What was the name of the village?"

"Oh, what was it? I remember it was near Tullow; umm… Ferrisfort, I think."

"OK, one of us needs to get to Ferrisfort and get that Tetros. You could cycle down tomorrow, Mark."

"What? No way; it's miles! It took us hours to get there in the Porsche."

"Well, maybe you could get Bree to drive you. Or maybe Niamh could go."

"There's no way Daddy or Martha will take me anywhere. I'm still in the doghouse."

"Didn't my mum tell them about the broken lighthouse key?"

"Yeah, but they still don't believe me. I don't think they want to believe it – it's too weird for them. God, they're so boring and ordinary."

"Don't you mind that they don't believe you?"

"Meh, not really. I worried about it for days and argued with them, but I don't care anymore. They're stupid."

Ferdia interrupted: "Mark, will you ask Bree to take you?"

"Yeah, she's still beating herself up about not believing me. I reckon she'll take me anywhere if I ask."

"Good, so that just leaves this Simon Magus character. I know that name. It occurs in biblical writings and Celtic mythology."

"How do you know all this stuff, Ferd?"

"I read a lot, Mark. I have a photographic memory. It comes from being *neat and organized!*" He looked pointedly down his webcam. Mark threw his eyes up to heaven.

"What I'm impressed with, is how well Niamh remembers what the priest said."

Niamh looked pale.

"I … didn't at first, but then I woke up from a dream and it was all there. I wrote it down."

"What kind of dream was it?"

"Well … this is going to sound crazy, but I dreamt that me and Mira flew to the Old Lighthouse, straight through the walls, and back to the night the priest died."

Ferdia looked pained. "'Mira and I'," he muttered, "not 'me and Mira.'"

Niamh ignored him. She looked thoughtful.

"You know what; that's the same night she disappeared."

Ferdia was reading the document again.

"This rhyme; is that all there was to it?"

Niamh nodded. "Yep, that's it. It sounds like a nursery rhyme. It's a bit dark for kids, though."

"Well, nursery rhymes were used to pass fables and warnings to children. They were often quite gruesome and scary. From what the priest said, this one is about Simon Magus coming to take over Ireland. Most nursery rhymes are well known, but I've never heard this one before. I wonder if there's anything about it on the Internet."

Ferdia googled the first line of the rhyme.

"Hey, I got a hit. There's only one match – *www.themagusconspiracy.com*"

He clicked on the link and the website appeared. The page title read:

THE MAGUS CONSPIRACY
How an ancient and powerful <u>cabal</u> rewrote history.

Further down the page was a link. It read:

'Spiteful, sinful Simon Magus.'
<u>The role of Magus as the bogeyman</u>

"Guys", he said, "you've got to see this."

He pasted the address into Skype and they clicked into it. As they explored the site for themselves, Ferdia clicked on the link containing the first line of the rhyme.

The page that appeared looked like an unrolled piece of old parchment with a rhyme inked on it in old lettering:

Spiteful, sinful Simon Magus
Brought his armies to enslave us
Opened gates from tír to tír
Rent and robbed and razed for years

Tír na nÓg and Tír faoi Thuinn
and Tír na mBan succumbed to him
But when he came to take this Land
He met with more than he had planned.

For in those days our minds were schooled
By four cabals that vied to rule
Clerics, Gentry, Templars, Masons
All with converse rhymes and reasons

Simon thought we'd be divided
Sinful Simon was misguided
Through common threat they found agreement
Simon was detained, defeated.

Now exiled in an empty tír
Simon counts the endless years
Held behind a sealed sidh
The death of kings provides the key

But we must ne'er e'er forget
This dread enchanter's mortal threat.

For if the factions break their trust
The lock will crumble into dust
And Simon Magus, evil seer
will once again invade our tír

Niamh's voice came through Ferdia's headset:

"Hey, have you seen that poem about Simon Magus?"

"Yes, I'm reading it now."

"All that stuff about tírs and sidhs – that's what the priest was talking about."

Mark cut in. "My dad used to talk about 'tírs' too. He talked about things happening in this tír and not happening in other tírs – whatever that means. What's a sidh, though?" He pronounced it '*sidge.*'

"It's pronounced '*she,*' Ferdia said. Niamh was nodding on the screen.

"Yeah, I read about them in children's story books. They were mounds of grass, or sometimes circles of stones or mushrooms. The faery folk used to use them to go between this world and places like Tír na nÓg."

"Yes, the poem mentions that – and two other places; Tír faoi Thuinn and Tír na mBan – The Land under the Waves, and The Land of the Women. All those places are from Celtic mythology."

"But if it's all just fairy stories, why has my dad disappeared? And your granddad? And why did a priest have to die? And why the secret room; and all the secrecy about the Tetroi?"

"Maybe it's not mythology, Mark. See what it says on the top of the page, 'How an ancient and powerful cabal rewrote Irish history.' Maybe all the old Irish stories about faeries and giants and monsters were true, and the cabal rewrote history to remove them. Maybe your dad and my granddad are mixed up in this cabal."

"What's a cabal?" asked Mark.

"It's a group of people with a particular agenda or goal. Secret societies are often called cabals. Maybe my granddad and your dad were part of a secret society."

"Or maybe the cabal is the men who locked me in the lighthouse," said Niamh.

"Maybe they're all part of the same cabal," said Ferdia.

There were a few moments of silence as Niamh and Mark digested the implications of this. Eventually, Mark snorted. When he spoke his voice had taken on an hysterical edge:

"I don't believe any of this. If some organization changed all the history books, which just sounds really stupid, where are all these faeries and giants now?"

"I don't know, Mark. We're just guessing. Whoever set this website up knows about it, though. I'm looking for contact details on here at the moment."

Ferdia clicked through several pages on the site then gave a sharp intake of breath.

"Mark, Niamh. There is something else here you need to see."

He pasted a link into Skype and they both clicked on it. They both gasped.

On their screens was a photograph of the website's owner. He was middle-aged and somewhat unkempt. He held his right hand out, palm-up towards the camera.

Sitting on his hand was the fourth Tetros.

There were several moments of silence then Mark said:

"He must be The Nobleman."

Ferdia shook his head.

"I don't think so. This website is trying to expose the cover-up the society perpetrated when they changed history. I think The Nobleman is dead and the person in this photograph acquired the Tetros somehow."

"What are we going to do?"

"I am going to contact him and arrange to meet him. We need to get our hands on that Tetros. You are going to go to Ferrisfort and get the other one."

"Ferdia, don't be crazy! This guy could be dangerous."

"No. I don't think he is. I've read the website. This man is a lone voice in the wilderness. He's looking for allies."

"You've read the whole website? When? We've only been looking at it for ten minutes."

"I speed read. Look, we need that fourth piece. I'm going to contact this person and tell him a little of what we've learnt; pique his interest. It looks like he lives in Dublin somewhere. I'll arrange a meeting and get that Tetros from him."

"How?"

"I'll figure that out when I meet him. There's no need to discuss this any further. I'm going after this Tetros; you get the one in Ferrisfort. Contact me when you have it. Niamh, I hope your cat comes back."

And with that, Ferdia disconnected.

CHAPTER SIXTEEN

JERE

A sonic boom echoed through the valley then rolled away like distant thunder.

"Well, there goes another one," said Sam, hands on hips, looking into the distance.

High in the air, a shimmering portal refracted the light at its edge, creating a ring of deeper blue against the cloudless sky. A multicolored contrail led from the portal to a huge wheel-shaped craft, speeding towards a distant snow-covered peak.

"That's, what, nine of 'em now?" said Sam. "Where they all going?"

The craft, now a dot in the distance, decelerated and came to a stop over the peak.

"That's *Schliew Unierren*; The Iron Mountain," said Fintan. "They all seem to be heading there."

As he spoke, the craft descended and disappeared into the top of the mountain."

"What're they doin' anyways?"

"I have no idea, Sam. Maybe a better question would be where are they coming from?"

"OK, well I got an even better question: Why the hell are we buildin' an oil pipeline in a place where there ain't no cars and there's boojums flyin' around all over the place by magick."

"Teic, not magick."

"Yeah, well whatever; they don't need gas, so none of this makes any sense."

"No, it doesn't, but if building a pipeline from Keher Kuhn-Ridh means I'm out here working every day and not in that cell, then I'm not complaining."

"Yeah, I hear that! What the heck's over there anyways? Hey Numbnuts!" He called over to the blond guard with the braids.

"It's Nemnet. What do you want Renstrom?"

"Yeah, whatever," said Sam with a wink at Fintan, "what's over there where all them boojums is flyin' to?"

"You'll find out soon enough; that's where this pipeline is going. Now get your crew back to work or do I have to give you some encouragement?"

Nemnet hefted his spear and an arc of energy crackled along the end.

"No boss, that won't be necessary," said Sam. "C'mon folks, let's get back to it. Baby, bring another length of pipe from that wagon, would ya?"

The woman Sam had called Baby stood up and walked over to where he stood grinning at her. She bent down to his level, blonde hair cascading down to her thighs, and placed a hand the size of a serving tray on his shoulder. He wilted under the weight, but kept grinning.

"Do you think it's endearing to get people's names wrong, Sam?" asked the giantess. "Are you actually that ignorant?"

"Oh c'mon, you know I only do it 'cause I like ya, Baby."

The giantess grinned back at him, teeth glinting like the snow. "Well, I don't particularly like you, Sam. You're a letch and a charmless oaf, and if I wasn't fettered by this mejrok, I'd pull your arms off."

"Baby, …"

"My name's Bewienn – as you well know – and if you call me Baby again I'll see to it no merchant in the city or surrounds will sell you that grain liquor you like so much, understand?"

Sam's grin didn't waver a whit. "Sure thing, *Baybeen*. Anything you say."

Bewienn sighed and stood up, pushing Sam down as she rose. He grunted under the force and almost cried out as she ground the bones and soft tissue in his shoulder together, but she let go before she did any actual damage. His grin returned as he watched her stride over to where the pipe segments were stacked. Something akin to a mooning schoolboy's expression appeared on his face as he watched the beautiful woman heft a two-hundred kilo length of pipe and place it over her shoulder.

Sam liked her - that was true - but the real truth was that Sam Renstrom had fallen head over heels in love with Bewienn the Giantess.

Jere the felkynd brushed past Sam to pick up a pickaxe.

{*Get your thoughts under control, Sam Renstrom. Your intentions towards Bewienn Mohr are polluting my mind. Put her from your notions, human; she'd snap you in two.*}

Sam stepped away from Jere. These tall fur-covered bipeds with their panthers' heads and their telepathy made him uneasy.

"Well, I don't see how that's any of your beeswax, Cat," said Sam from a safe distance. "Go clean out your litter box."

Jere walked past with the pickaxe over his shoulder and bared his teeth at Sam.

"Ok, Ok guys," said Fintan, "let's get back to work before Nemnet loses his patience."

*

They worked on into the late afternoon, clearing snow, rocks and soil, sinking foundations and erecting stanchions for the pipeline just like they had done the day before and countless days before that.

It amazed Fintan they could accomplish so much without optics and heavy machinery. He took on the roles of engineer, surveyor and draftsman and was able to explain his requirements to Jere who took levels with his bare eyes and, amazingly, did the complex calculations in his head. Fintan had taken to calling him 'The Walking Theodolite.' Bewienn did the heavy lifting and between them all they did the spadework and the welding of the sections using tiny teic welding rigs. Between them they did more work every day than Fintan would have believed possible.

Just around the time the sun was disappearing behind Schliew Unierren, Nemnet called a halt and a shuttle disc arrived to ferry them the two hundred kilometers back to Keher Kuhn-Ridh. The journey took over an hour and Fintan watched the pipeline they'd spent months building pass beneath them. Sam and Bewienn bantered with flirtatious enmity and Jere sat with his eyes closed, a faint purring coming from his throat. Eventually it got too dark to see and Fintan put his head back and closed his eyes.

He awoke from his doze as the shuttle landed with a crunch on the snow outside Keher Kuhn-Ridh. The lights from the city and the floating globes of teic illuminating the gates glowed through the transparent canopy. A group of guards approached the shuttle to escort them inside. Bewienn and Sam talked quietly to each other, but there was something up with Jere. Normally the felkynd would remain in his meditative state until the canopy opened, but tonight he was sitting bolt upright, his blue-grey fur standing on end and his muzzle pulled back in a silent snarl. He looked around, this way and that, his eyes wide as if sensing a threat. As Nemnet opened the canopy Fintan said, "Jere, what's wrong?"

Jere sprang from his seat and vaulted out of the shuttle. He ran into the night, his paws leaving big tracks in the snow and was almost out of sight when Nemnet reached into his shirt and touched his mejrok. There was a shriek and a snarl, and Jere fell headlong into the snow and lay still. Nemnet ordered the guard detail to retrieve the felkynd and kept the others at spearpoint. The guards dragged Jere back like a ragdoll and threw him in the snow. He snarled weakly and after a couple of attempts stood up, reeling like a drunk. Nemnet grabbed him by the front of his jerkin and snarled into his face, "If you try that again, Stray, I'll skin you alive, understand?"

Jere threw his head back and shrieked a howl of anger toward the stars, but he held both forepaws out before him, crossed, with the pads upwards in a gesture of submission. Satisfied, Nemnet indicated to the guard detail to take the four prisoners into the city.

"Jere, what's the matter?" said Fintan quietly as they walked. "I've never seen you like this."

{*A terrible thing, Øsul McHewell. Many of my kynd brothers and sisters crying out in great fear somewhere nearby.*}

"Why didn't you explain to Nemnet, rather than letting him zap you?"

{*Alas, we cannot communicate with any of Kuhn-Ridh's guards. Their mejroks block out our thoughts. They fear us being able to overpower them mentally.*}

"And could you?"

{*Were they not wearing those accursed stones, certainly. But whilst they do, they cannot hear our thoughts and we cannot hear theirs. That is how they capture felkynd in the first place; we are not aware of their approach.*}

"But surely you can hear them, even if you can't sense their thoughts."

Jere's eyes drifted towards a bend in the western road. Fintan became aware of a distant mewling sound, like many people keening quietly. The cries increased in volume until a prison transport – a large cage on a floating platform – came into view, accompanied by a group of guards. In the cage were felkynd of all ages, some sitting, some standing, but all staring out with large terrified eyes. Their mental cacophony filled Fintan's mind:

{*Help us!*}

{*/fear/*}

{*Where are we?*}

{*/pain/*}

{*What is going to happen to us?*}

{*Help us!*}

Jere stood with his eyes wide and his teeth bared. Fintan could feel the waves of telepathic frustration and anger emanating from him. Nemnet shouted over," Hey, you lot; keep moving toward the city."

One of the guards pushed Fintan and Jere in the back. The felkynd snarled and stood his ground. Fintan pulled on Jere's arm.

"C'mon, don't give them an excuse to hurt you again."

"That's it, McHewell; get that maggot-ridden stray moving before he earns you all half-rations for the next week."

"I'm doing my best, boss. He's just concerned about his people. What do you want with them, anyway?"

Nemnet walked over and placed the tip of his spear under Fintan's chin.

"You ask a lot of questions, McHewell, but I'll tell you anyway. All the chieftains have been ordered to double their efforts to track down the Lebor Stara, and Kuhn-Ridh wants to be the one to find it."

Nemnet turned to Jere with gleeful contempt. "He's going to perform a *taghairm*."

At the word 'taghairm', the felkynd in the cage started screaming and pulling at the bars. Jere snarled and his mind screamed {*NO!*} He leapt onto Nemnet knocking him onto his back and sank his fangs into his shoulder. Nemnet screamed and struggled beneath Jere, but the felkynd held on and tore at Nemnet's belly with his rear claws. Fortunately for Nemnet, his leather armor took most of the damage and he managed to get his arm free and reach for his spear. He brought the spear up to Jere's face and discharged it. There was an explosive crackle of energy, and Jere fell back in the snow and lay still.

The smell of burned fur and flesh filled their nostrils and a wisp of smoke rose from the charred ruin of Jere's left eye socket into the chill night air.

*

Later that night, as Bewienn tended to Jere's wounds, Sam hissed across to Fintan, "What'n the hell's a taghairm?"

Fintan stood at the front of his cell facing Sam's, gripping the bars and looking over at Jere and Bewienn. "I have no idea," he whispered, "but whatever it is, it scared the bejesus out of Jere and his people."

{*Why are you whispering, humans?*} Jere's thought-voice filled their heads. {*Do you forget I hear your every thought?*}

"Sorry Jere," said Fintan. "No offense intended. Humans have a tendency to whisper around people who are injured or being tended. How are you doing over there, anyway?"

{*I let my emotions get the better of me, Øsul. The fear and pain of my kynd, and the taunts of that accursed guardsman caused me to lose my control. My temper has cost me my eye.*}

Jere hissed inwards as Bewienn placed the poultice Fintan had traded his useless iPhone for on Jere's face.

"I'm sorry, Jere," she said as she tended the wounded felkynd through the bars that separated their cells. "I'm doing my best not to hurt you, but this wound is grave, and I need to remove the remains of your eye lest it fester."

{*I thank you deeply Bewienn Mohr. The giants and the felkynd have not always been the best of allies, but you are a great ambassador for your people.*}

"Thank you. Now lie still. I don't want to make this any worse."

The felkynd lay back while Bewienn continued her treatment. Unbidden, he said,

{*A taghairm is a divination ritual. It is a cruel and brutal rite used to raise daemons.*}

"But why? And what does it have to do with cats?" asked Sam.

{*In a taghairm, thirteen felkynd are roasted alive, one after the other.*}

Bewienn gasped and her hand went to her mouth. Jere sat up and looked over at Fintan and Sam.

{*As each felkynd suffers, the energy of his mental screams is captured in a device called a* føtta. *If it is timed properly, as the thirteenth felkynd dies, his final scream merges with the others and the mental resonance invokes a fire-daemon that becomes trapped in the føtta. The daemon cannot return to Iofrin until it answers a single question truthfully. If the divination works, Kuhn-Ridh will ask the daemon where the Lebor Stara is. And then we are all lost.*}

"What's the Lebor Stara?"

{*An ancient artifact. A book of great power. Kuhn-Ridh wants it badly enough to torture thirteen of my kynd to death for it.*}

"Oh Jesus," said Fintan. "That is appalling. When will this happen?"

{*At the feast of Sauwan. In twenty-one days.*}

"Does he have enough felkynd to do this? How many were in the transport?"

Jere lay back and closed his remaining eye. He gave no answer for a moment then said,

{*There were twelve.*}

*

Sam was about to knock on the door of Mug-Ruit's office when he heard raised voices inside. Ignoring the glare of his guard chaperone, he leaned closer to the door and listened.

"Are you crazy, Nemnet? Do you have any idea how difficult it is to find felkynd with engineering skills and that are susceptible to obedience patterns on their mejrok? In the last fifty-five raids we've caught exactly one. And now you want to put him in a taghairm?"

"Look," said Nemnet, "he's a troublemaker. He tried to escape last evening and when I restrained him he almost disemboweled me."

"So you were able to subdue an unarmed fettered felkynd with your spear." Mug-Ruit's voice was heavy with sarcasm. "Good for you."

"Hardly unarmed; they have claws and teeth. Anyone would think you were on the cat's side."

"I don't have sides in this. I just want a safe and peaceful city for everyone. And I know what you're like, Nemnet; always taunting the prisoners and harassing the maidens – my daughter amongst them. You have a nasty streak and it's a mile wide. You didn't need to tell Jere his people were being used for a taghairm. You didn't need to do anything but keep your mouth shut and make sure the prisoners made it back to their cells."

"They need to be …"

"Shut up, Nemnet. Just shut up and get out of my sight. Jere is too valuable as a teicnoir on the pipeline. He's not to be put in the taghairm, and that's the end of it."

"But he's half blind now; what good is he?"

"You're clutching at straws; he'll be perfectly fine working on the pipeline with one eye. Now get out and organize another raid. Find me another felkynd for the taghairm."

The door was wrenched open. Sam jumped back and Nemnet strode out gritting his teeth. He saw Sam standing there looking guilty and shook his head in disgust.

"Aliens! You're as bad as that cat. Too useful on the pipeline, my arse-rag! Let's see how useful he is when he loses the other eye."

"I heard that," shouted Mug-Ruit. "Ah Renstrom, there you are. Come in, come in."

Nemnet stomped down the tower stairs. Sam's chaperone stood to attention and cleared his throat.

"I have to report that this prisoner was eavesdropping at the door, *Tieschach*."

Sam started to bluster and profess innocence, but Mug-Ruit looked pained and waved his hand at the guard. "Yes, yes; terrible behavior. The whole tír's going to the dogs, now shut that door and wait outside until Mr. Renstrom is ready to go back to his cell."

The guard gave Sam a dirty look and swung the door closed.

"And no eavesdropping," called Mug-Ruit.

There was an embarrassed cough from outside the door and a shuffling of boots as the guard sidled away.

"Now Renstrom, how are you doing today?"

"'Bout the same as usual, I guess. What was all that about?"

"Oh, this taghairm that Kuhn-Ridh wants. Frightful business. Nemnet has some grudge against Jere and wants me to put him in as the thirteenth felkynd."

Mug-Ruit walked over to the window. Far below in the courtyard, an area had been fenced off where the teicnoiri were erecting the gantry for the fotta.

"Well, I ain't so fond of him myself," said Sam. "He's kinda hoity-toity, and not particularly friendly."

"Is he indeed? I find him quite pleasant to deal with. Have you had dealings with any other felkynd?"

"Well no, I guess I haven't."

"They're certainly more reserved than your average human, I'll give you that, but they're smart and hard-working, and honest to a fault. Jere is actually one of the more approachable of them."

"Jeez. Well I hope I never meet a real unsociable one."

"Perhaps you should try and get to know Jere better. He really is quite an extraordinary fellow."

"I don't get it. Why do you have such a soft spot him?"

Mug-Ruit looked in the distance for a moment. When he spoke his voice was quiet and carried the weight of distant memories:

"He saved my life once."

Sam look startled. "He saved your life? When?"

"Oh, a long time ago. When I was quite a different man. Well, look, fascinating as this all is, it's not why I asked you up here. I need to make a report upstairs. How is progress on the pipeline?"

Sam wanted to ask more about Mug-Ruit's past with Jere but the security chief fixed him with a look that stated in no uncertain terms that the topic was off limits. Reluctantly, Sam let it go.

"Er, pretty good, I guess," he said. "We're managing a major section every two weeks now, so if the sections stay the same length we should be at Schliew Unierren in about three months."

Mug-Ruit looked askance at Sam. "Who told you the pipeline is going to

Schliew Unierren?"

Sam shifted uneasily. "Nemnet mentioned it yesterday. Are we not supposed to know?"

"No, you're not supposed to know; as evidenced by the fact that I've never told you." Mug-Ruit sighed. "Oh well, we were going to have to tell you sooner or later, I suppose. Still, damn that Nemnet and his big mouth. Kuhn-Ridh has already given me a carpeting for other security leaks. If he hears about this, he'll flay me."

Mug-Ruit looked out the window, his brow furrowed. Sam cleared his throat.

"Can I, er… can I ask you a question?"

"Well, I may as well be hung for a sheep as a lamb, I suppose. Ask away."

"Far as I can see, you're opening these holes in my universe and using them to steal oil and bring it back here, right?"

"You make it sound so iniquitous, but that's about the size of it, yes."

"Well, if you can open holes anywhere you like, why do you need a pipeline? Why not just open the hole on this side exactly where you need it?"

Mug-Ruit looked at Sam with admiration.

"That is indeed an excellent question. I never thought you'd have the nous to come up with that. Well, I'll tell you what I know, but the underlying technical hocus-pocus is a bit beyond me, I'm afraid. It's to do with the spatial geometry of sidhs that link our respective tírs. The natural laws of your tír are framed within what you call physics. The corresponding discipline here is called teic; somewhat of a superset of your physics. Think of physics, throw in higher-order mathematics and add a good dash of what you call magick and that's Teic in a nutshell.

"But to answer your question, there are teic laws governing how sidhs are opened between tírs, and what can pass through them. The prime governing factor seems to be gravity. For example, within certain geometrical constraints, it's possible to open a sidh from this tír to anywhere in your tír, but if the sidh on your side is far within the gravity well of a massive object such as a planet or a star, living creatures cannot pass through it from here to there. I believe it used to be possible to open sidhs to your side with impunity and all manner of creatures used to travel over there, but the laws were rewritten to prevent it a long time ago."

"Huh? You mean the laws of physics here can be rewritten just like criminal law back home?"

"The laws of teic, to be precise, but yes, you have the idea. Apparently, there are artifacts that can do such things. But going back to your original question and how gravity affects things, when we open a sidh between tírs, near, or on, a planet's surface, we can only specify the exact location on one side or the other, but not both. Sidhs that open from the surface of your world tend to bunch up into smaller areas here. For example, every sidh opened on your side, anywhere on your planet, opens into the island of Eyron on this side. And in fact, every sidh we have that opens from your American continent, opens on this side into an area outside Keher Kuhn-Ridh no bigger than a small village. The gravitational effect is so strong that if surface sidhs on this side were not contained in a very strong teic field, they would drift around within their geometrical parameters and cause havoc."

"But you said living creatures can't pass through from my side, if the sidh is on the planet's surface. Ain't that how I came through?"

"Ah, what I actually said was that living creatures can't pass through from here to there. There's no law saying they can't pass through in the opposite direction. They didn't tighten that one up for some reason."

Sam looked glum. "So I really am stuck here. There's no way back."

"Well in theory, if you knew how, you could open a sidh into the space above your planet where the gravity is weak. The laws don't prevent that. If you had some way of surviving the journey to the surface, you'd be home."

"Which is another way of saying I'm stuck here."

"Oh come, come, Sam! Is it really so bad? You don't want for anything, and in a few weeks the pipeline will be completed and you'll be released from your work contract. You'll be able to roam the island to your heart's content, seek adventure, become a bard, or a mercenary, or a farmer – whatever takes your fancy. Or you could stay here and work for us. I'm sure there'll be other pipeline projects."

"Well, it's not like I got much to go back to anyhow – and there's another thing; how come you need oil anyways? I ain't seen no motor vehicles, and all your flying doohickeys seem to run on water."

"Ah, now that *would* be telling. Some things I really must keep to myself if I'm to retain my job – and my head."

Sighing, Sam walked over to the window and looked at the activity far below.

"What's goin' on down there?"

Mug-Ruit stood at his shoulder. "Preparations for the taghairm. See that large cauldron-like thing they're floating onto the top of that gantry?"

"Yeah, that thing that looks like a huge copper bath?"

"Bronze actually, but yes; that thing. That's the føtta. Quite horrible."

The føtta was a semi-spherical bronze crucible, big enough for several men to lie end-to-end in, and just about big enough to contain an enraged fire-daemon. Several rods went from the lip of the føtta and converged at a metal ring several meters above it. It looked to Sam like a place to attach a hoist but that clearly wasn't its purpose given the teicnoiri were maneuvering it on a floating platform. The gantry was surrounded by thirteen evenly-spaced iron cabinets, vaguely humanoid and reminiscent of iron maiden torture devices.

"What are those things standing in a circle around the whatchamacallit?" asked Sam.

"Those are called *eijen*. They're the ovens the felkynd will be placed in before the ritual. Ghastly devices."

"How does it all work?"

"They'll place a large crystal lens on the top of the tower here, and another in that ring over the føtta. As the sun rises, the lens on the tower will catch the rays and focus them onto the lens above the føtta. The lenses are cut in such a way that as the sun transits the sky, its rays will be concentrated on each eijen in turn, roasting the poor creature within. It takes hours. Many hours. Absolutely gruesome.

"Well, anyway; I've talked enough. Too much probably. It's good to hear that the pipeline is on schedule. Enjoy your day off, Renstrom. You can go now."

Sam headed for the door. *Yeah, enjoy my day off in captivity in a place I can't get home from. Gee thanks.* He opened the door and went through.

"Er, Renstrom?" called Mug-Ruit.

Sam poked his head back around the door.

"Don't share any of what I told you with anyone. It wouldn't do either of us any good."

Sam nodded and closed the door behind him. With a heavy heart and his chaperone in tow he headed back down the stairs to his cell.

*

From his tower window Mug-Ruit watched the progress of the føtta as the teicnoiri guided it into place. One of them took off his helmet and leaned his head back, mopping his brow and neck. He saw Mug-Ruit watching and saluted up at him. Mug-Ruit returned the salute.

That fellow has sharp eyesight. I must be a hundred meters above him and he could see me clearly enough to deliver the correct salute. Extraordinary. He must have the sight of a felkynd. Or at least the sight of a felkynd with two good eyes. Alas Jere. What am I doing to you and your people?

Despite what Mug-Ruit had said to Nemnet, Jere's future on the pipeline was very much in doubt. A teicnoir needed both eyes to take accurate levels and angles so it was only a matter of time before Jere was terminated on the project.

Not that it would make any difference to his ultimate fate.

Mug-Ruit hadn't been entirely honest with Sam either. In fact, he was appalled at how glibly he could lie to people these days. He had spoken to Sam about being released from the project and becoming an adventurer or what have you, but that was never going to happen.

Mug-Ruit didn't like it and in fact he thought it would increase tension among the races, but Kuhn-Ridh had sent down orders that morning that once the pipeline was completed everyone working on it would be executed.

*

{*Øsul, we have to help them*}, said Jere. {*The youngest is only a cub. It is unthinkable. The others have not explained the taghairm to him, but he can sense the danger. He is frightened beyond fear.*}

Fintan gripped the bars of his cell and looked over at Jere. Every erg of the anxiety radiating from Jere was reflected in the lines on Fintan's forehead. The bitter acid of impotent anger filled his craw.

Bewienn had her arm through the bars holding Jere's paw. His claws sank into her hand and retracted as he fretted, but she barely felt them break the skin. The tears on her cheek spoke of an empathic pain that was far more profound than a few puncture wounds.

Sam was lying on his bunk in the dark of his cell drinking *Ischkuva* and staying quiet.

"How can we help, Jere?" asked Bewienn. "What can we do?"

{*We must free them, Bewienn Mohr; free them and get them far away from here.*}

"But how can we hope to do that? We're all fettered with mejrok obedience patterns. We can't act against any of Kuhn-Ridh's people. Even if we could, there are too few of us. We'd be recaptured or killed in no time."

{*With enough willpower it is possible to overcome the effects of the mejrok for a few moments. I proved that when I almost gutted that vile guardsman yesterday. However, your point about our numbers is well taken. We need reinforcements.*}

"Where could we possibly get reinforcements from?" asked Fintan.

{*From the* Ord Kommarlu – *the high council of the Felkynd*}, Jere replied. {*They will not ordinarily interfere in the affairs of humans but if they hear of the taghairm they will besiege this accursed place and lay it low.*}

"Ok, how do we get a message to them? Can you reach them with your mind-voice?"

{*No, that is not possible. One must go to the Ord Kommarlu in the flesh to solicit their help. They live in a place where the thoughts of others cannot reach them and from where their thoughts cannot be heard. The gift of mind-voice comes with great responsibility and great consequences and our kynd do not take it lightly.*}

"So the only way to get help from the felkynd high council is to go there and ask for it. That means some or all of us have to escape. How are we going to manage that? As Bewienn said, we're all fettered. Perhaps you have the mental capacity to resist the mejrok, but I doubt I do. How about you, Sam?"

{*Waste not your time asking Sam Renstrom to help my kynd. He cares nothing for us.*}

Sam said nothing for a moment then swung his legs down and shambled to the front of his cell on unsteady feet. His voice was thick with the effects of the Ischkuva.

"I don't know nothin' much about you or your folk, Whiskers, but I know what's gonna happen to them and that ain't right; and there's a kid among them and that sure as *hell* ain't right! I don't like you, but I'll help you. Ain't no-one should sit back and let a kid die."

The words were no sooner out of his mouth than Sam fell to his knees and burst into racking sobs. The open bottle of Ischkuva rolled from his hand and spilled its contents in an arc on the floor. Fintan stood in shocked silence.

"Sam, what's wrong?" asked Bewienn.

Jere made a mewling sound and put his ears back. {*Ah, such anguish*}, he said. {*Sam Renstrom I had no idea you were carrying such a burden, you poor devil.*}

"What? What is it?" asked Fintan.

{*It is not for me to tell, Øsul. Sam Renstrom must unburden himself if he so chooses.*}

Sam looked up, his face a picture of grief. "Tell them. Just tell them, God damn it!"

"Tell us what?" asked Bewienn.

{*Much of what I'm seeing is unfamiliar to me but I see Sam Renstrom's mate and their child trapped in a vehicle. He has been ejected from the vehicle and is lying on the thoroughfare. His leg is broken and he cannot get to them.*}

"Oh my God, your wife and child were injured in a car crash?"

Sam used the bars of the cell to drag himself to his feet. "Killed. They were killed in an auto wreck. I was driving – drunk off my ass. I hit a barrier and spun the car across the other side of the freeway. I got thrown clear 'cause I wasn't wearing a seatbelt. Irony is, I always made sure Bobby was strapped in, and Hayley was in the habit of putting hers on automatically. She was always chewing me out for not wearing mine but I hated it. So I got flung out of the car and they were trapped – go figure. I'm pretty sure Hayley got hers off 'cause when I came to she was turned around in the car trying to get Bobby out of his. Then an eighteen-wheeler came round the bend and went clean over the top of the car. Bang. Just like that they were gone. Bobby was five years old. God damn it."

He forced his head against the bars and wept through clenched teeth.

"Oh Sam," said Bewienn. "I do not understand everything you said, but I understand your pain. How awful."

Fintan was shaking his head in sympathy. "Sam, I had no idea. I'm so sorry for your loss."

Sam wiped his eyes and nose with the backs of his hands. "Yeah, well it was a long time ago and it only comes to the surface when I drink this shit."

He kicked the bottle on the floor and looked over at Jere. "I'll help you rescue your kin."

Jere inclined his head. {*I thank you Sam Renstrom.*}

"Sorry to keep harping on about this, but how are we going to override these mejroks? There's no escaping as long as we're wearing them. Even if we could, we'd never make it out of the city."

Sam cleared his throat and looked out through the bars, his eyes and cheeks glistening.

"So we don't escape when we're inside the city – we do it when we're on the chain gang. Listen, tomorrow we'll switch places in the transport. Just as we're coming in to land at the pipeline, I'm going to yank the mejrok off Bewienn's neck. That'll free her. She'll do the same to Jere's and Fintan's. Then we're going to beat the tar out of those two guards, take their spears and make a run for it."

There was a stunned silence.

"Hold up, Sam," said Fintan. "How can you remove the mejrok from Bewienn's neck? The obedience pattern in yours won't let you."

Sam shrugged. "I ain't fettered."

There was another long silence.

"What do you mean, Sam?" asked Bewienn.

"Just what I say. I ain't got no obedience pattern. Don't know whether it was an oversight or because they knew I had nothing to go back to, but they never fettered me."

"But, but … why didn't you escape?"

"And go where? When I first got here all I wanted was to go back through that portal and back to my life in Alaska, empty as it was. Then I realized I was probably stuck here and I had to make the best of it. Either way, I figured I was better off sticking around here than going out into the wilds to take my chances with God-knows-what. Then today old Mug-Ruit pretty much confirmed to me there's no way back. So as things stand, I'm hangin' around a place out of choice where they burn innocent folk alive to raise demons. Well screw that! Tomorrow I'm out of here and you guys are coming with me. We're going to go see Jere's high council, bring an army back here and free his people. Then we're going to string Mug-Ruit and Kuhn-Ridh from that gantry they've built down in the yard."

"Oh Sam," said Bewienn, "it's a wonderful idea, but I'm afraid neither Jere nor I can go with you."

"Why the hell not? Don't you wanna get out of here? Don't you wanna help Jere's people?"

"Of course I do, Sam, but you're not going to be able to take my mejrok off. Look."

Bewienn unlaced her tunic and opened it down to the top of her breasts. She leant forward so that Sam and Fintan could see where the leather thong joined the top of the mejrok.

176

"Jesus!" said Sam. "How did it get under your skin?"

Where the mejrok should have nestled in her cleavage, the thong disappeared into her skin as if grafted there.

"This is what happens when you wear a mejrok for a long time. Jere's is the same. Yours will too after a few years. Haven't you ever noticed it sticking against your skin?"

"Yeah, but I just thought I was allergic or somethin'. It kinda sticks sometimes and leaves a raw patch when I yank at it." He looked over at Fintan. "Don't tell me yours is dug in too."

"No, it irritates my skin sometimes, but I can still move it around. Although, if I try to take it off, my arms refuse to work. If you're planning on cutting it off me, I hope it doesn't fry my brain or something."

"God damn it! So only me and Fintan can get these suckers off. Can we cut yours out maybe? I got plenty of alcohol to rub on the wounds."

Bewienn shook her head and looked at Sam with eyes like pools of regret. "No Sam, once the mejrok is under the skin it sends tiny filaments into the organs and nerves. It's as much a part of me now as my heart. I am bonded to Kuhn-Ridh until he terminates my contract."

{*It is true, Sam Renstrom. I can tell you and Øsul McHewell how to locate the Ord Kommarlu but you must travel there without us and convince them of the plight of our kynd.*}

"Ah shoot! OK, well what's the plan then?"

{*We shall adapt your plan, Sam Renstrom, for it is a good one. As we alight at the pipeline tomorrow I shall subdue the accursed Nemnet and relieve him of his spear. At that moment you will remove the mejrok from Øsul McHewell's neck. One of you will then take charge of the spear and dispatch the guards. I do not believe I can overcome the mejrok for long enough to manage that.*}

"Then what?"

{*Then you will both take to your heels with the spears and not look back. You will*} *find the Ord Kommarlu and return before the feast of Sauwan with an army of felkynd* Kommanlak *to tear this midden apart and free my kynd.*}

"But what about you and Bewienn? Won't you be punished?"

"We'll take care of ourselves, Fintan. You must get away quickly because they'll send guards after you. We'll send them in the wrong direction of course, but they'll eventually pick up your trail."

"Yeah, speakin' of directions, where is this Ord whatchamacallit anyways?"

{*Alas, I do not know, but …*}

"What? You don't know? What was all that baloney about goin' there and bringing them back then?"

{*Only enlightened felkynd know where the Ord Kommarlu is, Sam Renstrom, however …*}

"Well, what the hell's that mean?"

{*You should let me finish, Sam Renstrom. Some felkynd dedicate their lives to* Diru; *the study of felkynd mind powers. If they attain* Worar *– the highest degree of Diru - they are eligible to be felkynd leaders. Many of them then assume places in the Ord Kommarlu.*}

"Do you know of any of these enlightened felkynd, Jere," asked Fintan.

{*I know of one, yes.*}

"And how do we find him?"

{*Her. She lives in an old Diru retreat which was partially destroyed by Midir a long time ago. Only the tower remains, and therein she resides.*}

"So what is she, some kinda super witch cat, or somethin'?"

{*She is very powerful, but far from a witch. She is my mother.*}

"Your mother?"

{*Yes indeed, Øsul. She attained Worar level three and would have become a great felkynd leader had she not become pregnant with me. She made a great sacrifice to have me. She is the one you must find, but do not speak to her of me or give any indication that it was her son who sent you.*}

"Why on earth not? We're going to be two alien humans arriving out of the blue asking for help. Surely she'll trust us quicker if we tell her we know you."

{*Alas not Øsul; I was a severe disappointment to her and she disavowed me many years ago.*}

"But you're her son. I mean, how disappointed can she be? And if it was years ago perhaps she's gotten over it."

{*There is no getting over it, Øsul. Disavowal is final and irrevocable. We call it* 'basbattak' – *the living death.*}

"Not that it's any of my business, but why did she disavow you?"

{*Ah, a common quarrel between parents and children, Øsul: She had plans for me; I had other plans for myself. Against her counsel I followed my own path. She was unused to such waywardness and reacted as she would with a recalcitrant Diru acolyte: She expelled me from her life.*}

"But it can't be as irrevocable as you say. Is there no way you could reconcile?"

{*It is not possible, Øsul. Basbattak involves a complete psychic disconnection of two felkynd. Even if we wanted to, my mother and I can never communicate with one another again. The connection is cut. You must understand it is not called basbattak merely because the exile is dead to the one who banishes him. When my mother disavowed me, I felt the cut. It was like someone had never existed, yet I still had the memories of a life with them. For her it is better or perhaps worse, as befits your viewpoint: She has no memory of me whatsoever.*}

Fintan shook his head and turned away. The unbelievable sadness of Jere's situation tore at his heart and drove a lump into his throat. Thinking about what the noble cat had suffered at the hands of Nemnet, and the anguish he must be feeling at the potential fate of his kynd made it all the harder to understand how he could cope. As tears stung the corners of

179

Fintan's eyes and spilled down his cheek, thoughts he had been suppressing for months rose unbidden to his mind. Memories of Bree and Mark flashed through his mind and he gasped as the sense of loss hit him like a hammer blow. He staggered and caught the bars to stop himself falling over.

"Fintan, are you OK, man?" asked Sam.

Fintan looked up, the grief in his throat now a very real pain – like a knife was thrust in there - and saw the others staring at him. With more self-control than he knew he possessed, he forced the lid back on his misery and said, "Yeah, yeah; I'm OK."

Jere looked over, his one good eye screwed in sympathy.

{*That is the first I have ever seen of your family, Øsul. I would never look into your mind, but the sheer force of your recollections tore through my thoughts. You must tell yourself that you will see them again. You must believe it with every fiber of your being, else you are lost.*}

"Thanks Jere. Yes, that's how I keep going; by doing exactly that. I just had a moment of weakness. I don't know how you manage though. I think your story is one of the saddest things I've ever heard."

{*It is my lot, Øsul, and mine to bear. It does however have an advantage for you: When you reach my mother, no matter how hard she looks into your minds, she will not be able to see any trace of me.*}

"OK, well I still think that's incredibly sad, but I can see how it helps us. Where is this tower where your mother lives, anyway?"

{*It lies far to the north of here. It is called* Dewenisch.}

"Dewenisch?" said Fintan. "I think I know where that is. Is it on an island in a lake?"

{*It is indeed, Øsul. How did you know?*}

"Because there is an island called 'Devenish' in my tír with a round tower on it. It was a place of study and meditation a long time ago. It's extraordinary how many similarities there are between this tír and the one

Sam and I come from."

{*Well, it is fortunate that you know where it is. It will make your journey somewhat easier.*}

"It will indeed, Jere. What's her name?"

{*Her name is Mieru, but her title is Worara Øsul Mieru-San. If you address her thus and hold your palms up whilst approaching she will be better disposed towards you.*}

Fintan nodded. "Thank you, Jere." He looked around at the group, his lips tight. "OK, tomorrow, if all goes to plan, we set off to find Worara Øsul Mieru-San.

{*May your gods and guardian spirits go with you.*}

"Amen to that," said Fintan.

*

Outside the cell-block door, Nemnet stepped away from his spy-hole and started back up the stairs, his face twisted in fury.

Treacherous bastards! I should report them to Mug-Ruit and have them flayed for their sedition. But no; I'll deal with the scum myself. Oh, someone is indeed going to get killed tomorrow, but it won't be me.

*

"What 'n the hell is he doin' here?" growled Sam.

Mug-Ruit smiled at the work gang as the four of them approached the shuttle disc.

"No idea Sam," said Fintan, "but something's going on."

"Good morning, my friends," said Mug-Ruit. "I trust we are all well today."

"Good morning," said Fintan. "It's unusual to see you out here so early.

181

Is there something wrong?"

"No, not at all, not at all," said Mug-Ruit slapping Fintan on the shoulder. "Sam here was telling me yesterday how well you are getting on with the pipeline and I thought I'd come and see for myself."

At this Nemnet started and turned to Mug-Ruit with his mouth agape.

"You're coming with us?"

"Yes, indeed I am. It's been a while since I got away from the city and even longer since I visited Makloklin, the chieftain up there. He has, after all, been kind enough to let us put the pipeline through his kingdom so I should go and offer my gratitude in person."

"But, but … "

"Oh for heaven's sake, Nemnet! Why is everything such an issue for you? One would swear you didn't want me along!"

"Tieschach, it's a long boring journey and the lands up there are dangerous. I don't want to have to be responsible for your security as well as the prisoners."

"Nemnet, might I remind you that I was a mercenary before I was head of security. I am well able to take care of myself. And might I also remind you who fills your coin-purse at the end of the week. No more protestations. I'm coming along."

Nemnet turned away and muttered under his breath.

"You do far too much of that, Nemnet," said Mug-Ruit. "Don't try my patience."

The four were looking at each other in alarm at this turn of events and Sam approached Mug-Ruit. "Listen Chief, I wouldn't ordinarily side with old Numbnuts there, but he's right. You probably don't want to come on this trip. It's a hell of a hike."

Jere came up alongside and nodded his head in agreement.

Mug-Ruit sighed. "If I were of a more sensitive persuasion I might be deeply hurt by all this rejection. No more discussion. Let's be on our way."

He turned and climbed into the shuttle, taking a seat at the rear. He stared at Nemnet and the four for a moment then he raised his eyebrows and gestured at the empty seats in front of him.

"Come on," Nemnet growled. "Get in." He pushed them towards the craft and they started to board. Jere was last and as he stepped into the craft Nemnet thrust his spear into Jere's side, burning a patch of fur. The felkynd paused and stared into Nemnet's eyes with his teeth bared. Nemnet leaned into him and hissed, "Today's the day, Stray. Mug-Ruit or no Mug-Ruit I'm going to skin you alive." He tapped his finger on the patch over Jere's eye-socket. "Maybe I'll take the other one first."

Jere turned away and stepped into the disc taking his usual seat behind the pilot. Disappointed at the lack of reaction, Nemnet climbed in beside the pilot and closed the canopy.

"Jolly good," said Mug-Ruit from the rear. "Enough dissembling. Let's be off!"

*

A few minutes out from their destination Mug-Ruit spoke up. "Jere, you look very uncomfortable up there." He patted the seat beside him. "Why don't you come and sit back here with me?"

Jere shook his head and pointed to the floor under his feet, making an *I'm quite happy here* gesture with his other paw.

"No, no; I insist. Come back and sit here."

Nemnet turned and glanced at Mug-Ruit then eyed Jere with suspicion. Jere looked at Fintan who shrugged and nodded his head. Jere rose, eyeballing Nemnet, and made his way to the back of the craft.

"Excellent. You'll be much happier back here."

Nemnet continued to scowl back at them. Mug-Ruit waved him away and he turned to face forwards again, muttering.

Jere, I know what you're planning.

Jere's heart missed a beat. He narrowed his one good eye and looked sideways at Mug-Ruit.

{*I can hear your mind-voice, Tieschach.*}

Yes. And I can hear yours. Amazing what's possible when you have control of the mejroks, isn't it? Now, as I was saying, I know what you're up to.

Jere hung his head. A great sadness and sense of futility came over him.

{*Is our luck never to change? Tieschach, I implore you; if you stop us you'll be sentencing my kynd to death.*}

My dear Jere, I merely told you that I am aware of your plans. I said nothing about stopping you.

Jere glanced at him again.

{*You are toying with me?*}

Not so, my friend. I cannot be party to any actual violence against my people but I shall not prevent the escape. Nor will Nemnet and his guards, I shall see to that.

{*I am perplexed, Tieschach. Why would you help us?*}

Drop the 'Tieschach', Jere; we are long past such formalities. I shall help you because I owe you my life, and because that taghairm is an abomination. It cannot go ahead.

{*I am very relieved to hear you say so.*}

Indeed. However, there are conditions attached to my helping you. Would you hear them?

{*Gladly.*}

Very good. Only McHewell and Renstrom can escape. If I report that two aliens were killed in an accident, I don't have to account for them. You and Bewienn Mohr would present more of a problem.

{*It is as we planned it, in any case.*}

Indeed. Secondly, I must not be implicated.

{*Agreed. We would keep your involvement confidential, even under pain of death.*}

Thank you, Jere. Thirdly, and most importantly, when your people come to the city, no harm must come to Keher Kuhn-Ridh, any of her people or to the oil pumping system. Is that clearly understood?

{*Then how shall we free my kynd?*}

Without violence. McHewell and Renstrom will bring representatives of the Ord Kommarlu and a division of Kommanlak to the gates of the city. I shall convince Kuhn-Ridh that we should come to a diplomatic solution and shall effect the release of your people in that fashion. There is to be no attack or siege of the city. Is that clearly understood?

{*It is. If Kuhn-Ridh frees my people, there will be no bloodshed. However, should you not honor this pledge, I shall not be able to prevent the Kommanlak from laying waste to your city.*}

When we have agreed these terms I shall give you my spoken word, as a man in your debt, that I shall keep my bond as long as I am alive to do so. Will you accept it?

{*If you offer it, I shall accept it.*}

Excellent. Here is the final condition: Since there will be no taghairm and therefore no fire daemon, the Ord Kommarlu must agree to assist us in locating the Lebor Stara.

Jere raised his brow.

{*They will never agree to that. The Lebor Stara is lost in time and that is how the Ord Kommarlu wants it. They would never allow Midir to regain it.*}

Nevertheless, it is a condition of this bargain. If it makes you happier, you should know that I have no intentions of letting Midir have it either; I want it handed over to me.

{*You? What do you want with it?*}

Oh come now, Jere. Why would I not want such a powerful book?

{*You are asking the Ord Kommarlu for a great deal of trust in taking stewardship of such a thing, however I shall ask Øsul McHewell and Sam Renstrom to present your conditions as you have set them out. I accept your contract.*}

Mug-Ruit held out his hand to Jere surreptitiously. Jere gripped it and Mug-Ruit said "*Gjällim*" under his breath.

Now, our bond is sealed. May the gods of darkness and the gods of light look favorably on our bargain.

{*May Bastet and Sekhmet grant it their blessing.*}

A shadow loomed over them.

"What are you up to, Stray?" Nemnet demanded. "Tieschach, you must know you can't trust this degenerate."

"Calm down, Nemnet. Jere and I are old friends. There is no issue here with trust. Retake your seat."

"I don't think you understand, Tieschach. You can't trust any of them. I overheard them talking last night. They're planning to kill us and escape. Renstrom isn't even fettered!"

"Oh for heaven's sake, Nemnet. Do you think you are the only one who eavesdrops? I know everything that goes on; I control the mejroks, you moron!"

Nemnet managed to look simultaneously cowed and provoked.

"I'm the head of the City Guard! If you knew about the escape why didn't you tell me? Why did you let them leave the city today?" A sudden realization - a fervent hope - entered his eyes. "Wait, you're going to kill them out here, aren't you? That was my plan too; kill them and say they were trying to escape."

"No-one is going to kill anyone, Nemnet. I *want* them to escape."

Nemnet's jaw dropped. "You want them to …"

"Escape, yes. Well, McHewell and Renstrom at least. Look Nemnet, Kuhn-Ridh is making a huge mistake with this taghairm. There are better ways of finding the Lebor Stara than alienating the entire felkynd nation, not to mention invoking a fire-daemon in the middle of a crowded city. I have a practical alternate solution. All you have to do is cooperate and no-one has to get hurt. Are you going to cooperate, Nemnet?"

Nemnet took several steps back looking dazed then he snarled "Traitor!" and raised his weapon. Arcs of teic energy snaked across its blade as it charged. Before Nemnet could fire, Mug-Ruit leaped from his seat and delivered a snap kick to the point of Nemnet's chin. The others, who had no idea what was going on, looked on in shock. Nemnet flew back and fell across the rows of seats unconscious, but his thumb was on the trigger stud as he landed. The weapon discharged upwards and blew out the center of the canopy. The energy from the discharge flowed out through the hole and wove itself into the teic field surrounding the craft. The pilot cried out as the controls stopped responding and the craft began to lose height. The canopy disintegrated and large chunks of it flew away as the craft hurtled along, angling towards the ground. The occupants clung to their seats, the wind whipping their hair and clothes and threatening to pull them out of the craft.

"Look," shouted the pilot over the wind, "I'm going to bring us in over that lake. Get ready to jump."

They looked where he was pointing, "We'll never make it," shouted Fintan.

The pilot wrestled with the controls. "We will. I have enough power to bring us in shallow over the middle of the lake, but we'll get only one chance. When she hits she's going to skip off the surface and go back in hard over the land. We can't survive that so we're bailing out over the water. When you go, jump from the rear of the craft; feet first."

They took positions along the edge of the craft.

"What about Nemnet?" shouted Bewienn.

"Leave him," said Mug-Ruit. "He's a liability."

Jere jumped back down into the craft and tried to lift Nemnet clear but the guardsman had slid under one of the seats and his armor was caught.

Jere pulled hard on Nemnet's leg but the straps on the armor wouldn't give.

The pilot jumped up from his seat and ran for the back of the craft. "That's it; that's all I can do," he shouted. "We're just over the lake; go as quickly as you can. Danu be with you." The pilot jumped clear and fell out of sight.

"Jere!" screamed Bewienn, "We have to go *now*!"

Jere gave one last mighty heave on Nemnet's legs but the armor straps did their job and stayed put.

"JERE!"

Jere felt Bewienn's hand grab the scruff of his neck then he was falling towards the lake surface. He saw Mug-Ruit, Sam and Fintan enter the water below him in quick succession then he crashed through the surface and all went black.

Just as the pilot predicted, the shuttle slammed into the water and skipped up again shedding pieces of fuselage and interior fitting. It soared over the edge of the lake and came back down demolishing a teic generator powering one of the portal ground stations. High in the air, the portal shimmered and wobbled at its edge then shrank to the size of a penny, compressing the energy within it to a super-dense disc. It stayed stable for nanoseconds then exploded into either tír in two horizontally opposed, tightly-focused beams of high-energy particles.

Fintan burst through the surface of the lake gripping the spear weapon he'd grabbed from the disc before he'd jumped. An iridescent beam of light shrieked across the sky and ionized the air around it. On the other side of the portal in Fintan's home tír, the beam smashed through a gigantic disc shaped craft and the GPS satellite near it, knocking them both out of orbit. Emergency systems kicked in on the craft and a spherical field of energy leapt out from its core, enveloping it and the satellite.

Now locked in a twirling embrace like doomed lovers, the two objects began the long fall to Earth.

CHAPTER SEVENTEEN

THE INCIDENT AT LIME KILN BAY

illy Austin loved walking. Hill walking, bush walking; he didn't care. As long as he had a pair of hiking boots on his feet and a pole in his hand, he was happy.

He had been a walker all his life but since he'd retired he had really started to stretch his legs. At sixty-six he did the Inca Trail in Peru with dozens of travelers half his age, and was no sooner back than he flew out again and spent months walking the Camino de Santiago in Spain. By the time he turned seventy, he'd spent so much time out of Ireland you could say he'd pretty much walked all of Europe and a lot of the rest of the world besides. But for all the wonderful places he'd seen, his favorite walk was right on his doorstep, and whenever he was at home in Wicklow he got up early and did the cliff walk from the Black Castle to Wicklow Head.

Apart from the sheer clear-headed, loose-limbed feeling of freedom, it was the hypnotic effect of walking that drew him. With a good pair of boots and a trusty walking pole you could forget about the terrain and let your thoughts take flight. Indeed, he was so familiar with the rocks and tussocks of Wicklow Head that he could likely have walked it with his eyes closed.

Not that he ever closed his eyes while walking; there was too much too see. And that was another draw: No matter how often you did the same walk, you always saw something new.

But nothing could have prepared him for what he saw at Lime Kiln Bay early one morning in June.

*

It was shortly after 6 a.m. and Billy was approaching the canyon that leads to the beach at Lime Kiln Bay. He stopped, as he always did, thigh-deep in a patch of grass and ferns, deciding whether to go straight through the canyon or make the short hike up onto the headland and drop back down to the beach further up.

But today, for the first time in countless rambles, his mind was made up for him.

He saw it before he heard it; a vast bubble of light streaking downwards from the heavens towards the ocean. It passed straight over him; how high he had no idea, but certainly a lot lower than the jets that normally occupied that space. Training his binoculars on the bubble he could make out a huge disc-shaped craft and beside it, a box-shaped metallic structure with flat golden arms.

Then he heard it; a shrieking, whistling cacophony of air being torn aside, cut through with an eerie electrical resonance that made his scalp crawl. He tracked the objects through his glasses until the bubble disappeared behind the ridge.

There was a moment of silence then the displaced air closed behind the bubble. A sonic boom thundered down the canyon nearly knocking Billy off his feet. Ears ringing, he sprinted through the canyon towards the beach, his rucksack bouncing on his back. He arrived at the beach and the eponymous crumbling lime kiln just in time to see the bubble disappear into the sea in a cloud of spray and hissing vapor.

"Holy God!" he said. "What the hell was that?"

It occurred to him he should call the crash in to someone and was fumbling with his cellphone when a rumbling, rushing noise made him look up.

"Oh Jesus!" he shouted and took to his heels again. He had just made it up the cliff path towards the lighthouses when a rolling tidal wave hit the beach and surged up into the canyon. The seething soup carried driftwood, stones and the bodies of seals inland, flooding the canyon to the top. It had almost receded when a second wave struck and it started all over again.

Billy's hands were trembling so much he barely managed to dial the emergency services.

"*Which service do you require?*"

He paused. "Er... Coastguard, I suppose – and whoever investigates flying saucer crashes."

As the operator lectured him about the demerits of hoax calls to the emergency services, the second wave receded leaving the boxy object with the golden arms wedged in the top of the canyon.

"Oh, and you might want to call NASA; I think the sons of bitches are stealing our satellites."

CHAPTER EIGHTEEN

FORGILL & FERRISFORT

B ree's SUV wound its way through the narrow country roads. Mark rested his head against the passenger window and watched the countryside slide past. Memories of previous drives with his father, and fears about the journey ahead filled his thoughts.

Bree glanced at him then looked in the mirror into the back seat.

"Are you all right back there, Niamh?" she asked.

"Yes thanks, Mrs. McHewell," said Niamh.

"You should call me Bree, Niamh. You're almost a young woman after all. And we young women have to stick together!"

Bree winked in the mirror, and Niamh's face lit up. She and Bree both laughed. Niamh envied Mark, having a mum like Bree. She had never known her own mother, and Martha was cold and stand-offish. She'd certainly never banter the way Bree did.

As if reading her mind, Bree said:

"How are you getting along with Martha? Not that it's really any of my business, but I think she can be a bit hard on you."

"Yeah, she can be a right cow, sometimes. I've tried to get along with her for Daddy's sake, but I don't think she really likes me."

"Oh, I don't know about that, Niamh. I think she's one of those people who find it hard to express their feelings, but I think she loves you all right."

"She's got a strange way of showing it. She'd never have let me come today if you hadn't convinced her. And she's got Daddy wrapped around her little finger too. Sometimes I don't even know him anymore. He's so different now."

Bree thought for a few moments then said:

"Have you ever considered the possibility that they've stayed exactly the same and it's you that's changed?"

She shifted the angle of the rear-view mirror slightly to see Niamh's face. Niamh looked a little taken-aback. She looked out the window, her brow furrowed then puffed out her cheeks.

"I never thought about it like that. I don't think I've changed that much though."

"Look at it this way; you're not a child any more. Your dad knew exactly how to relate to your older brothers when they were teenagers, but now he has to come to terms with you not being his little girl any more. He doesn't know how to deal with it."

"Maybe. But what about Martha? She must have been fourteen once. She must remember what it's like."

"Oh she remembers, all right. She remembers only too well. She's jealous of you, Niamh."

"No way!"

"Oh, yes. It's obvious from the way she deals with you. It's the same combination of admiration and jealousy you see in schoolgirls that leads to bullying. She wants to be like you, but knows that part of her life is over. You're becoming a beautiful woman, and let's face it, poor Martha is no oil painting. You might think she is some stern older woman, steady and boring, but I promise you this; under the surface, she is just another young woman living in an older woman's body."

"But how do you know?"

"Because every woman is like that! When I was your age, I thought there was some special switch that would flick in your head when you hit twenty-one, or got married, or had children, and *CLICK*; you'd be an adult and have all the answers. There's not. Or if there is, I'm still waiting for it. Women don't feel much different whether they're fourteen or forty-four."

"Really?"

"Really. Men too. Men more so! Isn't that right, Mister?"

She looked over and nudged Mark who was still staring out the window. He hadn't said a word in ages.

"Wha...?"

"I was just saying that men never really grow up. You're all just a bunch of kids with expensive toys!" She grinned and nudged him again.

"Uh, I suppose. Sorry Mum, I wasn't really listening. Anyway, how would I know, I'm only fourteen?"

Bree made a mock-serious face at Niamh in the mirror, and Niamh chuckled quietly into her hands. Bree rolled her eyes at Mark.

"All right, Mr Grumpy! Sheesh, you're very serious today. So tell me; why are we going to this place... what's it called...?"

"Ferrisfort."

"Ferrisfort. Why are we going to Ferrisfort, again?"

Niamh shifted in the back seat and looked uncomfortable.

"It's one of the places Dad and I used to go to on our drives. I just wanted to see it again."

"Anything special there?"

"Not really. It's just a small village. I just wanted to walk around, maybe go to the shop; visit the church."

"Visit the church? Why would you want to do that?"

"I dunno, it just looks kind-of interesting."

Bree looked at him with an expression of utter puzzlement.

"Are you becoming religious since your father disappeared?"

"No, I don't think so. It's just something I'd like to do."

Bree looked at him again then looked at Niamh in the mirror. Niamh looked away.

"Why do I get the impression I'm not being told the full story here?"

They both started to speak but Bree interrupted them.

"Look, I don't want to know. Whatever you're up to must be important to both of you. Let me just ask you this: Is it dangerous, or will it get you into trouble?"

"No," they chimed.

"Ok, then I'm up for the adventure too whatever it is. Are we still on the right road?"

She nodded her head at the portable GPS in Mark's hand. He consulted it.

"Yeah, just follow this road. We should get there in twenty minutes. You're right about this gadget, by the way Mum – it *is* an awesome present. Thanks!"

"You're welcome Kiddo," she said, and they continued on their way.

*

Ferdia rested his head against the bus window and watched the leafy suburbs of South Dublin slip by. A quiet sense of anticipation bubbled in his stomach.

The previous four days had been some of the most satisfying of his life. After the Skype conversation with Mark and Niamh, he had written a well-crafted email to Del Forgill, the owner of the *Magus Conspiracy* website. As expected, Forgill was skeptical and wrote a curt response. Over the following days, Ferdia engaged Forgill in a battle of wits during which he fed out bits and pieces of the story like a fishing line. Forgill was interested but wary, and Ferdia knew he had to play him carefully. The contest continued daily and Forgill's interest waxed as his wariness waned. The coup de grâce was perfect: Ferdia emailed Forgill a photograph of the two Tetroi sitting on a copy of that day's paper. Forgill was hooked. The next email was an invitation to Forgill's home in Churchtown, and an entreaty to bring the Tetroi along for examination.

A smile played on Ferdia's lips. He was good at manipulating adults, but the victory over Forgill was his most successful joust yet. He ran his hand over the soft leather briefcase on his knee, tracing the edges of the Tetroi inside. He had no intention of showing them to Forgill, but had brought them for leverage should the need arise.

The bus bumbled along in the sunshine and Ferdia closed his eyes. He didn't know how he would separate Forgill from his Tetros, but was confident he would figure it out as the meeting progressed. He played several possible scenarios out in his mind as to how things would develop, and prepared himself mentally for the impending battle of wits. Soon the bus turned onto Lower Churchtown Road and Ferdia pushed the 'Stop' button. The bus trundled to a halt and he alighted. Squinting against the sunshine, he got his bearings and made for Del Forgill's house.

*

Bree parked the Volvo outside a store in Ferrisfort. There was a wide sidewalk out front with three ancient gas pumps that hadn't worked in years, and an old drinking trough, now converted to a flowerbox, exploding with summer blooms. Attached to the store was a pub with traditional frontage. The store had probably been a cozy country shop with similar frontage to the pub, but had been redeveloped into a franchised mini-market. Bree thought it was a shame: Ferrisfort was a beautiful little town and this store was an eyesore.

She shut off the engine and they stepped out of the air-conditioned SUV. It was like stepping into a sauna.

"Oh my God, is there no end to this heat?" said Bree. "Who wants an ice-cream?"

Mark and Niamh both declined and looked eager to be on their way.

"Well, there's a first; turning down ice-cream! Right; off with the pair of you. I'll probably meet you walking around, but if not, we'll meet back here at the car in an hour, OK?"

They both nodded and headed down the street. She watched them go, shaking her head slightly. In the distance was the spire of a church. They were heading straight towards it.

What ARE they up to?

Still shaking her head, she went into the deliciously cool interior of the store. When she came back out, ice-cream in hand, there was no sign of the teenagers.

I've got to find out what's going on.

She put on her sunglasses, adjusted her hat and followed the route Mark and Niamh had taken to the church.

*

Forgill's house was down a narrow lane, beside a grand old mansion on Lower Churchtown Road. Ferdia walked past it twice before noticing it, then made his way under a red-brick arch and down the pea-shingled lane to a small courtyard overhung by leafy branches. A single oak stood in the center of the quad.

It was like going back in time. The courtyard was bordered on two sides by old stone buildings that had once been the mansion's stables, but were now converted into a striking cottage. A tall privet hedge bordered the third side and the fourth was the rear wall of the mansion's grounds. An old Jaguar sports car, long and low, crouched in the shade of the oak.

Ferdia entered an ivy covered porch and rang the brass bell affixed to the granite surround. He heard shuffling noises behind the arched wooden door, and an eye glinted in the peephole.

"Mr. McMurnagh?" said the voice through the door.

"Yes, it's me, Mr. Forgill."

Three heavy bolts shot back, and a security chain rattled into place. The door opened just enough for Ferdia to make out the face of a middle-aged man with an unkempt grey beard. His hair was grey and straggly; not long but bushed out like a shaggy grey dog. The man peered at Ferdia.

"My God, you're only a boy! What is this? Who sent you?"

He looked over Ferdia's shoulder into the courtyard, nostrils flaring.

"Are you alone?" he snapped.

"Yes, I came on my own, as agreed."

Forgill looked unconvinced and started to shut the door. Ferdia knew he had seconds to salvage the situation. He held up the briefcase.

"I brought the Tetroi."

Forgill looked at the briefcase and the look in his eyes changed to something like lust. His tongue flicked out for a second and spittle glistened on his lower lip. The overall effect was deeply unpleasant and a wave of revulsion thrilled down Ferdia's spine. He almost turned and ran, but at that moment Forgill unlatched the chain and opened the door. He beckoned Ferdia inside, looking out into the courtyard and up the lane like a nervous ferret. Ferdia hesitated then gritted his teeth and entered the house. Forgill peered out into the courtyard for a few moments longer then swung the door shut. He slid the bolts into place, and latched several security chains.

Ferdia felt trapped and anxious.

Forgill gestured him to a leather armchair and seated himself opposite. For several moments he regarded Ferdia in silence, then stood up and walked to a cabinet covered in liquor bottles.

"Drink?"

Ferdia stammered. He'd never been offered a drink before. Before he had a chance to answer Forgill slapped his own forehead.

"God, what am I thinking? You're only a kid. How old are you anyway?"

This situation hadn't come up in any of Ferdia's mental scenarios. He needed to get control of the conversation.

"I'm … look, never mind how old I am. I'd much rather talk about the Magus Conspiracy, and the cabal."

"All right, all right. Keep your hair on, young Teetotaler!"

Forgill looked over the top of his whiskey glass at the briefcase on Ferdia's lap. He nodded towards it.

"Can I see them?"

Ferdia pulled the briefcase a little closer to himself.

"Tell me what this is all about, first – and your link to it."

Forgill sighed and walked slowly to his armchair. He sank into it and placed the glass on a small table.

"How long have you got, kid?"

"As long as it takes."

"OK kid, I hope you're ready for this."

Forgill leaned forward in his chair and said:

"Many thousands of years ago, this land was inhabited by a race known as the *Tuatha Dé Danann* - the Tribe of the Goddess Danu. They settled here for many years, presiding over a golden age of peace and prosperity, until a warlike race of humans called the Milesians arrived and set about displacing them. Rather than go to war - a practice they had long since eschewed - the Danu saw this as part of the natural cycle of things and opted to leave this tír. A much older race of beings, the felkynd, had given the Danu devices that could open gateways – or *sídhe* - between the tírs. Thus the last of the ancient godlike races abandoned this tír and left it to the humans.

"About twelve thousand years ago, one of the Danu, Midir, came back. He had wanted to stay in this tír originally, and had campaigned for a war against the Milesians. When he and his followers came back, had no compunction about taking on the Milesians and soon subjugated them. And he didn't stop there.

"Over the next two thousand years he built a vast empire that spanned the Earth. His seat of power was on an island in the Atlantic, variously called Hy Brasil and Atlantis. On the face of it, it was an erudite civilization with great advances in science and engineering, but it was rotten to the core. The ordinary people worked themselves to death to keep the empire going. Dissidents were imprisoned and tortured. Children were kidnapped and sent to other tírs as slave labor.

"The Danu turned a blind eye; after all, they didn't concern themselves with human affairs, and Midir was one of their own. But when the Danu king Dagda found out Midir was planning to expand his empire to other tírs, and that he had a deadly new weapon, he called a summit. With the approval of the felkynd, the races of all tírs agreed to intervene and stop Midir. They assembled an army and prepared to take him on.

"The felkynd opened a sidh on the island of Atlantis and Dagda's army poured through. They laid siege to Atlantis for weeks but were unable to take it, or to capture Midir.

"One day Midir appeared on one of the towers of Atlantis and projected an image of himself into the midst of the besieging army, right in front of Dagda and the members of the felkynd council. He ordered them to leave Atlantis. If they didn't he would unleash his secret weapon and wipe out millions of beings across all the tírs simultaneously. King Dagda believed Midir was bluffing, but the felkynd, who were the only race that lived in all nine tírs - and who had stewardship of the security of them - couldn't take that chance. Overruling Dagda, they ordered the army to retreat back through the sidh. Once the army was clear, they gave Midir one last chance to give himself up and hand over his secret weapon. He refused, and in fact, said he was going to use his weapon anyway to wipe out the felkynd completely. The felkynd, following what they believed to be the lesser of two evils, then took a terrible decision."

Forgill sat further forward in his seat, and his eyes flashed in the dim interior of the cottage.

"Survivors of the catastrophe described a vast shimmering disc over Atlantis. The felkynd altered the sidh they had opened, you see - widened it until it obscured the sky. Then they opened another sidh just as massive in *Tír faoi Thuinn* - The Land under the Waves - and joined it to the one over Atlantis."

He paused for a reaction from Ferdia.

Ferdia shook his head. "So what?"

"They opened it under the water."

Forgill paused again to let the significance of this sink in. He continued in a quieter voice:

"Water cascaded through the sidh onto Atlantis. The water levels all over the earth rose by tens of meters. In a matter of days, this tír was inundated and Atlantis disappeared under the water forever. Millions of humans, animals and other beings died, and the threat of Midir was erased."

Ferdia snorted and looked wholly unimpressed.

"That's a fairy story, Mr. Forgill. I mean, if it were true, and everyone in this tír was wiped out, how could you possibly know about it?"

"I didn't say everyone was wiped out - I said there were survivors. A man called Nú gathered as many people as possible, along with animals and possessions, and set off in a flotilla of ships before Atlantis was completely engulfed."

"Well, if there were survivors, how come it doesn't appear in the historical record?"

"Well, it does, in a way. I'm sure you've heard of Noah's Ark and the great flood."

Ferdia's mouth curled, and he was about to pour scorn on the whole idea when Forgill pre-empted him:

"Have you never wondered why every major civilization has a catastrophic flood in its mythology? Each of these myths is based on the drowning of Atlantis. Mind you, if we'd had our way, there would be no record of it whatsoever."

"What? What do you mean 'we'?"

Forgill sighed and took a long pull on his whisky.

"We rewrote history, but we didn't do a good enough job. The persistent myths of Atlantis and a great flood are a testament to how bad a job we did."

"You keep saying 'we'. Who are 'we'?"

"I'll get to that. The felkynd were still trying to find out if Midir had survived or escaped. They located Nú's flotilla, brought the survivors to dry land, and interrogated them. Midir wasn't amongst them, and no-one knew what had happened to him - or if they did, they weren't saying. But one of the survivors was Midir's master *scrievnor*. The felkynd focused on him since he'd be the most likely survivor to know about Midir's plans. It turned out he knew no more about Midir than any of the other survivors, but under interrogation he revealed he had saved one of Midir's most prized artifacts from the flood. At first, the felkynd thought they could use the artifact to coax Midir out of hiding, but when they realized what they actually had, they came up with a new plan: They would rewrite history – edit Midir, Atlantis and the flood out of existence."

"And how would they do that, exactly?"

"The artifact the scrievnor had brought was the Lebor Stara – the Book of History – one of the most powerful artifacts that has ever existed."

"What's so powerful about a book?"

"Oh, what the Danu called 'books' were far more than books as you know them. These were incredibly powerful objects created by a Danu guild known as the *Scrievnorí*. Like all Danu guilds, The Scrievnorí used a combination of science and magick – called teic – to create powerful machines and artifacts. The books they created were devices with a purpose, not repositories of facts or stories, and the Lebor Stara was the Scrievnorí's greatest achievement: It could actually change history."

"So what? All the great dictators revised history to suit their own ends. Disreputable newspapers do it all the time to promote certain political messages."

"Oh, but what I'm talking about is not some damnatio memoriae. Dictators rewrite history then use torture and murder to make sure the old truths are suppressed. What they can't do is fix it so that the events never actually happened."

"You're telling me this book could literally rewrite history. How is that possible?"

"It could manipulate timelines. A master scrievnor could write a series of events into the Lebor Stara, as if writing a story. If the Scrievnor wrote it in enough detail, the book would create a new thread of space-time in which those events actually took place. It would then insert that new thread into history, overwriting the previous version of events."

"But that's impossible! People would remember things as they had happened before. You'd have to tamper with the memory of every person who was affected by the changed events."

Forgill was nodding at Ferdia, his eyes gleaming over the rim of his glass.

"I told you it was powerful. A scrievnor could rewrite a period of history; kill off people, create others, erase events, places, you name it. The Lebor Stara would unwind history back to the starting point of the time thread, and roll out the revised history, like a red carpet, overwriting what was there before. And this would happen in an instant; so fast that people didn't notice it. The new history literally *became* their past, as if they had lived it."

Ferdia was staring at the floor and shaking his head.

"I can't believe it. It's too incredible ..."

"That's not the half of it. Some of the technology the Danu and felkynd had was truly staggering, even by today's standards. It's no wonder people thought they were gods."

"Who are these felkynd you keep mentioning?"

"They're an ancient race of beings; guardians of the nine tírs, if you like. They're the only race to live in all nine tírs simultaneously."

"But they don't live in this tír anymore, do they? I mean, I've never heard of them, or seen them."

"Oh, yes they do – and you certainly have seen them."

"No, I haven't!"

"You've never seen a cat?"

"Wh … felkynd are cats?"

"In this tír, yes. When I said they live in all nine tírs, I meant that quite literally. Each felkynd has a consciousness that spans all tírs, but has a different physical form in each. In this tír, we know them as cats. That's where the old legend about cats having nine lives comes from."

Ferdia was looking into space.

"I heard about a Felkynd Allegiance, recently. Whatever it is it seems to be mixed up in whatever's going on with the Tetroi."

"Where did you hear about the Felkynd Allegiance?"

Ferdia told Forgill about Níamh's encounter with the priest in the lighthouse.

Forgill bowed his head, and when he spoke his voice was grief-stricken.

"Ah. He is dead, then. Poor Patrik. I wish I could have seen him once more before he died."

Forgill was silent for long moments then he sat up and took a long drink from his whisky tumbler.

"Did you get his Tetros?"

Back to the Tetroi. Ferdia decided there was no point in stringing Forgill along any longer.

"The priest told Niamh where it was as he was dying. At least he tried to, and I pieced it together from what he said. It's in a church down the country. Some friends of mine are getting it today. In Ferrisfort."

Forgill leaped from his chair.

"What? Your friends are going to the church in Ferrisfort? We have to stop them. They're in terrible danger!"

Ferdia looked at his watch.

"Well, they're there about now. Why are they in such danger?"

Forgill ignored him.

"Do your friends have a phone? Call them immediately and tell them to stay away from that church. Oh, you stupid children; you have no idea what you're tangled up in."

Forgill's anxiety galvanized Ferdia and he stood up and fumbled his phone from his pocket. The briefcase fell to the floor. He dialed Mark's number and waited.

"It's gone straight to voicemail."

"Try him again. You must …"

At that, Forgill jumped. The reaction was so intense that Ferdia jumped in sympathy. Forgill dropped to his knees and stared out the window, waving Ferdia away towards the other side of the room.

"There's someone outside," Forgill hissed. "Stay quiet."

Forgill's head bobbed this way and that as he looked through the window.

"There are four of them. Magus's people – The Cabal."

"Wha …"

"Quiet! They're coming towards the house."

Sure enough, Ferdia could now hear soft footsteps as several people crept across the pea shingle. Forgill shrank back from the window, dropped to a crawl and scurried across the room towards Ferdia. With that, a face appeared at the window and several heart-stopping bangs came on the front door.

"FORGILL!" a woman's voice screamed. "You've gone too far this time. Let's get this over with."

Forgill's face was ashen. Another loud bang on the door spurred him into action: He jumped to his feet, seized Ferdia by the shoulder and dragged him towards a large bookcase. He wrenched the bookcase aside revealing a stone stairway leading downwards. Tendrils of dank air groped at Ferdia from the stairway. He pulled back but Forgill pushed him towards the opening and halfway down the steps.

"The briefcase!" Ferdia shouted.

"I know," said Forgill, and ran back towards into the room.

Ferdia hesitated on the cold steps, trying to decide the best course of action. In the room above he could hear Forgill dashing about, knocking things over and – surely not – opening the security chains and shooting the bolts back.

Ferdia had started back up the steps when Forgill appeared in the opening and ran down towards him. He thrust the briefcase into Ferdia's arms and ushered him down the steps.

"Hurry; go through the basement. There's a door leading to the outside. Don't worry; the exit is well hidden. When you get outside, follow the hidden passage to the end and wait for me there."

"But why did you open the security chains?"

"I have to lure them into the house to trap them, now go!"

He pushed Ferdia towards the basement and scampered back to the top of the steps.

Ferdia descended to the basement entrance and in the dim light from above, he could make out a door in the far wall. He hurried through the basement and unbolted the door revealing a staircase leading upwards to another door. Like the front door, this one had many bolts and chains securing it. Ferdia unlatched them all and pulled it open.

He emerged into what seemed like a jungle, with sunlight - blinding after the dark of the basement – boring through thick vegetation. He was disorientated until he realized the door opened into the middle of the privet hedge. The hedge was hollow and concealed a passage that lead along the edge of the courtyard to the back wall of the mansion.

He crept along the passage to the wall. Through the hedge he could see the old Jaguar and by pressing his face to the vegetation he could make out the front of the cottage.

Forgill's attackers were four blonde women, their hair tied back in severe ponytails. Two were in the porch in fighting stances with long blades in their hands, peering into the house. Two more held back, one at the window and one near the oak tree. They were all dressed in fitted black leather armor that showed in no uncertain terms how lithe and purposeful they were. Ferdia's heart beat a little faster.

There was a sudden noise from inside the house and the two women in the porch rushed inside screaming an ululating cry in unison. The other two came forward to take their places and drew their blades. There was another loud crash from inside the cottage and a scream of anger. The two in the porch charged inside issuing the same strange cry. Their voices waned as - Ferdia guessed - they ran down into the basement.

Terrified, he looked down the passage towards the exit door. He was sure Forgill must be dead. He was also sure that at any moment the women would pour out through the door, down the passage and hack him to pieces. Suddenly, there were two metallic crashes from the basement, and the voices of the four women were muffled to near silence. The door from the basement opened and Del Forgill ran out and down the passage to Ferdia.

"Wha…?"

"No time. Come on!"

Forgill squeezed through the gap between the end of the hedge and the wall and dragged Ferdia after him. Forgill jumped into the Jaguar and Ferdia followed suit. The engine roared, and with pea shingle spraying, Forgill accelerated the car across the courtyard and down the lane.

Halfway down the lane a shimmering disc appeared in front of them and a leather-clad woman stepped out of thin air into their path. She aimed a weapon at the windshield. It looked like a spear, but from the way she was holding it, it must have been a projectile weapon. Ferdia threw his hands up before his face, but Forgill swerved the car and, with a sickening series of thuds and bangs, ran straight over the woman. Ferdia shouted in horror and caught sight of the woman in the mirror, rolling to a bloody, broken stop. He squeezed his eyes shut and fought to keep his breakfast down.

The Jaguar shot out of the lane onto Lower Churchtown Road, narrowly missing a bus, and fishtailed down the road as Forgill wrestled with the steering. Once the car was under control, Forgill glanced at Ferdia's lap.

"You still have the Tetroi?"

Ferdia nodded. He had to swallow several times before he could speak.

"That woman ... she's ...?"

"I certainly hope so. I'm only sorry I couldn't do for the rest of them too. Best I could do was trap them in the cellar. I had it specially fitted with shield doors; they're not going anywhere for a while. If they can't open a sidh and get out they'll starve – and good enough for them; mercenary harpies!"

"They were all women."

Forgill looked at him in puzzlement.

"Of course they were. All the Marfori are women; assassins from Tír na mBann, recruited by Magus."

"Why were they after you?"

"Because I'm trying to expose the cabal, and tell the truth about what happened when we rewrote history."

"There's that 'we' again. You say it like you were there."

"Well that's the point; I *was* there. I was Midir's master scrievnor."

"In a past life?"

Forgill laughed without humor.

"Oh no; in this life. This long, awful life. Because of my involvement with the Lebor Stara, I'm immortal. I'm over twelve-thousand years old."

Ferdia's mouth fell open. "You can't be serious."

"Sadly, I am deadly serious. After they interrogated me, the felkynd ordered me to write the Flood, Midir and his empire - including me and the Lebor Stara - out of existence. I was to be my own executioner.

"I was quite willing to die, but I screwed up. Perhaps on some level, I didn't want the story to be forgotten. Anyway, I only managed to relegate Midir and Atlantis to the realm of myth, and I disrupted my own timeline, causing it to loop back on itself. I haven't aged a day since then."

Ferdia drew breath to ridicule Forgill's story, but he snapped his mouth shut. All he had seen today had made him a lot less arrogant and sure of himself.

"What happened to the book?"

"When I activated the new timeline, the book disappeared. Magus and the felkynd have been looking for it ever since."

"OK, so what's Midir's connection to Simon Magus?"

"Magus was a creation of Midir's. He literally crafted him in his own image, like a flesh-and-blood simulacrum. We're not entirely sure if Magus is an autonomous being or just a shell for Midir's *Animus*."

"Animus?"

"His persona, his essence. His soul, if you will. We know Midir used the Magus corpus to travel to different tírs, but not if there was a Magus personality independent of Midir."

Forgill stopped the car at a red traffic light and peered about, his face worried. Ferdia did the same.

"Do you think they can follow us?"

"I have no idea what they're capable of these days. I only hope they've given up; or that they'll wait at the house thinking I'll come back eventually."

"Aren't you going back? That's your home!"

"It's one of my homes. One tends to amass a lot of property and accoutrements over twelve thousand years."

Forgill pulled away from the lights and turned right.

"Where are we going?"

"To Ferrisfort. Keep trying to get your friends on the phone. One way or another, we have to get them away from that church. Pray we're not too late."

*

Bree stood in the pleasant cool of the chapel porch and waited for her eyes to adjust to the dimness. The door from the nave opened, and an old woman in a headscarf walked out into the porch. She dipped her hand into the stoup, and looked Bree up and down with disdain as she crossed herself and shuffled out into the sunlight. Bree caught her own reflection in the glass of the chapel door as it swung closed and supposed she might look out of place with her designer sunglasses on top of her head and her summery blouse and shorts.

Movement inside the church broke her focus and through the glass door she saw Mark and Niamh walking up the left aisle, examining the wall.

What are *they looking for?*

Bree climbed the stairs to the gallery, took a seat near the front and watched them. They were examining the exterior of the confessional. It was a carved wooden panel with three doors built into the inner church wall.

"Where do you think it is?" Niamh's voice carried clearly in the bright acoustics of the church.

"Well, what did the priest say exactly?"

Niamh took some paper from her pocket and unfolded it.

"He said it's 'hidden in plain sight' and it's 'right there under their noses'."

"Whose noses?"

"The penitents; people going to confession."

Mark thought for a second then looked around the area in front of the confessional. The pews there were shorter than the rest to make room for two small rows of benches with kneelers, perpendicular to the main seating, facing the confessional. Mark knelt down on the nearer one and studied the carved wooden fascia of the confessional. Up in the balcony, Bree stood up and leaned over the edge to see what he was doing. After a moment a huge grin spread across Mark's face.

"What are you grinning at, you loon?" asked Niamh.

Mark pointed at the front of the confessional, near the floor. On the fascia was square inset into the wood, and in the square was a pattern of sixteen alternate black and white marble tiles.

"I'll bet you a year's allowance, that's the top of the Cleric's Tetros," said Mark.

"Wow!" said Niamh. She knelt on the floor and examined the top of the Tetros. Just above it was a wooden flap, and under it three brass dials in a row, with the numbers one to fourteen embossed around their edges. On each dial was a rotating pointer.

"I guess we have to set these pointers to the correct numbers before we can release the Tetros."

"Yeah, but what numbers? Hang on; didn't the priest say something about a key?"

"Yeah, he said 'the falls are the key; the falls along the way'."

Mark wrinkled his nose. "What does that mean?"

"Well, we're looking for a three-digit number, right? Is there three of anything in here that might relate to falls? Waterfalls? Maybe it means Fall as in Autumn."

Mark ran his hands through his hair and blew air out through pursed lips. "God, I haven't a clue. The only thing that's falling here is us; at the final hurdle!"

"Wait a minute," said Niamh. "Maybe they are actually falls, as in someone falling down. Each of these dials has fourteen numbers, and there are three of them, right? Well, there are fourteen Stations of the Cross, and in the stations Jesus falls three times. Look."

Niamh grabbed Mark by the arm and lead him up the gap between the pews and the wall, towards the front of the church. Bree sat back in case they noticed her, and watched them proceed to the first row of pews. Niamh pointed up at the wall.

"The Third Station: Jesus falls for the first time. The Stations are also called the Way of the Cross, and the priest said the key was the 'falls along the way.' I think the first number is three, and the other two numbers are the numbers of the other stations where Jesus falls."

Mark stood for a moment with his mouth open then turned to her and grinned.

"You're a genius, Dot!"

They dashed back to the confessional and knelt on the floor. Bree stood up again and leaned over the edge to watch them. Behind her in the balcony, a shimmering disc appeared in mid-air.

Mark lifted the flap hiding the brass dials and held it open.

"Go head, Dot: Set the dials."

"OK, Jesus falls in stations three, seven and nine, so let's set these to three … seven … and nine."

As Niamh set the third dial, there was a click and the square of wood holding the Tetros in place slid away, leaving the Tetros accessible in a small recess.

Behind Bree in the balcony, a leather-clad figure appeared in the shimmering disc.

Mark let the flap close and reached into the recess. With great care he placed his hands on either side of the Tetros and lifted it free.

Just as he placed it in his rucksack, a shriek came from the balcony. Mark's and Niamh's heads snapped up. Standing on the balcony, her back to the ten-meter drop, was Bree, her arms flailing as she fought to get her balance. A woman clad in leather gripped Bree by the throat and was forcing her over the edge.

"Mum!" Mark shouted, and he started for the back of the church, but before he'd gone more than a few paces the leather-clad woman won the battle and Bree fell screaming, head-first, towards the tiled church floor.

"Mum!" screamed Mark, "Oh God, no!"

He wanted to turn away but couldn't. With bile rising in his throat he watched his mother fall to certain death.

But Bree never hit the floor.

A large shimmering disc appeared on the floor beneath her and she fell straight through it and disappeared. As Mark stood gawping, the leather-clad woman howled a cry of fury and dived head-first off the balcony towards the disc. Just before she reached it, the disc faded and disappeared. The woman had time to emit a very short, terror-laden shriek, then hit the floor with a sickening crunch, spasmed for a moment and lay still.

Mark screamed, "Mum," and ran to where the disc had appeared. He stopped short of the pool of blood expanding from the dead woman, hesitated then ran back to Niamh.

"What happened? Where did my mum go? Who is that woman?"

"I don't know, but I think we need to get out of here."

"But my mum …"

"Mark, your mum's not here. She went through that hole in the floor, whatever it was. C'mon, we have to get out of here."

Mark edged towards the woman's body and examined the floor as if it might give some clue as to Bree's whereabouts.

"Hey!" he said, and took something from the dead woman's hand.

"She had my mum's handbag!"

With that, two more of the women appeared at the top of the church. One of them shouted "Oisín!" and they started down the center aisle.

"Come on," shouted Niamh and pushed Mark towards the entrance.

They ran out into the glaring sunshine and pelted up the road towards the store.

"Where are we going?" gasped Mark.

"Are the car keys in that handbag?"

Mark struggled to hold on to the bag and open it as he ran. He jangled the car keys at Niamh.

"That's where we're going then," she said.

"What? To the car? But I can't drive!"

"No," said Niamh as she snatched the keys, "but I can."

Niamh pressed the unlock button on the key as they approached the 4x4 and the signal lights flashed. As they reached the car, a shimmering disc appeared in the road near them. A leather-clad woman stepped from it and swung at Niamh. Niamh ducked and side-stepped the woman, angling across the road towards the driver's side of the Volvo.

"Mark, jump in the back," she screamed as she wrenched open the door. She jumped into the driver's seat, and slammed the door shut, as Mark leaped into the back. She hit the lock button on the key and just as the woman reached for the door handle, the central locking engaged. The other two women arrived and banged on the windows.

"Oisín! Come out we need to talk to you."

"Mark, don't you dare open that door," said Niamh as she started the engine.

Mark was numb with shock and grief. Tears rolled down his cheeks. He just shook his head.

Niamh slid the key into the ignition lock and started the engine. She jammed the transmission into *Drive* and floored the gas pedal. The Volvo screeched away from the sidewalk, leaving the three women screaming in anger outside the store.

As they sped through the main street, it became obvious that things had gone to hell in Ferrisfort. Crashed cars littered the street, and several of the stores were on fire. A group of villagers ran from one of the buildings and, as Niamh watched in horror, several shimmering holes appeared in the air near them. Leather-clad women stepped from the holes and cut the villagers down. Niamh stifled a cry and pushed the gas pedal further to the floor.

Mark sobbed in the back seat. He was repeating something to himself, too quietly for Niamh to hear at first, then it sent a chill through her. He was repeating:

"I'm an orphan. They're both gone. I'm an orphan ..."

It took all her concentration to keep the car on the road. She wanted to say something to comfort Mark, but nothing seemed appropriate. She drove on, her heart aching for him; her own grief for Bree pushed aside out of necessity.

A few kilometers outside Ferrisfort they saw several police patrol cars with sirens and lights heading in the opposite direction. *I pity the poor cops going into that chaos*, thought Niamh. *I wonder if they're armed. I wonder if it would make any difference!*

As she contemplated the fate of the police officers, Mark shouted something and shocked her back to alertness.

"What?"

"Look, there's a police roadblock up ahead."

Sure enough, several hundred meters up the road, two police patrol cars with flashing blue lights blocked the road. Numerous uniformed and plain-clothes police officers milled around, turning back cars that were trying to enter Ferrisfort, and searching cars that were leaving.

Niamh pulled over and chewed her lip.

"What are we going to do?" asked Mark. "We can't go back."

Niamh thought for a moment longer then said, "I'll tell you what we're going to do: We're going to drive up there and talk our way through that roadblock."

"But you're not ..."

"Yeah, I know, but I have a plan. Where does your mum keep her makeup?"

"What? Makeup? I don't think she has any makeup in the car."

"Don't be stupid, Mark; every woman has makeup in the car. Check the glove-box."

The glove-box revealed a collection of rather expensive cosmetics which Niamh took and applied to her face. A few minutes later, with a scarf on her head, and a pair of Bree's sunglasses perched on her nose, she drove up to the roadblock.

Two officers stood in the middle of the road, one with his hand in the air. Niamh drew to a stop and the two officers walked to either side of the windshield. The one on the left, a cynical looking middle-aged type, checked the tax and insurance, then proceeded along the side of the SUV checking it out. The other officer, a younger man, approached the driver's window. Niamh let it down. Before he had a chance to speak, Niamh started babbling:

"Oh my God, I have no idea what's going on back there. There are houses on fire and cars crashed in the street. It's awful. My brother and I are just on our way back from visiting our aunt, and … and … Oh God, what's happening anyway?"

The officer was nodding his head and making calm-down gestures with his hand.

"I wouldn't like to say, now, what's happening in Ferrisfort. We're in attendance up there and things are under control, that's all I can say. What were ye doing in Ferrisfort today anyway, folks?"

"We were just passing through, Officer; on our way from our aunt's house in Carlow."

"Right. And where are ye heading to now?"

"Back home to Wicklow, Officer."

"All right. Do you mind if my colleague takes a quick look in the back, there?"

"Er, no; go ahead, I'll unlock it." She pressed the central locking switch and the doors unlocked.

As the older policeman opened the tailgate and looked inside, the officer at the window said, "What's your name, Miss?"

"Bree McHewell."

Mark's heart did a little dance and his eyes rolled sideways.

"Would you have a license, there, Bríd?"

Mark's stomach turned over and he thought he might vomit.

"It's 'Bree' Officer, and I'm afraid I don't have my license with me. I must have left it in my other bag when we came out."

"You know you're supposed to keep it with you when you're driving?"

"I do, Officer; I'm very sorry."

"Is this your car, Bree?"

"It is, Officer. Our father bought it for me for my eighteenth birthday."

Mark ears started burning and he thought he might pass out from the nerves. *What the hell was Niamh up to?*

A hint of irritation flashed across the young officer's face, tinged with jealousy. It was clear he thought little of spoilt rich kids. He started to ask Niamh for her address, but was interrupted when the older officer closed the tailgate and walked up the driver's side of the car shaking his head. Whatever he was looking for, he didn't find it in the back of Bree's SUV.

"Let them go," he said. "They've nothing to do with it."

The young officer looked undecided then said, "Ok, that's grand. You can be on your way, but make sure you have your license with you in future."

Niamh thanked the policemen and pulled away, maneuvering between the patrol cars. When they drew clear of the roadblock Mark let his head fall back on the seat and blew air out of his mouth.

"I have *never* been so nervous. I thought I was going to explode!"

Niamh's hands were shaking on the steering wheel.

"Me too. The thing is though; I think we have bigger things to worry about than the police, like why those women are after us."

"Yeah," said Mark, "and what's happened to my parents." The edges of his mouth quivered and he rubbed a tear away with the back of his hand. He sniffled, then looked over at Niamh with candid admiration in his face.

"Dot, that was amazing, though. You're the bravest person I know."

Niamh smiled tightly and reached over to put a hand on his knee.

"Let's get back to your house. We can start planning what we're going to do next. Why don't you give Ferdia a call and find out where he is."

As Mark pulled out his phone, Niamh slowed down to allow a car in the other lane to make a U-turn. There was a long line of cars waiting to approach the roadblock and drivers were getting impatient. She let a few more cars go then continued along the line of traffic. Just as they drew alongside an old-fashioned sports-car, the road bucked beneath them as if an earthquake had struck. The phone flew from Mark's hand onto the floor. Niamh gasped and gripped the wheel. A glimmer appeared in the air between the cars. In the blink of an eye, it expanded to a huge shimmering disc. Niamh hit the brakes stopped short of the disc, which had now started to engulf the back of the sports-car. The doors opened and an unkempt man bolted from the driver's side; a youth from the other.

"That's Ferdia!" shouted Mark.

"Ferdia!" shouted Niamh from open window.

Ferdia looked over, did a double-take, and then jumped the long bonnet in a smooth leap. The disc had now swallowed the rear half of the car, and was making another bid for the front of the SUV. Ferdia grabbed Forgill's arm and propelled him towards the back door of the Volvo. They jumped in and Niamh floored the gas pedal, swerving onto the verge to avoid the disc.

Forgill looked back in time to see the sidh collapse in on itself, taking the car with it.

"I loved that car," he said in a strangled voice.

"But at least we're safe. And you must have more cars," said Ferdia.

Forgill fixed him with a stare.

"That was a very rare Jaguar XK150 Roadster with a five-liter engine. Took me years to find it. Damn them all, and damn Midír to the far reaches of hell. Oh well, it's one of a kind now in whichever tír it's gone to, and we are, as you say, safe."

Mark was looking back at Forgill with raw distrust.

"Who's this, Ferdia?"

"This is Del Forgill – the man I went to see about the Tetros."

"Does he have anything to do with the disappearance of my mother… or my dad?"

"No, he's on our si… wait, your mother's disappeared?"

Mark gave a brief and tear-stained account of the recovery of the Tetros, Bree's fall and the death of the assassin. "God, I hope she's not dead."

Forgill interjected.

"Bree's not dead, young man – she's gone through a sidh to another tír."

"Are you sure."

"Did it look anything like the sidh that took my car?"

Mark nodded, wiping his eyes. "So those women have her?"

"No they'd just have killed her. Someone else opened that sidh to save her."

"But who?"

"I have no idea, but whoever they are, they saved your mother's life."

"You're sure she's alive?"

"I'd bet my life on it."

Mark managed a little smile. Niamh looked over and rubbed his knee.

"Let's get back to Almha."

"Yes, we should get away from here," said Forgill, "they'll be back. Oh, I almost forgot, I have something for you, Ferdia."

He reached into his coat pocket and held something out.

Sitting on Del Forgill's palm was the final Tetros.

CHAPTER NINETEEN

THE HUNTER

Niamh trudged into the study in Almha, where Ferdia and Forgill were sitting at the desk examining the four Tetroi.

"How is he?" asked Forgill.

She shook her head. "He's not doing well, but that concoction you gave him has knocked him out for now."

In the journey back from Ferrisfort, as they exchanged their experiences, Mark had swung from bouts of hyperactivity - talking rapidly, even telling jokes - to deep depression. Forgill had taken over the driving and Niamh had sat in the back with Mark, doing her best to keep him on the level. By the time they reached Almha, he had sunk into a profound silence, wide-eyed catatonia, his head in Niamh's lap. She had brought him indoors and put him to bed while Forgill foraged in the kitchen. He brought a drink made of hot milk and spices up to the bedroom. Niamh had gotten Mark to drink it and stayed with him until he fell asleep.

She sat between Ferdia and Forgill at the desk and indicated the Tetroi. "I hope this has all been worth it."

Forgill looked into her eyes for a moment, then back to the cubes on the desk. "It will be. I'm sure it will be."

He shook his head in wonderment. I can't believe they're all here together. I've dreamt about this for years."

"OK, well what are we supposed to do with them?"

"Put them together, obviously," said Ferdia.

"Then what?"

"Let's find out."

Using the pen from Mark's backpack, Ferdia released the spring-loaded dowel on the first Tetros and joined the second to it. As before, a further set of dowels sprang out of the second cube to which Ferdia attached the third, releasing three more dowels.

Ferdia moved the fourth Tetros into position to attach it and paused. He looked at Niamh and Forgill and said "Ready?"

"I'm not sure," said Niamh, chewing her lip. "What's going to happen?"

They both looked at Forgill. He looked back at them in astonishment.

"Don't look at me!" he said, "I have no idea what's going to happen any more than you do. All I know is that this thing is supposed to open a sidh to the tír in which Magus was exiled."

"Now, wait a minute," said Niamh, "do we really want to do that? I mean, what if we're releasing him?"

Forgill shook his head. "From what I understand, the sidh is tuned in such a way that Magus cannot use it. Some very clever *teic* was employed to make it possible for the Sentinels to move to and fro, but to make it impassable to Magus."

"Are you sure?"

"That's what I understand."

"There's only one way to find out," said Ferdia, and connected the last Tetros.

"Wait," shouted Niamh, but it was too late.

The fourth Tetros snapped into place and a rhythmic clicking sound like a carousel projector loading slides came from within the device. Then there was a loud click and several of the lenses on the chessboard squares lit up with a dazzling blue light. They all jumped back and froze. Niamh realized she was holding her breath.

After several moments the lights went out. There was another click and the Tetroi sprang apart with a loud snap. They all jumped again and Niamh gave a little shriek.

Nothing happened for several moments. They looked at each other then back to the inert Tetroi on the desk.

"Is that it?" asked Niamh, a little disappointed, despite her earlier misgivings.

"So it would seem," said Forgill, quite disappointed himself.

Ferdia was looking thoughtful.

"There's obviously more to this," he said. "There's a particular set of circumstances under which the Tetroi must be joined, and I believe the poem holds the key."

Forgill nodded. "I think you're right."

"I've already transliterated the runes," said Ferdia.

He put his iPad on the desk where they could read the poem. Niamh read it out:

Against the sable backdrop of the night,
The starry actors glide across the stage.
In jeweled costumes sewn with threads of light,
They read their parts, then turn tomorrow's page.

The earthly audience watches from the dust,
As cosmic players tread Forever's boards.
Our bearing on our travels we entrust,
To these bejeweled heroes of the Gods.

The Hunter leads the lambent stellar ranks;
His faithful Dogs attending his foray.
His hunting grounds are Danu's fertile banks;
The Unicorn and Hare his timeless prey.

The Hunter tempers Man's conceited traits,
And teaches him the limit of his worth.
And Man in turn has sought to emulate,
The august Hunter's works on austere Earth.

And thus on Earth the Hunter can be found,
In structures placed to emulate his form.
Where Vikings and St Patrick came aground,
The Hunter's shape conceals a secret door.

Prone, he spans the village like a plan,
From which the ancient builders drew their schemes.
They plotted out his measure on the land,
And placed their covert lodges at his limbs.

Three hallowed houses sit along his belt.
His sword affords a haven from the seas.
His shoulders rest up high along the hills.
His head is where they hid the secret key.

Above a lofty crag, a Regal keep
surmounts a grotto hid by time and tide,
wherein the key is placed to then reveal
the secret door that's hidden Saiph inside.

Niamh looked around the desk at the others.

"What does it all mean?"

Ferdia picked up the tablet.

"We already know the first four stanzas are something to do with the constellation Orion. What's all this about St Patrick and the Vikings, though?"

Niamh furrowed her brow, looked into the middle distance for a moment, then exclaimed:

"It's Wicklow! St Patrick came ashore at Wicklow when he returned to Ireland, and Wicklow was founded by the Vikings."

Ferdia pursed his lips.

"OK, let's work on that assumption and see if it fits," he said. "If we're interpreting the fifth and six stanzas correctly, someone - the original Sentinels presumably - put up a series of buildings in Wicklow town, arranged according to the location of the stars in Orion."

"How do you mean?" asked Niamh.

"I think we need to overlay Orion on a map of Wicklow town, and a pattern should appear."

"There are thousands of buildings in Wicklow," said Forgill. "Even if you're right about Orion, how would we know how to orientate the constellation over the town?"

Niamh, who had taken the tablet from Ferdia and was reading the poem again, piped up:

"I know how."

Ferdia and Forgill peered over her shoulder as she pointed at the seventh stanza.

"It says 'Three hallowed houses sit along his belt'. Hallowed means holy, right?"

Ferdia nodded. "I see where you're going with this. There are three stars on Orion's belt, and you reckon they apply to three holy houses; churches, in other words?"

"Exactly," said Niamh.

"But are there three churches in Wicklow along a straight line like Orion's belt?" asked Forgill.

"Not exactly," said Niamh, "but there are two churches and another place that might fit. Let me show you. Can you get Google Earth on this thing?"

"Of course," said Ferdia. He loaded Google Earth on the tablet screen and navigated to Wicklow town. Niamh zoomed and rotated the aerial view of Wicklow for a moment then placed the tablet back on the desk and pointed at the screen.

"OK, here's St Thomas's church on Church Hill, and here's St Patrick's church on St Patrick's Road. Now, look here: In between the two churches is a ruined Franciscan abbey – another holy place. Do you reckon they might fit the pattern of Orion's belt?"

"I do indeed," said Ferdia, his interest piqued. He took the tablet from Niamh and downloaded an image of the Orion constellation from an astronomy website. He overlaid the image on the aerial view of Wicklow and manipulated it, trying to align the stars on the belt with the positions of the three places.

But it wasn't working.

When he scaled the image so that the two churches aligned with the two outer stars on the belt, the middle star did not align with the abbey.

"I don't think we have this right," Ferdia said, his voice heavy.

"You're forgetting something, son," said Forgill. "The sixth stanza says Orion is 'prone', meaning he lies over the town face-down, as it were. You need to use a mirror-image of that picture, I believe."

Ferdia thought about it, then, annoyed that it hadn't occurred to him, grudgingly said, "You're right."

Using Photoshop, he flipped the image of Orion, and overlaid it on Google Earth again. Niamh and Forgill moved in close as he aligned the two outer stars with the churches. The middle star fell precisely over the location of the abbey.

Forgill grinned and slapped him on the back, and Niamh whooped and punched the air. Ferdia just looked stunned.

"That's it. I don't believe it"

"There's more," said Forgill. "Look at the stars that make up his sword."

The stars of Orion's belt fell directly over the North Pier in Wicklow harbor. "'His sword affords a haven from the seas'," quoted Forgill.

"Oh my God," said Niamh, "It's all true. So Wicklow town was built according to a plan; to match the constellation Orion?"

"So it would seem. There are several other constellations mentioned in those first few stanzas, so they might have been factored into the design too."

"But if the stars of the belt align with the churches and the abbey, does that mean the churches were involved in all this?"

"Quite possibly," said Forgill. "Don't forget that one of the Sentinels is always a cleric. It's likely that some or all of the churches were part of the conspiracy to suppress the truth about Magus and Midir."

"Oh, this is big," said Niamh. "Do we really want to get involved in this?"

"I don't think we have much choice at this stage," said Ferdia. "Fintan and Bree have both disappeared, and circumstances have chosen us to be the people to see this through."

"So what do we do now?"

Ferdia pointed at the tablet screen.

"We find the secret key mentioned here and open the secret door. I have a feeling once we do that we'll know what to do with this device."

"Well, it says the secret key is located at Orion's head. Which star is his head?"

Ferdia indicated the screen. "These two stars, Betelgeuse and Bellatrix are his shoulders; and this one, Meissa, is his head."

"That's right on Ashtown Lane; on the outskirts of the town. Look, Meissa is right over a huge house with a wall around it. I have no idea who lives there, though."

"So let's say we get this key," interjected Forgill, "what do we actually do with it?"

"The answer is in the last stanza," said Ferdia.

Forgill read through it.

"Why is the word 'regal' capitalized – and why is 'safe' misspelled? Did you make a mistake in the transliteration?"

Ferdia gave him a withering look.

"Certainly not. It's a play on words. The two stars at Orion's knees are called Rigel and Saiph. We use the key at Rigel and the door will open at

Saiph."

"All right then," said Forgill, "Niamh, you have the local knowledge; what's located where the star Rigel is?"

She peered at the tablet screen for a few moments, looking for obvious landmarks, then exclaimed:

"It's the Black Castle!"

"What's that?"

"It's an old ruined castle on the cliffs near Wicklow Harbor. It stands right over a beach called 'Travelahawk' where St Patrick is supposed to have landed when he came back to Ireland."

"Is there, by any chance, a cave beneath it?"

"Yeah, at the bottom of the cliff. You can only get to it at low tide. There are steps cut into the rock at the back of the castle that lead down to it. People call them 'The Danes' Steps'. My dad always told me not to go near them, 'cause they're slippery and dangerous. There's supposed to be a tunnel in the cave that leads somewhere, but my dad says that's just an old rumor."

Forgill looked at Ferdia. "Sounds like our 'grotto hid by time and tide.'"

"Yes. There must be a lock in there that takes the secret key. Once we use it, the door located at Saiph will open."

"Guys," said Niamh. "If I'm reading this right, the star Saiph is out in the middle of Wicklow Bay. If this is correct, the door is underwater. That doesn't make any sense."

"I shouldn't worry, young lady," said Forgill. "I suspect the tunnel will run under the ocean floor to the location of the secret door."

"Then what?"

"Well, let's not get ahead of ourselves," said Forgill. "First of all we need to get the key."

"When are we going to do that?"

"Well, tomorrow, I should think. I don't know about you, but I'm bushed. It's late, and even if it were safe to go back to Churchtown, I have no way of getting there without taking Bree's car. Do you think Mark would mind if I stayed here on the sofa?"

"I guess not," said Niamh, looking at her watch. "Omigod, it's after ten! I'm gonna be killed! Mr. Forgill, could you drive me home? It's only five minutes away."

"Of course, young lady. I'm sure I can stay awake another few minutes. Shall we go?"

Ferdia raised a cautionary finger. "Don't say anything about what's happened to Bree."

"No, of course not."

"Don't you need to get home, Ferdia?"

"No. I'll send my mother a text and tell her I'm staying with friends. My parents don't really care what I get up to – as long as I stay away from my grandfather."

"Very well. We shall see how Mark feels in the morning," said Forgill. "If he's up to it, we'll all go and reconnoiter the place on Ashtown Lane. If not, one of us can stay here with him, and the others will check it out. Agreed?"

Niamh and Ferdia both nodded.

"Good. Right then, young lady. Let's get you home."

Niamh and Forgill went out of the study, leaving Ferdia alone with the Tetroi - and a load of unanswered questions.

CHAPTER TWENTY

THE DREAM

Morning sunlight crept across Mark's pillow, and onto his face. As the brightness glared orange behind his closed lids, he grunted and began to emerge from a deep sleep.

He surfaced gently, his brain untangling reality from dreams, then his stomach lurched and his eyes snapped open as he remembered the events of the previous day.

He groaned and rolled onto his back, shading his eyes with his arm. Images of his mother falling from the balcony were interspersed with memories of the leather-clad women and flashes of the journey back to Almha. His heart ached, and the feelings of helplessness and loss made him want to roll over and bury his head in the covers.

Then he remembered the dream.

"Don't fret, Oisín," a musical voice had said, "Bree Redhair is safe. We translated her to our *heimtír* to save her from the Marforí."

"Who are you?" he had asked.

"We are the felkynd."

"Can you bring her back to me?"

"No. She must stay here until you have travelled between the tírs and completed your quest."

"What makes you think I can do it?"

"You are a *Taevnor*. You can use sidhs to navigate the dead zones between tírs where time and space have no meaning. Not even the felkynd can do that."

"I can't do that! I don't even know what you're talking about."

"You can; you just don't know it yet. You already have the capability, but you will meet someone who will tutor you in the ways of the Taevnorí"

"Who?"

"We do not know that. We only know you will meet them when you cross over to save your father."

"Do you have him too?"

"No, but he is alive in a different tír."

"Can you help me?"

"We will help as much as we can, but this is your burden."

"What do I have to do?"

"Your friends already know. They will help you, but they need your help too, especially Niamh Goldenhair."

"Why, what does Niamh ..?"

"It will become clear. Oisín, I have one last important message: Be careful of Del Forgill. We do not trust him."

"Why?"

"He has his own agenda. We cannot be sure of his loyalties."

"But how can I…?"

"Sleep now."

As the voice had faded, Mark had had the strangest image of Niamh's cat Mira sitting on his bed covers, dissolving to nothingness.

Niamh needs my help!

Mark jumped out of bed, grabbing his cell from the bedside locker. He dialed Niamh's number.

To his surprise, he could hear the muffled ringtone coming from within the house. He opened his bedroom door and followed the jangly tone downstairs. Just as he reached the living room, it went to voicemail.

From within the living-room, he could hear Niamh's voice, the words punctuated with sobs and sniffles. He entered and stopped dead in the doorway. Niamh was sitting on the sofa, her back to him, crying. Del Forgill sat beside her, his arm around her shoulders.

Mark rushed into the room. "What are you doing to her?" he demanded, his fists bunched.

Forgill looked over his shoulder and put his finger to his lips. He stood up and steered Mark out of the living room into the kitchen.

Mark glared at him.

"Calm down, young cavalier, and allow me to explain. Niamh asked me to drive her home last night. When we got there we found the place abandoned; all the lights on. Someone – the Marforí, presumably - opened a sidh in the wall of the Kinnear's living room – tore a circular hole right through it. There were drops of blood leading from the armchair to the hole. The rest is guesswork, but it looks like the Marforí took Niamh's parents through the sidh to God-knows-where."

"Oh, Jesus!"

"There's more. There was a police patrol car parked outside. I think Niamh's parents had reported her missing again. The two officers were still in the car. The interior looked like an abattoir. Their heads were missing."

Mark paled.

"Was it a man and a woman?"

Forgill nodded. "I think so."

Mark felt a twinge of remorse about how he'd spoken to Detective Kelly and Officer Ryan. They'd only been doing their jobs. And now their jobs – and this mess he was caught up in – had cost them their lives.

Forgill continued: "That's a typical Marforí technique: Open a sidh around the neck of a victim and translate just the head. Very nasty."

Mark's head was spinning. "Why should I believe you? Why should I believe any of this? You seem to be up to your neck in this, and I don't know if I should trust you."

"Niamh was there, Mark. She can verify everything I've said. Now, I can't make you trust me, and I don't blame you if you don't, but I assure you, I mean you and your friends no harm.

"Now, I think you should go and speak to Niamh; she needs you."

"Where's Ferdia?"

"He's in the study on the computer researching a mansion on somewhere called Ashtown Lane."

"Huh? How'd he log in? He doesn't know the password. How did he even get into the study?"

"Ferdia already knew the code to the study – something to do with some comic book page, unlikely as that sounds. As regards the computer, I don't think passwords are any impediment to that young man. If he wants to use someone's computer, he'll find a way to get in. He is a deeply strange character. If I'm honest, he unnerves me more than anyone I've met in a very long time, and that's saying something. Are you sure he's only sixteen?"

"So now you're trying to make me distrust Ferdia, is that it?"

Forgill sighed, and in a resigned voice said: "Go and comfort Niamh, son. I've been up with her all night. I'm going to see how your teenage man-robot is getting on."

CHAPTER TWENTY-ONE

THE SIGNS

Clodagh Daly was a good cop. She was young and just months out of the academy, but she had a startling memory for detail and a mathematical talent for analyzing data. She also recognized the work of Satan when she saw it.

And Satan had been busy lately.

The omens weren't exactly as the Revelation had predicted, but she acknowledged you'd probably have to refract a first century prophecy through the prism of two thousand years to see the spectrum of signs in a modern light. And while she wasn't so prideful as to second-guess the minds of God and the prophets, the Apocalypse was coming; she was damn sure of that.

She had been taught in bible class the Apocalypse would start with the beasts of the Earth and that certainly seemed the case: In early June, missing cat posters had started to appear in Wicklow town and now every lamppost and store window was festooned with them. Clodagh's own cat Alfie, a venerable and domiciliary ginger tom, vanished from her apartment. Weirdest of all, the volunteers at the local pound had arrived one morning to find all the cat cages still locked but empty, all the other rescues in distress. Soon after that it became apparent that all cats were gone.

She'd been looking at a picture of Alfie on her phone in the station when several of the other officers had come on duty.

"What've you got there, Clodagh?"

She held up the phone, tears glistening on her cheeks.

"Ah, there's no need to cry about it. He'll turn up – they all will. It's some kind of stunt someone's pulling."

"It's not just that he's gone. I mean that makes me sad of course, but what does it all mean? It must be some kind of portent."

She crossed herself, kissed the crucifix on the chain around her neck and dropped it back inside her shirt.

One of the officers snorted. "There goes Sister Clodagh, seeing the devil everywhere. Jesus, loosen up, girl!" They laughed and went to the locker room. *Heathens*, she thought. *When God comes to save the righteous from Satan's hordes, you're all going to burn.*

Then a satellite came down just off Wicklow Head. At least that was the official story. But Clodagh was on duty when the Americans arrived with an Irish army escort and winched that weird wooden UFO out of the sea. She'd taken a peek inside the forensics tent at the mangled remains of the occupants and didn't sleep for nights afterwards.

At that stage Clodagh was sure that evil was afoot. She tried to warn her friends and colleagues but they ridiculed her.

And the signs kept coming.

On the last day of her old life – her 'profane existence', as she would later call it – serious and inexplicable disturbances occurred simultaneously in Ferrisfort in County Wicklow and in Churchtown in Dublin. People reported murderous women in strange garb appearing out of thin air to massacre dozens of people and lay waste to buildings. The women were variously reported as having red eyes, fangs and the ability to discharge fire from their hands. Many of the reports were contradictory, but the streams of fire came up consistently. All of it was discounted by her colleagues as hysteria.

That evening, Officer Ryan, who had taken a fatherly shine to her, confided (*"and you didn't hear it from me"*) that the military had found something bizarre on one of the bodies in the UFO; an iPhone belonging to a well-known and missing Wicklow local, Fintan McHewell. That name resonated with her for some reason and she puzzled over it during her shift. On her break, she went to the church to pray for inspiration and (praise Jesus!) it came to her. She hurried back to the police station and logged in to her computer.

After the earlier madness in Ferrisfort, the squad car video from the roadblock and the officer's notes had been uploaded to the police database. Clodagh had skipped through them looking for things out of the ordinary. While she didn't find anything, her uncanny mind had processed and stored it in minute detail. In the serenity of the church, her brain had made the connection.

An SUV had been stopped coming out of Ferrisfort and the driver had given her name as Bree McHewell. The registration matched up to the name but that was where it started to get suspicious. The database listed Bree McHewell as being in her early forties, but the driver on the video was a young woman accompanied by a teenage boy. Clodagh had been stepping through the video frames to get a good still of their faces when Detective Fiona Kelly peered over her shoulder.

"Those two! What have they been up to now?"

"What?! Do you recognize them?"

"I do, unfortunately. Pair of degenerates. That brassy little madam ran away from home recently and got that young idiot to cover for her. Wasted no end of our time."

"Ran away from home? How old is she, then?"

"About fifteen, I think."

"Very interesting. Too young to drive, and she lied about her name."

"What do you mean?"

"This video is from the roadblock near Ferrisfort earlier. She gave her name as Bree McHewell."

"McHewell? That's that young guy's name. Mark McHewell. Bree is his mother, if I remember correctly. The husband is that rich guy that disappeared last year, remember? Actually, I think it was before you arrived."

"What's the girl's name?"

"Er, Niamh Kinnear."

"The cheek of her! She drove right up to that roadblock and you can hear her on the video telling the officer her name is Bree McHewell, that the boy is her brother and that the car is hers. What the hell are they up to?"

Detective Kelly's teeth made a grinding noise. "I'm going to get Pat Ryan now, and that's exactly what we're going to find out!"

And that was the last time Clodagh had seen them alive.

Kelly and Ryan hadn't returned when Clodagh was going off duty so she looked up the Kinnear's address and drove out the coast road. As she pulled up at the Kinnear's driveway she saw the squad car parked at the house, engine running. From the moment she stepped out of her car she knew something was wrong. She gripped the crucifix at her throat and sidled up to the passenger door.

Nothing in her police training could have prepared her for the butchery inside the car. The sheer amount of blood indicated the victims had been decapitated where they sat, but there wasn't enough room inside the vehicle to swing a weapon or even to use a cheese-wire garrote. In other words, these murders were impossible.

She backed away from the car and looked around in a daze. The side of the house and been blown open and there were blood trails in the living room, but no further bodies.

The brutality of the killings left Clodagh almost insensate with horror but she prayed to Jesus and channeled her shock into decisive action. She'd never had much time for Fiona Kelly but Pat Ryan was like a father to her and she wanted to do right by his memory.

She knew her colleagues would not take the threat seriously and they were beyond redemption anyway, so calling this in was not an option. It took her all of ten seconds to decide what she should do.

She took out her cell.

"Hi Killian? It's Clodagh."

…

"Yes, I'm in good health, praise Jesus, but we are all in mortal danger."

…

"Have you not seen the signs? It's happening Killian, just as Papa always said."

…

"Killian, I really don't have time to explain but you do trust me don't you?"

…

"OK, does Joshua Morton from the prayer group still have his car transporter? Can you borrow it from him?"

…

"When? Right now, Killian! We have a chance to thwart Satan and his hordes, but we have to act now."

. . .

"Just meet me at this address as soon as possible."

She gave the Kinnear's address and rang off with a *"Praise Jesus."*

As she sat in her car waiting for Killian, all that had happened played and replayed in her mind. Each cycle of the events climaxed in her finding her colleagues butchered in their squad car. The sense of Satan's immediate presence disturbed her and she prayed to Jesus for guidance and strength. She felt terror at the coming Armageddon and she wailed in her car, pulling at her hair and knocking her head against the steering wheel. The waves of horror she felt eliminated any possibility of rational thought and thus it was that as Clodagh sat in her car, weeping and wailing and waiting for her brother, she had her epiphany.

Every omen was linked to those young antichrists, Kinnear and McHewell, and that was exactly what Clodagh believed them to be; demonic little harbingers of the End of Days.

The fear lifted from her and she stopped crying. In fact she started to smile, then grin, then shriek with laughter. She finally realized exactly why she had been put on this Earth and exactly what she had to do.

By the time her brother arrived and found her in her car screaming with laughter, Clodagh's beautiful mind had finally, after many years of flirting with it, succumbed to complete and irrevocable narcissistic madness.

CHAPTER TWENTY-TWO

ASHTOWN LANE

I t was the middle of the afternoon and Ashtown Lane was quiet. The sun had softened the road and the smell of melting asphalt finessed its way through the air conditioning filters of Bree's SUV. The entrance to the mansion shimmered in the heat, the name '*Abydos*' picked out in gold across black marble gateposts. Forgill and the teenagers sat in the capsule of cool air, engine running, and watched the gates.

Further down the road, in a nondescript dusty little car, Clodagh Daly watched and waited.

Mark's humor had improved greatly with the cracking of the puzzle and Niamh felt reassured by Mark's dream, inferring from it that her parents and Mira were alive somewhere. Now she was focused on getting through the sidh and rescuing them. Mark withheld his opinion that there was a world of difference between being rescued by the felkynd and being abducted by the Marforí. He hoped Kenny and Martha were still alive but, if he were honest with himself, he thought it unlikely. Still, not finding their bodies at the house was a good sign.

But now he and Niamh were essentially fugitives. Once the police found their dead colleagues, the first place they would go looking for answers was Almha, and although he and Niamh were innocent of any wrongdoing, if the police realized their parents were missing, they would be taken into care and all hope of rescuing the adults would be lost. From now on they had to stay under the radar.

Ferdia's research had revealed the mansion on Ashtown Lane was called *Abydos* and belonged to a businessman who spent most of his time out of the country. If the sources were correct he was in Asia, but they were taking no chances. The plan was for Forgill to buzz the intercom on the gate and masquerade as a TV license inspector. Ferdia had run up a convincing laminated ID card in the business center in Wicklow and this would get them into the grounds if there was someone at home. But when Forgill called there was no answer, so they were staking the place out and considering their next move.

"That wall goes all the way around the property," said Forgill, "and it's topped with razor-wire. I don't fancy trying to climb over it, so the gate is our only option."

"There's a keypad on that intercom," said Ferdia. "I think we should try to hack the code."

"And how do you propose to do that?" asked Forgill, "Pull it off the wall and hack it with your pocket computer, I suppose."

Ferdia looked confused.

"No, of course not. I'll use probability. Most people don't change their access codes regularly, so I just need to examine the keypad and see which buttons are the most worn. That will tell me the digits in the PIN code which will limit the permutations considerably. The keypad has a manufacturer's logo and model number on it, so I'll look up the security system on the Net and see how many digits are in the PIN code for that particular model of keypad. Next I'll cross-check the most used digits on the pad with important numbers and dates in the guy's life. I reckon I'll have a match in a couple of hours."

"You've been watching too much CSI," said Mark.

"I have no idea what you're talking about," said Ferdia, "but this will work."

Despite himself, Forgill was impressed.

"Ok, Boy Genius," he said, "here's another one for you: How are we going to know what the secret key looks like?"

"That's obvious. It'll look like it fits the lock. I'm amazed no-one has brought this up already."

"How do we know what the lock looks like?"

"Well, obviously we go into the cave underneath the Black Castle and look for it. Actually, one of you needs to do that; I'll be cracking the PIN code on that keypad."

They debated for several minutes then decided Mark and Forgill would go into the cave, while Ferdia and Niamh stayed in the SUV and worked on the access code.

"Give me one minute," said Ferdia. He jumped out and ran up the road to the gate of Abydos, disappearing around the nearest gatepost, tablet in hand. Several minutes later he reappeared and ran back to the SUV.

"Ok," he said breathlessly as he jumped into the passenger seat, "it's going to be a bit trickier than I had hoped. Six different digits are worn on the keypad, and according to the manufacturer's specs," he brandished the tablet, "that model of keypad uses a six-digit code. The good news is that people generally use dates for six-digit pin numbers. With a little bit of digging into his family, cross-referencing the worn digits on the keypad, I should come up with a shortlist of candidate codes."

"Jolly good," said Forgill. "You work on that. Now, let's be away to the Black Castle. Could someone give me directions, please?"

CHAPTER TWENTY-THREE

THE CRYSTAL GROTTO

Fifteen minutes later, Forgill turned the SUV into the small car park on Castle Street and parked in the first space.

"That's quite a view," he said.

Stretched out before them was Wicklow harbor, behind it the bay and the mountains. Small boats, cradled in the arms of the two piers, bobbed in the harbor, fittings glinting in the sunshine, and sails of all colors flapping in the lazy breeze. To their right was an elegant sandstone wall which ran along a set of wide concrete steps, down to the quay and a boatyard. At the top of the steps, near the car park, a stone arch was built into the wall. Beyond the stone arch, a well-kept grassy area extended to the castle and the cliffs alongside it.

Niamh pointed out into the bay, through the opening of the two piers.

"If we're right about the gate being at Orion's left knee, it's out there somewhere, under the seabed."

She shivered at the thought.

"That really creeps me out, but if it means getting Dad and Martha back – and Bree and Fintan, of course," she squeezed Mark's hand, "then I'm totally going out there."

"We'll discuss who goes and who doesn't when the time comes," said Forgill. "Let's get to the bottom of this first."

Mark looked askance at him.

"I'm going, no matter what happens."

Forgill nodded. "That's a given, Mark. You're right at the center of this. Now, shall we take a look in that cave?"

Forgill stepped down from the SUV, walked a short distance towards the stone arch, and beckoned to Mark. Mark took a flashlight from the glovebox of the SUV and joined Forgill. They headed through the stone arch into the grounds around the castle, leaving Ferdia and Niamh to work on the access code.

Mark was eyeing Forgill as they walked, looking away when Forgill almost caught him. Eventually Forgill stopped, turned to Mark and said:

"All right, son; out with it."

"Out with what?"

"You've obviously got something on your mind. Let's have it."

"Oh, I've got loads on my mind about you. Like, where did you get that Tetros you had? And why did the felkynd tell me not to trust you?"

"Well, one thing at a time. I've had the Tetros ever since …"

"Hey McTool! What are you doing down here?"

Mark started, then groaned. Coming towards him from the direction of the castle was Christopher McCabe flanked by his cronies. McCabe had a can of cheap lager in his hand and judging by his demeanor, it wasn't his first of the day. He walked up to Mark and Forgill and looked them up and down.

"What's going on, Psycho? Come down to do some drinking with your boyfriend?"

"Who are you, young man?" enquired Forgill.

McCabe stood toe-to-toe with Forgill, eyes watery from the alcohol. He was considerably taller than the older man.

"Who are you, young man?" mimicked McCabe. "I'm the young man that's going to kick your head in, that's who."

"C'mon," said Mark, pulling at Forgill's sleeve, "let's come back later."

"No, no. I'd like to hear what this young ruffian has to say for himself."

"Ruffian!" sniggered McCabe, taking a swig from his can. "Who are you calling a ruffian, you old spastic?"

"Look," exploded Mark, "just leave us alone!"

McCabe bared his teeth and grabbed Mark by the hair. Forgill moved like lightning. He grabbed McCabe's other arm, pulled it straight and drove his open hand into McCabe's solar plexus. McCabe released Mark and doubled over wheezing for breath. The rest of McCabe's pack circled, not knowing what to do.

"Time to leave, gentlemen," Forgill said.

They were too afraid of McCabe to abandon him, but they moved back several paces. Mark turned for the car but Forgill took his arm.

"No, no. Don't let these brigands intimidate you. We came here to do a job, and do it we will."

McCabe stumbled to his feet and bared his teeth at Forgill. "I'm going to kill you, you old bastard," he hissed. He pulled a knife from his pocket and flicked the blade open. He started towards Forgill, still unsteady on his feet.

Forgill sighed. He reached inside his jacket and pulled out an automatic pistol.

Mark was horrified. He'd never seen a gun before and it looked shockingly purposeful. Forgill pointed the pistol at McCabe's face.

"Piss off now, son," he advised. "You're in over your head."

McCabe's face blanched and his knife-hand fell to his side. "C'mon," he muttered to his cronies, and they slunk away to their makeshift camp of discarded lager cans and fast food wrappers.

Forgill took Mark's arm and lead him towards the castle at a fast walk.

"Friend of yours?"

Mark didn't answer. He walked beside Forgill for several paces, staring at the ground, shaking his head; then looked up at him and said:

"I can't believe you're carrying a gun! That's a really big deal – especially a hand-gun. What if they tell the police?"

"A gun? I don't know what you think you saw, young Mark, but I certainly don't carry a gun."

"But ... I saw it. You pointed it right at McCabe's head."

"So that's his name. What is he to you, then – the local bully?"

"Something like that," Mark muttered, "and stop changing the subject. You're not going to trick me into forgetting about the gun."

"Oh, you mean this thing," said Forgill, reaching into his coat. He withdrew a black object and held it out to Mark. It was a black walking stick, with a clever telescoping shaft that retracted almost entirely into the pistol-shaped grip. Mark eyed it with caution, then raised his eyes to Forgill's face:

"That's not what I saw."

"Oh! Isn't it? Oh, well, never mind. There must have been a mistake, then."

"What? Are you completely nuts? I'm not going to mistake a walking stick for a gun!"

"Mark," said Forgill, a twinkle in his eye, "There's no gun. One does not get to my age without learning a few tricks; a bit of sleight of hand; some legerdemain here, a touch of prestidigitation there ..."

"All right," shouted Mark, "there was no bloody gun. Forget I ever mentioned it!"

"I don't know why you're so upset, young fellow. You were about to get a hiding; I sent the cove packing. Does it matter how I did it?"

"Not really, I suppose. Anyway, we're here."

They had arrived at a deep ditch, separating the mainland from the promontory on which the castle stood. The ditch ran the entire width of the castle and fell away to the cliffs on either side of the promontory. The remains of the castle stood stark against the backdrop of sea and sky, like a trio of rotted teeth.

"That's it? There's not much left, is there," said Forgill. "I mean, when you said 'castle' ..."

"Well, it was built nearly a thousand years ago," said Mark, local pride creeping into his voice.

"And the pyramids were built four and a half thousand years ago, and they're in decent order," countered Forgill.

Mark muttered something rude under his breath. Forgill erupted into deep laughter.

"Oh, come on, young Mark; I'm just pulling your leg. I'm sure this was a proud and impregnable bastion in its day. It's quite a setting, I must admit."

The castle stood on a natural outcropping, protected on three sides by sea cliffs. The spit of land leading to it, at which Mark and Forgill now stood, was narrow and easy to defend. Forgill looked down into the ditch.

"Is this fortification natural or man-made, young McHewell?"

"Dunno. I always thought the bit of land the castle is on had slipped out to sea a bit and made this trench, but I suppose the people that built the castle might have dug it out of the rock, and put a drawbridge over it, or something. Those steps are definitely man-made, though."

He indicated a series of steps cut into each side of the ditch, leading down the counterscarp from their feet to the bottom and up the scarp on the other side to where that main door of the castle would have been, were the walls standing.

"Those steps must have been added more recently. There would be no point in having steps in a defensive ditch. It would defeat the purpose."

"I never thought of that," said Mark. "I'm glad they're there today, though, 'cause that's where we have to go."

He started down the steps. Forgill followed, and they soon stood in the heart of the derelict stronghold, out on the promontory. So little of the castle remained that they were exposed to the Irish Sea, and the breeze nipped at their clothes. Despite the heat of the late afternoon, they both shivered.

"Where's this cave, then?" asked Forgill.

"Back here," said Mark, heading for the cliffs to the east side of the outcrop. He jumped down from the remains of the east wall, and made his way to where the cliff fell away to the sea and rocks below. Forgill followed cautiously, picking his steps.

One part of the cliff was less steep than the rest, and a series of horizontal notches could be seen cut into the rock, leading down to where the tide seethed and roiled around the base of the cliff. Mark pointed down the series of carved footholds and said, "The Danes' Steps."

Forgill raised his eyebrows.

"Steps? I think we could have them under the Trade Descriptions Act on that one. I don't like the look of those, one bit."

Mark shrugged. "They'll be OK until we get to the high-tide mark, then they'll get slippery. It's low tide, so we'll be able to reach the cave but we won't have long; it's on the turn."

"Have you ever been down these steps before?"

"Only halfway, when I was younger. Then I got scared and turned back."

"And you're sure this cave is actually there?"

Mark nodded. "I've seen it from my dad's boat."

"But you've never been in it?"

Mark shook his head and stared nervously at Forgill.

Forgill expelled a great breath of air then clapped his hands together in a loud crack that made Mark jump.

"Right then," he said rubbing his hands together, "faint heart ne'er won dank cave, to misquote William Camden."

"What?"

"Never heard of William Camden? What are they teaching you youngsters in school, these days? Well, never mind. All I meant was, let's get on with it, young adventurer."

Mark gave him a '*God, you really are an old fossil*' look, then said: "OK. The best way to go down is like this."

He sat down and placed his feet on the top step. He scooted forward on his backside and moved to the next step. When he had gone five steps down, to where the steps got steeper, Forgill sat down and followed in like fashion.

They picked their way down the steps slowly with relative ease until they reached the high tide mark. Here, the steps became slippery, partly overgrown with seaweed, and dotted with sharp barnacles. The steps were more eroded here and hard to find. Mark sought out the deeper parts of the steps with his heels and shouted instructions back up to Forgill. Once or twice, their feet slipped and the barnacles nicked their hands, but after a few minutes of careful descent, they stood in the mouth of the cave.

Mark switched on the flashlight and shone it around the interior. It was quite large at the entrance, but got lower and narrower towards the rear. It didn't appear to extend very far back under the castle, and seemed impassable.

"Wow, I always thought it would be bigger than this," he said. "I'm a bit disappointed."

"Indeed," said Forgill, "and I'm not seeing anything that looks like a lock. Could I have that flashlight for a moment?"

Mark handed him the flashlight and Forgill went to the back of the cave. He stooped, then got down on his knees as the roof got lower. He played the flashlight beam around the back of the cave then exclaimed:

"Ah! There's a passage at the back. We just need to squeeze through here."

He crawled forward, pushing the flashlight before him until he and the light disappeared.

"Hold on, Mr. Forgill. I can't see you anymore."

"Just give me a moment, Mark. It's too small for two back here."

Mark waited for several minutes. At first he could hear Forgill grunting as he maneuvered his way through the tight passage, but soon he could hear nothing over the sound of the waves breaking outside.

"Mr. Forgill?" No answer.

Mark crawled after him, following the passage as it curved to the right. After a few meters, the light from the cave entrance no longer penetrated the gloom. He crawled forward in darkness until his outstretched hand met a wall. It was a dead-end, but where had Forgill gone? *Did I miss a fork in the passage?*

He waited in the oppressive dark for a few moments, eyes straining to perceive the rock around him, then started to feel claustrophobic. Panic welled up in him and he called out in a shaky voice:

"Mr. Forgill? Where are you?"

Strange scratching and shuffling noises emanated from the top of the passage and he was suddenly illuminated from above. He looked up and, to his great relief, saw Forgill's head poking out from another tunnel some distance above his head.

"I'm terribly sorry, Mark. I got carried away and forgot you didn't have a light."

In the beam of the flashlight, Mark saw the passage ended in a vertical shaft several meters in diameter. He got to his feet and looked around. A series of corroded metal steps were driven into the wall of the shaft and led up to the tunnel where Forgill stood a few meters above. Mark climbed the steps and joined Forgill.

This tunnel was bigger. They could stand up with height to spare, and it was wide enough for them to walk side-by-side. It sloped downwards away from them and to the right, back out to sea.

"How far does this go?"

"I don't know, son. I'd only gone slightly further than this when I heard you calling. I'm sorry to have left you in the dark like that."

"I was actually really scared for a moment."

"Indeed. I could hear it in your voice. I really am sorry, Mark. I've been on my own and living on my wits for so long that I've become selfish. I promise it won't happen again. What do you say? Can you forgive me?"

Mark eyed him.

"Can I carry the torch?"

Forgill laughed and handed it to him. "Of course you can, my boy. Shall we press on?"

They followed the tunnel as it curved and descended for several minutes. After one particularly sharp bend, Mark said:

"Where do you think we are – in relation to the castle I mean?"

"I've been trying to keep my bearings - not easy when one's underground - but I believe we are under the seabed somewhere beyond the end of that pier with the lighthouse on it."

"The East Pier."

"Yes, I believe we are somewhere off the end of that. Not far, in fact, from where the star Saiph was when Ferdia overlaid Orion on the map. If I'm right, just around this bend we should ... oh!"

As they rounded the bend, Forgill stopped talking. Then he said in a small voice: "Oh my!" His eyes were fixed on something in the tunnel ahead.

Mark had been looking at him as he spoke, but now turned to see what had left Forgill speechless.

"Oh wow!"

"Indeed."

The tunnel ended a short distance ahead in a chamber slightly wider than the tunnel. The chamber itself was remarkable, walls of jagged purplish glass like the inside of a geode, but its rear wall was exquisite:

Multi-colored shards of crystal covered the entire wall, scintillating in the beam of the flashlight. They were translucent and seemed to glow with an inner phosphorescence.

"It's ... amazing," said Mark. "It's like a huge stained-glass window. No; it's like someone found a broken rainbow and tried to put it back together in the dark."

"That's a very apposite and poetic analogy, young man. I'm impressed."

"Uh, thank you, but that's just what it looks like to me. Do you think that rainbow wall is the door?"

"That would be my guess, yes."

Mark approached the crystal wall and rubbed his hand over it. The surface was uneven, the crystals layered over each other.

"Hey, Mr. Forgill, these crystals feel kind-of warm."

Forgill came over beside Mark and touched the wall.

"Indeed they do. And have you noticed that they glow slightly, every so often."

"Really? I hadn't ... oh, yeah!"

When Mark raised his voice, the cyan and blue crystals dotted randomly through the wall glowed brighter, as if lit from within. They also seemed to move away from each other slightly.

"Did you see that?" he squeaked, his voice rising in excitement. "They're moving!" The blue and purplish crystals glowed even more brightly and made a grinding sound as they slid against the facets of their neighbors.

"That is extraordinary!" said Forgill. As his voice echoed through the chamber, the red and orange crystals glowed and creaked.

"Mark, they're not moving; they're shrinking. And have you noticed that certain crystals respond to my voice, and different ones respond to yours?"

"Yeah! Why does it do that?"

"I think it responds to frequencies. My voice is deeper than yours, so it activates the colors with a lower frequency in the visible spectrum."

"Wow! What does it mean, do you think?"

"I think this whole chamber is the lock. The key will be something that generates sound across the audible sound spectrum, and lights up all the crystals."

"What then?"

"Then they will shrink back and reveal the passage beyond, I hope."

"Hey, look at the floor here." Mark pointed to the cave floor in the center of the chamber. "It's smooth, like the stone tiles in our kitchen. The rest of the floor is more ... crinkly."

"You're absolutely right, young Mark" said Forgill crouching for a closer look. "The stone here has been ground down in a perfect circle and polished like marble. Look, you can see amazing patterns in the rock."

He brushed aside sand and pebbles with his palm to better see the patterns then said "Oh! There's something else here. Holes. Several of them."

Mark helped to clear away the detritus. When they were done they had uncovered seven holes drilled into the polished floor, each about two finger-widths in diameter, spaced evenly around the perimeter of the circle. The holes were filled with sand and small pebbles.

"These are most certainly not natural," said Forgill.

The first two holes were circular in cross-section, the third ovoid, the fourth triangular, the fifth pentagonal, and the sixth and seventh, octagonal and thirteen-sided, respectively.

Mark scrunched up his face as counted the sides of each hole. It reminded him of something and he was in the process of counting them again when it hit him.

"Encyclopedias!" he shouted.

The crystal wall glowed and creaked.

"Pardon," said Forgill looking blankly at Mark.

"This is the *fibbernadgy* sequence," he said, "same as with the encyclopedias in my dad's study."

"I'm sorry; I don't follow."

"You see, you take the last two numbers and add them together ..."

"I know what the Fibonacci sequence is, young man; but what does it have to do with encyclopedias – or any of this?"

Mark told him about his and Ferdia's discovery in Fintan's study.

"Impressive," said Forgill.

"Yeah, and these holes follow the same sequence. Look; these two holes are circular, so they have one side each, the next one has two curved sides, then three, then five, then eight, then thirteen. 1, 1, 2, 3, 5, 8, 13 –

Fibbernadgy!"

"Fibonacci."

"Whatever."

Forgill examined the holes more closely.

"By Jingo, you're right. Well spotted, young mathematician. Well, this should narrow down the search for the key considerably."

"Do you have any idea what it is?"

"Not specifically, but I think we're looking for a series of large tuning forks or similar that fit into these holes."

"Oh yeah, that would make sense."

"Indeed. Well, I think we've found what we came for. Let's make our way back to your friends. If we describe this to young Ferdia, I'm sure he will figure it all out."

Forgill turned and headed out of the chamber. Mark paused, playing the beam of the flashlight over the crystals and the holes in the polished floor.

Imagine, this has been here all this time. I wonder what's on the other side. And that fibbernadgy thing again. I wonder how my father got mixed up in this.

"Come along, Mark; I can't see a thing," called Forgill.

Mark turned and followed Forgill out of the chamber.

"Yeah, well now you know what it's like."

"You're not going to let that go, are you?" chuckled Forgill.

He put his arm around Mark's shoulder and they headed for the surface.

CHAPTER TWENTY-FOUR

DEWENISCH

Three days after their escape, Fintan and Sam, disheveled and hungry, crested a dawn-drenched hill and looked north. In the valley before them was a vast lake dotted with islands, like rough emeralds sewn onto a shimmering blue cloak. Some way off the southern shore lay a large island covered in dense forest throughout which derelict stone buildings were dotted. At the forest's center was a clearing in which stood a gleaming stone tower.

"Dewenisch", said Fintan.

It took them the rest of the morning to reach the lake and another hour to hike along the shore to a jetty where an old man wearing a jester's hat was dozing on a crate. He raised his head at their approach and regarded them serenely. Sam's step faltered. In the center of the old man's forehead was a third eye.

"Fintan, I don't like this, man," hissed Sam pulling at Fintan's sleeve. "Let's find another boat."

A goofy grin lit up the old man's face.

"Oh, there are no other boats, Dearie," he said. "No other boats, no, no. Hee hee hee!"

Fintan patted Sam's arm. "C'mon. Let's talk to him at least."

"Talk, talk. Yes, yes. Let's talk. Hee hee! Come closer, dear friends. We're all friends here, we three. Hee hee!"

The jetty creaked as Fintan and Sam stepped onto it and they picked their steps across the weathered boards to where the old man sat.

"Yes, yes. Come closer. Come closer to me. So I can see. Hee hee!"

Sam couldn't tear his gaze from the man's forehead.

"You've got three eyes!"

"Yes, yes. Very wise. Three eyes. Hee hee, eyes of three!"

He leaned conspiratorially toward Sam. "Just as well I do, Dearie; just as well I do. There are cataracts in the other two. Hee hee! Cataracts, cataracts; you'll soon be planning cat attacks. Cat attacks, cat attacks, you wish to find the Kommanlak."

He stood up and removed the jester's hat. All trace of mirth drained from his face.

"You would seek the aid of the cat folk in your quest."

"How could you know that, Øsul?" asked Fintan.

The old man chanted and tapped his head, cheeks and forehead in a well-practiced ritual gesture.

'The eye of the mind to see the past
'The eye of the left to see your face

"The eye of the right to watch you pass
"The eye of the brow to see your fate."

"See our fate? Are you telling me you can tell the future?"

"I can see *all* futures." He put one hand over his two lower eyes and looked over the lake with his third, pointing towards the island.

"I can see you disembarking at the old quay yonder." He barked a short laugh. "You just missed your step and stumbled onto the dock."

He pointed to a place in the lake, midway between the jetty and the island.

"Your friend's hand is dangling in the water. A luus comes from beneath and takes his arm with a single bite. In the same spot, I see the same fish do the same to you and your friend gets away scot free. Over there, we hit a rock and we all join the luus for supper."

"I see."

"No, Dearie; no, you don't see. Not like I do. Given an arbitrary starting point I can see all possible futures branching and branching again, all overlaid on my vision."

"But the possibilities are infinite. How can your mind cope?"

"Those of us from the northern isles born like this are sent to the felkynd at an early age to learn to control and use the ability. When it becomes too much to bear or we want to sleep, there's always the hat." He waved the jester's hat in the air.

"That's extraordinary! With a gift like that you could have been anything; a great leader, or a military tactician or an advisor."

"Or a gambler," added Sam.

"Ah, but I was something far greater, Dearies. I was a *lungschohr* – a navigator. I once guided flotillas over vast expanses of ocean, but then I started to lose the sight in my lower eyes. A lungschohr needs his full sight. I was pensioned off and came here to live on Inischkoppel, the most beautiful island on all of Lokeirn. The felkynd pay me a retainer to service the islands with transport."

"So you, what, come here every day and wait for passengers?" asked Sam.

"Oh no, Dearie; I only come when someone needs ferrying."

"So how did ya know we were coming?"

The old ferryman leaned forward to Sam and keeping his lower eyes perfectly still, rotated his middle eye in its socket.

Sam took a step back. "Don't do that again," he said.

The old man cackled. "You're a meek one, aren't you, Dearie?"

"Øsul, can …" started Fintan.

"Berentos," said the old man.

"Sorry?"

"My name is Berentos. Grand titles like *Øsul* and I are poor bedfellows."

"Berentos it is then. I'm Fintan and this is Sam."

Berentos replaced his hat then immediately swept it off and bowed deeply. "At your service," said Berentos.

Sam could have sworn that as Berentos replaced his hat for that split second the same goofy grin flashed across his face.

"Berentos, can I ask you a question?" asked Fintan.

"I believe you just did."

"Aha, very droll. Can I ask you another?"

"Again, you just di…"

"Berentos, where's your damn boat?"

"I thought you'd never ask."

Berentos stooped to the jetty and picked up a long rod made of some pliable wood. He flexed it like a fencing foil a few times then stooped and ran it in a graceful curved pattern on the surface of the lake. He had just lifted the tip of the rod from the water when bubbles started to break on the surface. In seconds the water around the jetty was seething like a hot spring. In the middle of the maelstrom, a circular coracle rose to the surface. Sam eyed it with blunt mistrust.

"That thing doesn't fly, does it?"

"I have no idea; I've never tried to make it fly."

"Well don't start today. I've had enough flying in weird boojums for one life."

"As you wish."

The coracle settled on the surface and the water flowed up and over its edge. The residual pools of water ran in self-propelled rivulets from the interior into the lake leaving the seats bone dry.

"That's a neat trick."

"My felkynd mistresses are not fond of water. I extend the same courtesy to all my passengers. Time is wasting, Dearies." Berentos gestured towards the boat.

Sam stepped down into the craft. Fintan threw him the spear then jumped down after him. The coracle stayed unexpectedly stable causing a sort of reverse sea-sickness.

"Oh man, that's weird," said Sam. "It doesn't rock at all. Damn, I hate this. Gimme a good ol' fashioned rowboat any day."

"I hear that!" said Fintan. "Wish I had my boat here."

"You got a rowboat back home?"

"Nah. Something a little bigger."

"Oh, one more thing," called Berentos from the jetty. "You'll need your strength and wits about you on the other side. I brought you some food."

He lifted the crate and pulled out a sack. He threw it into the boat where it landed with a dull thud. Sam and Fintan looked at each other for a moment then both lunged for the sack. They'd been living on leaves, berries and water for three days but the sack contained a variety of cheeses, bread and meats which they set upon with relish. When they had eaten their fill they realized they were halfway to the island. Sam belched and lay back in his seat, his arm dangling over the side.

"Oh man, I'd never been so hungry. Thanks Berentos."

"Watch your arm, Dearie," called Berentos from the rear.

Sam snatched his arm out of the water and looked down. He caught a glimpse of a huge silver fish and a flash of needlelike teeth. The creature passed beneath them creating a swell on the surface which the coracle rode smoothly.

"Was that a pike?" he asked.

"Looked like it," said Fintan. "But I've never seen one that big."

"That was a luus, Dearies. They keep me in business, so they do. The occasional brave heart decides he doesn't need a ferry to reach Dewenisch and swims for it. Very unwise."

"Yeah, well if I had my marlin rod we'd show them who's boss," said Sam, but he still moved away towards the center of the boat.

And all the while Dewenisch loomed closer.

Eventually Berentos maneuvered the coracle alongside a mooring point. The water lapped around a flight of alga-carpeted steps leading up to the top of the quay.

"Now Dearies, all ashore that's going ashore."

Sam stepped out onto the slippery stone gripping Fintan's shoulder then returned the favor as Fintan disembarked. They picked their way up the greasy steps using each other for support. Just as they reached the top, Fintan's foot caught on the lip of the quay and he sprawled forward dropping the spear.

"Easy there, Tiger!" Sam caught him just before he fell.

Fintan looked back at Berentos who nodded and did the weird eye trick.

"I told you, Dearie," he called. "One more thing; ware the forest, and be sure to follow the path of righteousness." With a final salute he spun the coracle around and headed back towards the lake shore.

"I wonder what he meant by that," said Fintan.

"Hell if I know," said Sam. "I didn't understand a whole heap of *anything* he said."

"Me neither. What a strange little man."

"Yeah, well are we going to hang around here all day or find Whiskers's mother?"

Fintan looked along the quay to the edge of the forest. There was a gap in the trees through which he could see an arched gateway in an imposing stone wall. He looked at Sam and indicated the forest with his head. Sam shrugged and said, "Let's do it." Fintan picked up the spear and they headed down along the quay.

They stopped at the tree line and peered into the forest shade. The stone wall stretched as far as they could see in both directions, and all there was through the gateway was more forest.

"We've come this far," said Fintan. "No going back now." He clapped Sam on the shoulder and entered the trees. After a moment's hesitation Sam muttered "Aw hell!" and followed.

"That's some stonework," said Fintan when they arrived at the gateway. "Some kind of white granite I've never seen before. These felkynd, or whoever built this for them, are fantastic stonemasons. What a beautiful wall!"

"And high," said Sam. "Jeez, that thing must be forty feet tall."

"Which is puzzling," said Fintan. "Why build such a wall and not put a gate in the entrance?"

The gateway was an ornate gothic arch that could have graced an abbey, and was entirely devoid of door or gate.

"Who knows," said Sam. "I've long since given up trying to figure out things here."

"Hey, look at this," said Fintan. He ran his fingers down along the left side of the gateway's surround. There was a series of notches on the edge of the stone.

"Mason's marks?" suggested Sam.

"No, this is Ogham," said Fintan, a hint of surprise in his voice.

"It's what?"

"Ogham. It's an old Celtic alphabet. The grouped notches on the edge form letters."

"Can you read it?"

"Actually, I can. It's an amazing coincidence but when I was designing buildings back home I always put a stone with an Ogham inscription in the design; some quote or such that suited the building."

"That sure is a coincidence."

"Except I don't believe in coincidences. Not anymore."

"Well, I already told ya how I feel about this place. Nothin' makes sense." Sam indicated the gate surround. "What's that say anyhow?"

Fintan ran his fingers over the markings again. "It says 'Follow the path of righteousness.'"

"That's what Three-Eyes said!"

"Yeah, it is. Maybe it's some felkynd motto."

"Well, if it's important we'll find out. C'mon, let's find this crazy cat lady."

"Wait…" said Fintan, but Sam had already stridden through the gateway and was heading for the trees beyond.

"Hold up, Sam." Fintan caught up with him and grabbed his shoulder.

"Hey, what the ..?"

"Sorry Sam, I didn't mean to manhandle you but I have a bad feeling about this."

"What's the problem? That tower we saw is right over there. Can't be more than a coupla hundred yards through the trees."

"I know, but I've got a weird feeling. That inscription on the gateway, and what Berentos said; it's got to mean something, right?"

"Follow the path of the righteous? Ok, we'll be righteous! We'll be righteously righteous."

"Look, let's think about this. There are four paths leading into the forest here. Which one should we take?"

Sam pointed to a path that went along the side of a derelict building covered in ivy. "That one. It's goin' in the right direction."

"Ok, we'll do it your way, but watch out for traps."

"Yeah, we'll be careful. C'mon."

Fintan raised the spear into a defensive position and followed Sam. They had just cleared the end of the old building when they heard a rustling behind them. Fintan whipped around raising the spear. The ivy on the building had come to life and was extending tendrils in the air and along the ground towards them. Fintan shouted in shock and thumbed the fire button on the spear.

Too late.

The ivy wrapped around his arm and twisted it. He screamed in pain and dropped the spear. The ivy continued to twist until he felt his shoulder dislocate. "Sam!" he screamed, "Jesus Christ, help me!"

Sam grabbed the spear and sprayed the ruined building with fire. The ivy in the air withered and turned to ash and the remaining tendrils withdrew. Fintan was kneeling on the ground whimpering and supporting his arm. Sam grabbed his other arm and got him to his feet. Further down the path, the grass was moving as if alive and roots were tearing up from the ground, writhing like snakes.

"The hell with that!" said Sam and propelled Fintan back towards the gateway.

"Oh Jesus. Oh God, this hurts. What am I going to do Sam? There are no doctors here."

"Here, gimme a look." Sam examined Fintan's shoulder with great care.

"Turn around so I can see it from the back," he said. As Fintan turned around, Sam grabbed his arm and kicked his legs out from under him. As he fell his own weight pulled his shoulder back into place with a loud *Snick!*

Fintan screamed and passed out.

A while later he woke up to find Sam making a sling from a piece of his shirt.

"Here, put this around your neck and support that arm in it."

"You bastard!" Fintan croaked. "Where did you learn to do that?"

"College football. How you doing?"

"It hurts like hell, that's how I'm doing, but at least it's back in place. Thanks Sam."

"Yeah, but what are we gonna do now? We can't go back down there; that creeper woulda torn us apart - and who knows what might be down the other trails."

"There's got to be a safe way of getting through those trees and it's got to be something to do with this 'path of righteousness'. Oh God, this is throbbing. Let me rest here a while and think about it."

"Sure, sure. Take your time, man. I'm gonna take a walk back out on that dock if ya don't mind bein' on your own for a time."

"Yeah, of course. I'm pretty bad company at the moment. Go ahead and take a look around; just be careful, Ok?"

"Yeah, I will."

Sam wandered off and Fintan lay back favoring his damaged shoulder.

When he closed his eyes the pain seemed to get worse but eventually his brain flooded with endorphins and the pain became manageable. The instinct to sleep after the injury was strong and he started to slide into the well of unconsciousness. As he fell into that pre-sleep slumber where you hear voices in your head and memories are almost eidetic, his thoughts took flight. He thought about the Ogham inscription and the almost mocking way Berentos had said it. The Path of Righteousness was clearly a reference to the safe path through the forest, but what did it mean? He slid further towards sleep. Snatches of music, smells, faces and a variety of random memories flashed through his mind. Eventually his thoughts found their way back to his college days and his first encounter with the Ogham alphabet.

His girlfriend had opened a design book at a page showing a photograph of an ancient Ogham stone. Written at the top of the page was *Beith-Luis-Fearn* and the alphabet was shown beneath.

"What do the Irish words at the top mean?" he had asked.

"Ogham is sometimes called Beith-Luis-Fearn because those are the names of the first three letters, just the same way that the word 'alphabet' is made from the Greek words Alpha and Beta."

"Oh yeah, I see. Makes sense. Actually, thinking about it, *beith* is also very close to the second letter of the Hebrew alphabet 'Beth' which means house. I wonder if they come from the same root."

"No, I don't think so. Beith means 'birch'"

"Birch?"

"Yeah, as in birch tree. All the letters in Ogham are named after trees or plants. So Beith-Luis-Fearn is Birch-Rowan-Alder."

Fintan came awake and sat bolt upright. He shoulder howled in protest but he ignored it.

"Sam!" he roared. "Sam! Where are you? I think I've got it!"

He got to his feet and shambled to the gateway. "Sam!"

Sam was sitting near the end of the dock looking into the water. He turned around at Fintan's voice. Fintan gestured to him, the movement sending darts of pain through his shoulder. Sam got up and came walking back down the dock.

"What's up?" he asked when he reached Fintan. "I thought you were going to take a rest."

"I was, and as I was falling asleep it came to me. Look."

He led Sam to the gateway and ran his finger along the inscription.

"Each letter in the Ogham alphabet is named after a tree or a plant. See the word for righteousness, '*firentagt*'?"

"Yeah?"

"If you spell it out in Ogham you get Fearn Idad Ruis Edad Nion Tinne Ailm Gort Tinne, or Alder Yew Elder Poplar Ash Holly Fir Ivy Holly. What I'm thinking is, if we follow the path of righteousness – or firentagt – letter by letter, we'll make it through the forest safely."

Sam's eyes were wide. He made several attempts to say something then just shrugged. "If you say so, man. I hope you know your trees. I wouldn't know a poplar from a parka."

"I should be able to recognize all of these, yeah."

"I guess we'll know soon enough. What was that first letter again?"

"Alder."

"Well, was there an alder at that first junction?"

"As a matter of fact there was."

"Ok then, we're off to a good start. Wanna give it another go?"

"Sure. But keep that spear at the ready, just in case."

The trail marked with an alder tree was second from the left. They crept down it like a pair of frightened birds, Sam following Fintan with the spear cocked. The trail took them on a circuitous route through the forest and led them a long way from the tower, but nothing attacked them. Eventually they arrived at another clearing with four trails.

Fintan breathed a sigh of relief.

"There's a yew tree here. Maybe I've got this right."

"Yeah, well I ain't gonna relax just yet. It could all still be fluke."

"Only one way to find out."

They headed down the trail marked with a yew tree and when they got to the clearing at the end of that, they followed the next trail.

The sun had peaked and was on the lazy downhill amble into mid-afternoon when they finally walked out of the forest into the well-kept grassy clearing at the center of the island. After the gloom of the forest, the brightness and openness felt like a curse lifting. The clearing was roughly circular and many hundreds of meters across, cut through with radial and concentric pebbled paths dividing the area into sectors and subsectors. The glistening white tower stood at the center like an enormous gnomon, its lengthening shadow pointing somewhere to the left of Fintan and Sam. Throughout the grounds were derelict buildings, overgrown with grass and wildflowers yet still at keeping with the landscaped feeling of the place. If Midir had indeed laid waste to the complex, he had failed to rid it of its essential essence: Dewenisch still had the atmosphere of a place of retreat and learning.

A door opened in the base of the tower and a tall figure emerged in a long robe, accompanied by several other creatures. As the figure drew closer they could make out an ageing female felkynd who radiated a tremendous aura of calm and power. The fur around her muzzle was graying and her whiskers and ear tufts were long. The iridescent blue of her robe shimmered as she walked, the front of it decorated by symbols reminiscent of Egyptian hieroglyphs.

In her arms was an exotic-looking domestic cat with blue eyes. The other creatures that walked and flew alongside her were vaguely feline but unrecognizable to either Fintan or Sam.

Fintan bowed as the stately felkynd approached and held out his hands in the supplicatory gesture Jere had taught him. He hissed out of the side of his mouth at Sam who made a diffident effort at doing the same.

"Good morning Øsul, I am Fintan McHewell and this is Sam Renstrom. We have come to seek an audience with Worara Øsul Mieru-San."

The felkynd lady stopped, her creatures arranging themselves around her feet.

{*Worara Øsul Mieru-San, you say? Your information is outdated, Øsul-ti. There is no longer anyone by that name here.*}

Fintan's heart sank and he heard Sam swearing under his breath.

"Øsul, we have come a long way to find her and to ask her help. Could you tell us where she is now?"

{*Oh, I am she, but I do not go by that name any longer. I am now Worara Mieru-Roku.*}

Fintan breathed a sigh of relief.

"Ah, I think I understand. The suffix on your name is a title indicating how far you've progressed through your Worar levels."

The felkynd inclined her head in affirmation.

{*Very good. You are somewhat familiar with Diru meditation. But what brings you here, may I ask? You said you needed my help?*}

"Yes Øsul. We need to petition the Ord Kommarlu for help."

Mieru stopped and cocked her head at Fintan.

{*And what makes you think I have any knowledge of the Ord Kommarlu, or their whereabouts?*}

"A felkynd who once knew you told me to come to you."

{*Indeed? And what was the name of this felkynd that I may verify your story?*}

"I'd rather not say, Øsul."

Mieru drew herself up to her full height.

{*Without candor we have no basis for parlay. Please leave my island.*}

She started to turn on her heel.

"Please! Please, Øsul... his name is Jere."

Mieru's muzzle twisted in a slight snarl. It was uncanny; just for a moment it could have been Jere standing there. He had exactly the same expression of bemusement.

{*Jere? It is a noble name but I do not know this felkynd.*}

The lump returned to Fintan's throat and tears pooled in the corners of his eyes, already watery with pain. How tragic that a mother could have no memory of her son.

"He explained that you might not remember him, but I assure you he was very important to you in your past. Could you take my word for it?"

{*The word of a stranger is easily given but not so easily taken. However, I can see a sincerity in your eyes. Why does this Jere wish to find the Ord Kommarlu?*}

"Kuhn-Ridh is holding Jere and twelve other felkynd captive at his city. He plans to perform a taghairm to locate the Lebor Stara."

A collective shock went through Mieru and her companions. The cat in her arms wriggled and started to mewl. Mieru placed it on the ground and it started to pace back and forward, keening and swishing its tail.

{*Come with me immediately.*}

Mieru strode back towards the tower with her entourage. Sam and Fintan exchanged glances then hurried after her.

CHAPTER TWENTY-FIVE
ABYDOS

When Mark and Del Forgill exited the cave and got back to the green area between the Black Castle and the car park, McCabe and his posse were gone – their litter still strewn about - but Niamh was coming towards them looking agitated.

"There's something up with Ferdia," she said. "He was trying to figure out the gate code on his tablet, and he suddenly went really pale and got out of the car. He's sitting on one of the benches and won't talk to me. He found something on the Internet that really upset him. He looks kind of sick."

Mark ran over to the car park and found Ferdia. He was looking into the distance, his iPad dangling in his hand. His expression reminded Mark of when he'd told him about the weird comic page. He looked downright scared.

"Ferd? Are you OK?"

Ferdia didn't answer for a moment then turned to Mark and said:

"I found the code for the gate. We should get going."

He stood up and started walking back to the car, his eyes unfocused.

"Hang on a minute, Ferd. Are you all right? Niamh said you found something on the Net that upset you."

"No, I'm fine. Let's go."

Try as he might, Mark could not prize what had upset Ferdia out of him. He tried a few more times on the drive back to Ashtown Lane, but Ferdia wasn't talking. Forgill watched them in the rear-view mirror, his expression unreadable.

There was still no answer at Abydos when Forgill tried the intercom again. He parked a little farther up the road and beckoned the kids out from where they were hiding in a nearby gateway.

They clustered around the keypad on the wall and Ferdia entered the code he'd gleaned from the Internet, blocking the others' view as he did so. Mark, puzzled by this behavior, asked Ferdia what the code was.

"It doesn't matter," he muttered, and pushed the star button to finish entering the code.

There was a pause, then a creak, and the heavy wooden gates started to ease open.

"Wow, Ferd! You nailed it first time!"

Ferdia didn't answer. He walked up to the gates, turned sideways and slipped through the opening gap. The others looked at each other, shrugged and followed.

A driveway of sandy pea-shingle curved up the hill, through a well-tended expanse of lawn, to a mansion that would have been entirely comfortable on a plantation in the American Deep South. It was an impressive pile of columns, garrets and balconies, and it dominated the landscape utterly.

"Wow!" said Mark, not for the first or last time that day.

"Yeah," said Niamh, "and I thought *your* house was awesome!"

Only Ferdia and Forgill seemed unfazed. Ferdia continued his solitary march up the drive; Forgill seemed more interested in the flower beds. He wandered along muttering things like *"Juniperus horizontalis" and "Cotoneaster japonicus"* to himself, and occasionally bent down to take cuttings from the plants and stuff them in his coat pockets. All the while, Ferdia got further and further ahead. It occurred to Mark it would be best if they stuck together, in case there actually was someone in the house.

"Hey Ferd," he shouted, "wait for us." He gestured to Niamh and Forgill and hurried up the drive to join Ferdia.

Soon they arrived at the porch.

"Very well, then," said Forgill, "Let's ensure we're alone in this antebellum monstrosity."

"We are," muttered Ferdia.

"Most likely, young man, but let's play it safe, eh?"

Forgill walked through the pillared porch – bigger itself than the average home – and tugged on the bell-pull beside the front door.

A bell rang deep inside the house and faded to silence. Forgill waited, straining to hear any noise from within. When there was no answer he tried the front door and, as expected, found it locked.

They left the porch and backed away from the house looking up at the windows and balconies for a way in. Seeing no obvious points of entry, they headed around the house to the left.

The long walk along the side of the mansion turned up only closed shutters, but at the rear they found at a wide ramp leading down into the earth.

"What's that?" asked Niamh.

"Judging by the tire tracks, I'd say it's an underground parking garage," said Forgill. "We should take a look; perhaps there's an access door down there that leads into the house."

"Good idea," said Mark.

They headed down the ramp into the gloom of the garage. At the bottom of the ramp a slatted metal security shutter barred their way. As Mark reached it, it lurched then rattled upwards.

"How did ...?"

He turned in surprise and saw Ferdia still at the top of the ramp, standing beside a security keypad on a metal pole.

"Same code," said Ferdia, looking gloomier than ever.

"Ferd, what *IS* the matter with you," demanded Mark. "I'm getting a bit tired of this. Either tell me what's wrong or snap out of it, OK?"

Ferdia said nothing and just looked at him.

"Suit yourself, but you're being a complete pain in the ass. C'mon, let's go."

They walked into the gloom, their footsteps echoing in the dim concrete bunker. After a few paces the lights came on automatically, making them jump. There were parking spaces for dozens of vehicles, and the four nearest the gate were occupied by cars under dust covers.

Forgill paused at the fourth car, and cocked his head to one side.

"That looks very familiar," he murmured.

He stooped and lifted the front of the cover.

"I knew it," he shouted, his voice edged with excitement. "Mark, grab this other corner, would you?"

Together they peeled back the cover and the long bonnet of Forgill's

Jaguar XK150 was revealed.

Forgill was shaking his head, tears in his eyes.

"I never thought I'd see her again. Keep pulling that cover back, Mark."

They dropped the cover on the concrete floor. Forgill walked around the car, rubbing his hand along the wings and stooping down to examine the body panels. He reached the driver's door and looked inside.

"Extraordinary! The keys are in her, and she's completely undamaged. The tires are a bit flat, but that's easily fixed. She's here! I just can't believe it!"

Then Ferdia spoke up.

"There's something wrong here. You only lost your car yesterday. Judging by the dust that came off that cover, and the condition of the tires, this car has been sitting here for months; years maybe. This can't be your car."

Forgill looked at him, shocked. A red tinge started at his neck and rose up into his cheeks.

"This is absolutely my car. I'd know her anywhere. That's my registration, and I'd bet my life, if we open the bonnet and check the VIN number, it'll be correct."

"How do you explain the dust?"

Forgill looked troubled.

"I can't. You're right about those tires too. But this is my car, and I can prove it."

He opened the driver's door and bent down to reach under the seat. When he stood up he was holding a road atlas. He took an envelope from between the pages and showed it to Ferdia. It was an electricity bill with Forgill's name and address on it."

"Satisfied, young skeptic?"

"Well, it's no weirder than any of the other stuff that's happened," said

Mark.

"Indeed," said Forgill. "I'm sure it will all become apparent in due course."

During this exchange, Niamh had been looking under the other car covers.

"Mark," she called, "what was the registration number of your dad's Porsche?"

"12-WW-27574. Why?"

"Come and look at this."

She pulled the dust-cover back across the bonnet of the second car, revealing a Ruby Red Porsche 911.

Mark's jaw fell. "That's my dad's car! This is where he must have come on Christmas day!"

Ferdia shuffled his feet and looked awkward.

"Ferd, do you know something about this?" asked Mark. "Is this what you found on the Internet?"

"No. Nothing like that."

Mark stared at Ferdia for long moments. He looked like he was about to say something else when Niamh interrupted:

"Look guys, there's a door over here. Let's see if we can get into the house."

Mark eyeballed Ferdia for another moment then strode over to the metal door and yanked on the handle. To his surprise, the door flew open and crashed against the inner wall of the garage. He staggered back off balance and fell on his backside.

"Well," said Forgill, "it would appear we've found our point of ingress. Shall we?"

He held his hand out to Mark. Mark gripped it and Forgill pulled him to his feet. Mark shot a sidelong glance at Ferdia and strode through the door into the mansion.

He found himself at the end of a narrow concrete corridor that turned immediately to the right and ran the length of the house. He started down the corridor and the others followed.

Dust motes danced in the flashlight beam as he played it over the bare walls and floor. There were no exits on either side of the corridor but at the end they found a spiral staircase.

They ascended, and emerged into grandeur.

"Wow!" said Mark.

The room was vast. The walls were painted a sumptuous red with paintings and busts in alcoves between the window shutters. The parquet floor was polished to such a sheen they could see their reflections. In the middle of the floor were seven life-sized marble statues in a large circle.

High above their heads, the entire ceiling was a vaulted skylight protected by metal bars. The sunlight streamed through and projected the shadow of the skylight frame onto the floor and the imposing double-doors at the front of the building.

Mark snapped off the flashlight and turned slowly in place, looking around and up.

"I've never seen a room this big in a house. This must be the whole inside of the mansion," he said.

"Indeed," said Forgill from beside one of the window frames. "These shutters are decorative. There are no windows, and there is no way to open the front doors. This is not as much a house as a vault."

"But what's supposed to be kept in it?"

"Perhaps it is designed to keep people out."

"Well, we got in pretty easily."

"Quite, but I don't believe that metal door in the garage was meant to be open. I think someone buggered up."

282

"But why would someone disguise a huge strongroom as a mansion?"

"Maybe it's something to do with this," called Niamh.

She was standing in the middle of the circle of statues, her feet far apart, rocking from side to side.

"What the hell are you doing?" asked Mark.

"The floor here moves; look."

They moved closer to see what Niamh was standing on.

"Good Lord!" said Forgill, "it's like a giant ship's compass."

A huge brass ring, several meters across, was set into the floor. The ring was at the center of an eight-pointed star, the arms of the star formed of hardwood inserts in the parquetry. The statues stood at the tips of seven of the arms.

The perimeter of the brass ring, inset into the wooden floor, was inscribed with radial lines, like the ticks on a clock-face. Outside the lines, at regular intervals were arcane symbols.

Within the ring was Forgill's giant compass: a glass-topped brass dial, almost as wide as the outer ring, the glass top level with the floor. There was a brass rim around the edge of the glass which also had periodic radial tick marks.

When they looked closer they realized the outer ring was an enormous brass crucible set into the floor. Between the edge of the crucible and the huge dial they could see mercury glinting in the sunlight. The disc was over a meter deep.

They stepped onto the glass to join Niamh and felt the disc rock very slightly under their feet.

"The disc is floating on the mercury," said Forgill, "Whatever it is, this is what the entire place was built to protect."

"Look what's inside it," said Niamh.

Beneath the glass, etched into the brass floor of the hollow disc, was a relief map of Ireland. Set into the map at various locations was a series of small old-fashioned electric bulbs. Some bulbs glowed an insipid yellow, but most were out.

"What do those lights mean?" asked Niamh.

"I have no idea," said Forgill, "but they seem to form a pattern."

"What pattern?"

"I don't know. It's vaguely familiar, but I can't quite get it."

"Hey Ferd," called Mark, "come over here and look at this. You might figure it out."

Ferdia was sitting at the top of the spiral staircase looking glum. He peered around at Mark, and with a look of resignation got up and joined them on the glass.

"Can you see a pattern in those lights, Ferd?" asked Mark.

"Or at least," interjected Forgill, "tell us what all the locations have in common."

Ferdia walked up and down the glass examining each bulb. The disc rocked very slightly in the mercury as he moved around. He looked puzzled at first, and then Mark saw the quick changes of expression ticking across his face as his brain made the connections. He looked back at the other three with a satisfied expression.

"You have it, don't you?" said Mark.

"Yes, I do. They're round towers. It was the islands that gave it away. There are lights on Ram's Island, Devenish and Inis Cealtra. Let me check the rest of them."

He pulled out his iPad and started Google Earth.

"Yes, those lights are all at the sites of round towers; Drumbo, Ram's Island, Clones, Devenish, Drumcliff in Sligo, Oran, Drumlane, Duleek, Clonmacnoise, Seir Keiran, Roscrea, Inis Cealtra and Ardpatrick."

"Very impressive, young Ferdia."

"But that's not every round tower, is it?" asked Mark, "I mean, there's a round tower at Glendalough here in Wicklow, and that one's not marked."

"That's correct," said Ferdia, "There are many more round towers than this in Ireland. Over fifty more."

"So what's so special about," - Mark counted them - "this thirteen, then?"

"I haven't figured that out yet."

"You know what this reminds me of?" said Niamh. "When my dad worked at the power-station in Turlough Hill, he brought me up there once. There was a big map of Ireland on the wall, with lots of places marked with lights. It was part of the monitoring system for the electricity grid. The lights showed if anything went wrong with any of the substations. I think this floating disc thing is like that?"

"But why would anyone want to monitor round towers?" asked Mark. "And what are they monitoring for?"

Ferdia's eyes glazed over for a moment then he said, "Oh my God; I've got it! Get off the disc, all of you."

Forgill was about to say something about this rudeness, but Mark stopped him.

"He doesn't mean it. He's just focused. Best to leave him to it."

Forgill nodded and they stepped off.

Ferdia put one foot on the glass, and the other on the edge of the crucible. He pushed against the disc until it started to move. It was slow work but after a minute it had rotated through several degrees. He stepped away and watched the disc. They all crowded around.

"What are we looking for?" asked Forgill.

"Watch," said Ferdia.

Slowly the disc revolved back to its former orientation.

"Now look at this," said Ferdia.

He bent down and pointed out ticks on the outer rim and on the disc that were in alignment. After several minutes the tick on the disc had moved a perceptible distance away from the outer tick.

"It's rotating!" exclaimed Niamh.

"Yes. It's very slow, but it's definitely rotating," said Forgill.

"What's moving it?" asked Mark. "I can't hear any machinery."

"You're all missing the point," said Ferdia. "It's not that the disc is rotating within the crucible; it's that the disc is fixed in space, and the Earth is rotating beneath it."

"Like a Foucault pendulum?" asked Forgill.

Ferdia turned and pointed at him. "Exactly."

"But if it's fixed in space, it must be fixed relative to something."

"Yes. Eridanus."

"The constellation Eridanus?"

Ferdia nodded.

"And how did you arrive at that conclusion?"

"Let me show you."

He pecked at the screen of his iPad for a minute then placed it on the floor to show them. They all hunkered around as he worked at the screen.

"This is an aerial view of Ireland in Google Earth, and these place-markers are the thirteen tower locations. I've downloaded an image of Eridanus and flipped it over. Watch what happens when I overlay it on Ireland."

"Good Lord. Every location corresponds to a major star in Eridanus."

"Oh my God!" said Niamh. "So it's not just Wicklow; all the round towers were laid out according to the stars too."

"Well, these thirteen at least, yes."

"Could it be a coincidence?" asked Forgill.

"Hardly. The towers and Eridanus are a perfect match. Taking into consideration the Orion connection with Wicklow, there's no chance this is coincidental. The thirteen round towers that are marked on here are part of a network of some sort, and this is where they're monitored from."

"Could this day get any weirder?" said Mark.

"Could this *life* get any weirder!" exclaimed Niamh. "This is awesome. You know, this means this whole business goes back to the time of St Patrick, at least."

Ferdia shot Forgill a sidelong glance. Forgill looked at his feet for a moment then sighed and nodded.

"It goes back a lot longer than that, young lady," he said. "I think it's time I told you my full history, and what I know about the background to this. Ferdia's already heard it."

Niamh and Mark looked at each other with apprehension as Forgill started into his story.

Ten minutes later, they sat around looking dazed. Niamh was shaking her head. "I can't believe you're that old. It's not possible."

"I'm very sorry to say that it is entirely true, young madam."

"I dunno if I've gone mad since my dad disappeared," said Mark, "but your story seems no weirder to me than anything else that's gone on. Maybe I'm lying in bed somewhere imagining all this."

"I assure you, this is real; as real as every moment of my last twelve thousand years."

Ferdia cleared his throat. "I, eh ... I've got something to tell you too. It's about what I discovered when I was cracking the gate code – what bothered me so much."

Mark sat forward, his eyes flashing with interest. "Yeah?"

"This place, whatever it is; it belongs to my father."

"What?!"

"That's what I discovered on the Internet. It was hidden under a few layers of corporate ownership, but the trail led back to Father."

"Jesus! Are you sure, Ferd?"

"Absolutely sure. The code for the gate is my birthday."

"Oh my God!" said Niamh.

Ferd looked close to tears.

"Well," said Mark, standing up and wiping his hands on his jeans, "So what. Another mystery to add to the pile. Big deal. We're all tied up in this somehow. Nothing's changed; now we know what *your* connection is, that's all. Don't be upset, Ferd."

"But Father never told me or Mother about any of this. How could he keep something like this from us?"

Forgill scowled at him.

"I think the clues are in the words 'conspiracy' and 'secret society'," he said. "Stop whining and show some backbone. You're no more unfortunate than these youngsters. In fact, they're worse off: They've had their parents abducted and you don't see them blubbering, do you?"

"Abducted!" Ferdia shouted, and leaped to his feet. He pulled out his phone and ran to the other side of the room, dialing frantically. They watched as he suffered the wait of the ringtone, then saw his shoulders relax as his call was answered. After a brief conversation he returned to the others.

"My mum is fine. She's at home, but my father's away on one of his" - Ferdia made air-quotes - "'business trips'."

"Well, you can count yourself lucky, young fellow," said Forgill. "Actually, I never suspected for a moment your parents might have been taken too. I do suspect, if this place belongs to your dad, he's involved in this thing somehow."

"Well, we don't know that," said Ferdia.

"No, but it's rather likely, don't you think?"

"We don't know that," repeated Ferdia.

There were long moments of silence, then Forgill took a deep breath and hitched his trousers. "Hmm. Well, fascinating as all this is, we still haven't located the secret keys we came for."

This perked Ferdia up.

"What did the lock look like?"

Mark and Forgill described the chamber and the geometric holes to Ferdia, and he raised his eyebrows in admiration as Mark described the relationship he had discovered between the holes and the Fibonacci sequence.

"How many holes?"

"Seven."

"Aha. And what can you see seven of in this room?"

"Err, I ..."

"Statues!" said Forgill. There are seven of them, holding tridents."

"Not tridents; tridents have three prongs."

"What do you call a fork with two prongs then?" asked Mark.

"Good God!" said Forgill, "they're tuning forks; large tuning forks. Those are our keys!"

"I believe so," said Ferdia. "If you check the cross-section of the shafts, I think you'll find they match the holes you found in the cave."

"Well, can we take them and get out of here?" asked Niamh.

"Good idea, young lady."

Niamh approached the nearest statue.

"This looks Egyptian."

"It is," said Ferdia.

"It's Seshat," said Ferdia and Forgill in unison.

They looked at each other, started to talk at the same time, then stopped and looked at each other again. Forgill laughed and gestured from Ferdia to

Niamh.

"Go ahead, young antiquarian. You probably know more about it than I do anyway."

Ferdia nodded.

"Seshat is the Egyptian goddess of wisdom, writing, astronomy, architecture and mathematics."

"Why does she have a star over her head?"

"It's not a star; it's a papyrus plant, symbolizing writing. Normally she carries a palm stem marked with notches to indicate the passage of time, but here she's holding a large tuning fork. I've never heard of that before."

Niamh looked at him, shaking her head.

"How do you know all this stuff? I'm going to start calling you Ferdipedia!"

Before Ferdia could retort, Mark interrupted from the other side of the circle:

"They're all the same. The statues, I mean; they're all the same person."

"Seshat," said Ferdia, "goddess of ..."

"Yeah, we heard," said Niamh.

Mark tried to pry the fork out of the grip of the nearest statue. As he wrestled with it, he spoke over his shoulder:

"You know, I was thinking; whatever we're caught up in - this conspiracy - the bits of it come together with this goddess. I mean, my dad is an architect, she's the goddess of architecture; all these fibbernadgy numbers, she's the goddess of math; then there's all the astronomy ..."

He broke off, panting. "Damn! I can't get this fork thingy out of her hand."

They each moved to a statue and tried to remove its tuning fork.

"You're right, young McHewell; this is stuck fast."

"This one too."

"Yep. Same here."

"There must be a way of releasing them. But there are no clues. Ah! There's an inscription on the base of this status. 'Seshat opens the door of heaven for you.'"

"This one says the same."

Mark checked the remaining statues. "They all do."

"It doesn't tell us much, does it, my young friends? It could merely be referring to the fact that she's holding the keys to the portal. What else do we know about Seshat, young Ferdia?"

"She was a scribe, and a measurer."

"What did she measure?"

"All sorts: Foundations for buildings, sacred alignments, time. She recorded the time allotted to the Pharaoh for his stay on Earth, by making notches on her palm."

"Now *that's* interesting, young Egyptologist. Everyone; check the statues' palms for notches."

"No, not the palm of her hand; the palm stem she's normally seen with."

"But they're not carrying palms, they're carrying those forks."

Niamh called out: "Guys, look at this. Mr. Forgill is right; this statue has markings on the palm of her free hand."

"A play on words," said Forgill. "Well, why not? What do those notches look like, young lady?"

"I think you'd better look for yourself, I can't describe them."

Forgill joined Niamh and peered at Seshat's outstretched palm.

"This is hieratic script. It is the number two-hundred and seventy."

"How do you know that?"

Forgill looked at Niamh, eyebrows raised, and pointed at himself.

"Twelve-thousand years old, my dear. I've watched entire civilizations –

including the Egyptian Empire – rise and fall in my lifetime. I've learned and forgotten as many languages and scripts as you've had hot dinners."

"OK, but what's the significance of the number two-hundred and seventy?"

"I think I know," said Mark. "These statues are at the points of that star on the floor, and that star looks a lot like a compass rose. Two-hundred and seventy degrees is west on a compass."

"You're absolutely right, young navigator," said Forgill. "I wonder …"

He grabbed the statue by the shoulders and tried to rotate it. It turned more easily than he had expected and he almost fell off balance. As the statue rotated, there was a detent at each of the major compass points.

"Well, it seems we have the right idea, but which way is north?"

Niamh pointed through the circle to the statue opposite the unoccupied compass point. "That's north."

"Righto then."

Forgill rotated the statue until its outstretched hand faced west. He then went to each of the other statues in turn, read the value off its palm and rotated it accordingly. As the last statue settled into its proper detent, there were seven simultaneous loud clicks and the seven tuning forks fell to the floor in a cacophony of metallic ringing. They all jumped then jumped again as the front doors sprung open. They watched the doorway with apprehension expecting someone to come through, but no-one did.

"I guess they were rigged to open when the forks were released," said Mark.

"Indeed," said Forgill. Well, we got what we came for – and a great deal more, besides. Time to leave, I dare say. Let's gather up these thingamajigs."

They moved through the statues picking up the tuning forks.

"Do we have them all?" asked Forgill. "I have three."

Mark held up two, and Ferdia and Niamh held up one each.

"That's seven. Very well, let's make good our escape from this dive."

They walked out into the porch, then all walked into each other as Mark stopped dead. Niamh bumped her nose on his shoulder.

"Hey, what the ...!"

"Oh my God!" Mark exclaimed.

They spread out to see what had prompted this reaction, then all let out a variety of exclamations as they saw what had stopped him in his tracks.

The entire lawn, on both sides of the avenue, right down to the gates, was covered in cats. This was bizarre enough in itself, but what made it truly unnerving was that the cats were all sitting still, staring at the four humans. None of them was prowling, or cleaning or interacting with other cats. They sat like statues, watching intently, as the humans crept out of the porch.

"Oh, this is freaky," said Niamh in a whisper. "What do they want?"

"I don't know," said Mark, his voice unsteady.

"It's almost like they're waiting for us to do something; and look at the way they're only on the grass, not on the driveway. They've left it free for us to pass."

"Yeah, that's really weird. And there's thousands of them! This must be every cat in Wicklow."

"More like every cat in Ireland!" said Niamh.

Forgill interjected, speaking quietly: "I think we should make our way to the gates. I believe they're here to protect us rather than hinder us."

Mark, his dream fresh in his mind, nodded. "I think so too. Let's go." They headed down the avenue, and as they passed, the cats turned to watch them go by.

They had made it halfway to the gates when an electric buzzing and crackling filled the air. Numerous glimmers appeared in the grounds of the mansion, and quickly expanded to shimmering discs. Dozens of Marforí spilled out of the sidhs and ran screaming for the group on the avenue.

The cats exploded into action.

In seconds the Marforí were engulfed by shrieking cats that tore and bit at them in swarms. The Marforí swung their spear weapons as clubs and discharged them into the feline hordes, but the cats had the numbers. The screams of mutilated Marforí and the howls of injured and dying cats filled the air. One of the Marforí, entirely mantled in a writhing mass of fur and teeth, staggered toward Mark, trying to aim her weapon. As she got closer, Mark could see her eyes were gone – clawed out – and the cats were working on her nose and ears. She took another step and collapsed, jerking on the ground. As she writhed, Mark screamed at the rest of the group, "Let's go. The cats will hold them off; we've got to get out of here."

They bolted for the gates and ran through the narrow gap onto Ashtown Lane.

"Where's Forgill?" shouted Mark.

"He gave me these and ran back towards the house," said Ferdia presenting the tuning forks. Mark ran to the gate and looked through the gap. Near the house he could make out Forgill in the grip of two Marforí, who in turn were covered in shrieking cats. As the Marforí struggled to hold onto Del Forgill and fight off the cats, a sidh opened around them then closed, taking Forgill, the Marforí and the cats to God-knows where.

Mark's shoulders slumped and he walked back to Niamh and Ferdia.

"They got him. It's just us again."

"We need to get out of here," said Niamh.

"Yeah. Are you OK to drive the SUV again?"

"Forgill had the keys."

"Ah, crap. OK, we're on foot; let's leg it."

The headed down Ashtown lane at a trot, putting the tuning forks into their backpacks. Soon they reached the bottom of the lane, crossed over the roundabout and headed down Marlton Road towards Wicklow Town.

Back in the grounds of the mansion, Clodagh watched from her hiding place at the end of the porch, mouthing the Prayer for Deliverance from Fear. The she-devils gathered their dead and wounded and disappeared in small groups into thin air. To her astonishment, the cats did exactly the same, keening over their dead and dying.

When it had gone silent, Clodagh crept out of cover and sidled along the porch. She screamed as the front doors of the mansion slammed shut then screamed again as two she-devils appeared out of thin air and reached for her. Her shriek was cut off as she and the Marforí disappeared with a noise like a whip-crack.

At the end of the avenue, the gates swung closed and locked.

CHAPTER TWENTY-SIX

THE SIDH

"Where are we going?" asked Niamh, struggling to keep up with Mark.

"Straight to the Black Castle. We're going to open that portal and go after our parents."

"There's no point," interjected Ferdia.

Mark stopped.

"That's easy for you to say, Ferd; your parents haven't been kidnapped. In fact, from what you said before, your father's probably responsible for all this!"

If this hurt Ferdia, he didn't show it. He just stared at Mark and spoke in a quiet, even tone:

"That's not what I meant. There's no point in going to the Black Castle now because it won't be low tide again for another nine or ten hours."

"Oh damn! Yeah, I forgot."

"So where will we go?" asked Niamh. "There's no point going home, is there?"

"No. There's nothing for us there now."

"We can't go wandering around the town either. I'm sure the police have found the bodies at my house by now, and they'll be looking for me."

"Yeah, me and all," said Mark, "but where can we go?"

"What about your father's boat?" said Ferdia. "That's moored in Wicklow Harbor. We could wait there."

"No, she's still in The Canaries. Dad wasn't around to have her sailed back when summer started."

"Actually, it's not. Mother told me Bree got the crew to bring it back last month. I think she was hoping you'd want to go out sailing over the summer. It's moored at the East Pier."

"For God's sake," shouted Mark. "Why does everyone think they know what I need? I didn't want any of this stupid child psychology crap; I just wanted to be left alone."

Niamh touched Mark's arm. "Well, what's done is done, Mark — and people only wanted to help. They were worried about you."

"I guess. OK, well let's go to the boat then. And by the way, Ferdia; it's not 'it', it's 'she'. Boats are never 'it'."

"I have heard that, but I don't agree with it. I'll be saying 'it' for boats and any other inanimate object."

"Suit yourself, you contrary git."

Twenty minutes later, having dodged police on foot and in patrol cars, they arrived at the East Pier. The boat, a twenty-two meter Bermudan Cutter, was moored alongside the pier in a cluster of other vessels. Mark hopped down and found the hidden emergency key. He unlocked the companionway and went down the steps into the saloon, beckoning to the other to follow.

"Welcome aboard *Vimana*," he said as they descended.

Niamh's eyes widened as she saw the yacht's interior for the first time.

"Oh my God!" she said, a hand on her chest. "This is like something out of a James Bond movie."

The initial impression of Vimana's saloon was of rich wood fitting, interspersed with sumptuous upholstery and high-tech equipment.

"It's so ... compact; so well organized. Not an inch of space is wasted," said Niamh.

"A place for everything, and everything in its place," said Mark. "That's what my dad used to say."

He picked up a remote control and pushed a button. With a low hum, a large TV slid up into view from behind a panel on the forward bulkhead of the saloon.

"Want to play some PlayStation?"

"Sure, but can I take a look around first?"

"Of course. Knock yourself out."

Ferdia, who had been on Vimana many times, stayed in the saloon while Niamh went forward to explore. He sat on one of the couches and tapped at his iPad as Mark set up the PlayStation. Over the next ten minutes, regular squeals of delight drifted aft to the saloon as Niamh discovered some feature or cubbyhole in the galley, or one of the cabins. When she appeared back, a smile from ear to ear, Mark was deep into a game of *Skyrim*.

He looked up across briefly as she stepped across the threshold into the saloon.

"What do you think?" he asked.

She giggled. "It's awesome. Can I live here?"

They both laughed as she settled down beside him on the curved seat.

"Do you want me to put on a two-player game; *Gran Turismo*, or something?"

"No, I like this game. It's cool to watch; almost like a movie."

"What are you up to, Ferdia?"

He grunted. "Checking the tide times. Low tide is at exactly midnight, would you believe."

"OK, that's really weird. The very night we're going into the cave to open a secret door, low tide is at exactly midnight. That gives me the creeps."

"Any weirder than thousands of cats turning up to fight off a bunch of crazy women who appear out of holes in the air?"

"Stop – I really don't want to think about that," said Niamh. "I keep wondering if Mira was amongst them, and if she was one of the ones that got hurt; or killed."

"Oh, I have something to tell you about that," said Ferdia. He related what Forgill had told him about the felkynd, their nine lives, and how they appear in this tír as cats.

"Felkynd!" said Mark. "That's the word your cat used in my dream last night! 'We are the felkynd', she said."

"What on earth are you talking about?"

Mark told them about his dream. Niamh looked like she might cry but she just bit her bottom lip and listened.

"I always knew there was something special about cats," she said when he had finished. "No wonder so many people find them weird. No wonder so many people find *me* weird! I always used to say, I couldn't relate to anyone that didn't like cats."

"I hate cats," said Ferdia. Niamh arched her eyebrows. "I rest my case," she said. He just snorted and went back to his tablet.

Many hours later, as midnight drew close, the teenagers locked the boat, hefted their backpacks and walked back along the East Pier towards the Black Castle. Niamh and Ferdia followed Mark into the castle grounds and down the Danes' Steps to the cave. Eventually they arrived in the chamber with the rainbow wall and Mark put down his backpack.

Niamh played her flashlight around the circular room and ran her palm in awe over the gently glowing crystals. Ferdia stood beside her doing the same, and it was the first time she had ever seen him so full of childlike wonder.

Mark gathered the seven tuning forks from the backpacks and started to put them in the correct holes in the floor. They chimed slightly as he maneuvered them into place, and Niamh and Ferdia stepped back from the wall in surprise as the crystals moved in response.

Mark chuckled. "Yeah, I didn't tell you about that. Pretty cool, isn't it?"

"Amazing," said Ferdia. "The crystals are reacting to the frequencies of the tuning forks."

"Yep. That's what me and Forgill figured. OK, that's the last one in place. What do you think we do now?"

"Make them all ring at the same time, I should think."

Mark walked around in a circle, striking the top of each tuning fork with his flashlight. The dissonant chiming increased in volume and complexity as each fork joined the cacophony. As the thickening sound wave filled the chamber, the crystals creaked and shifted, then shrunk back completely, revealing a smaller chamber beyond.

The youngsters walked through in silence to the chamber. In its center was a polished stone plinth, up to Mark's chest, with a square indentation on the top. A fine spray of water jetted over the top of the plinth from small holes all around the edge of the indentation.

"I think I know what we need to do here," said Mark. "Grab those rucksacks, and let's get the Tetroi together."

They connected the Tetroi, and as the mechanism started whirring and clicking, Mark placed the assemblage into the indentation on the plinth. Lights appeared on thirty-two of the squares and projected the images of chess pieces into the mist of water like holograms; one set blue, the other red.

"That is too cool for words," said Niamh. "But now what?"

As she spoke, the whirring got louder and was accompanied by a click. One of the blue pawns disappeared and, with another click, reappeared one square forward. The whirring subsided.

Mark gestured at the device. "We play a game, I guess."

He pressed the square under one of the red pawns. It depressed easily and stayed depressed. He then pressed the destination square. The clicking inside the machine sped up for a moment and the whirr intensified. The square the pawn was on popped up with a loud click, and the light went out. The destination square did the same and the pawn reappeared at that position.

"Cool!"

The clicking and whirring changed tempo again, and one of the blue pawns disappeared and reappeared two squares away.

"OK, it looks like we have to play this out. Ferd, you're the chess-master; how quickly do you think you can get this thing to checkmate?"

"One move. Don't you recognize the gambit? It's the Fool's mate. The machine is playing to lose. All I have to do is move the queen from here" - *click*- "to here" -*click*- "and it's checkmate."

As the destination square popped up and the queen moved to her new position, the whirring and clicking stopped abruptly and the lights went out. The Tetroi sprung apart and fell away from each other to the floor of the chamber. The fine diffusion of water ceased and the plinth slid with a rumble into the ground.

Mark had just finished gathering up the Tetroi when a shout echoed across the main chamber:

"McTool! What are you geeks doing in here at this time of night?"

Mark's stomach turned over as he saw Christopher McCabe, his sister Veronica and a variety of their lowlife cohorts stroll into the chamber. Ferdia, less concerned by McCabe's presence, noticed a glimmer of light, no bigger than a marble appear in mid-air in the midst of the tuning forks.

"I couldn't believe it when I saw you freaks running around the castle a few minutes ago. Followed you down the steps and found this rathole. Is this where you take your little slag for a bit of McTool-time, or are you both doing her?"

"You shut your mouth, you filthy scumbag," screamed Niamh.

That was the first Veronica McCabe had noticed of Niamh. With a shout of, "You're dead, bitch," she bared her teeth and ran across the chamber to grab Niamh's hair. Ferdia, one eye on the nascent sidh, grabbed Niamh and Mark by the sleeves and pulled them sideways to put the tiny glowing ball between them and the attacking harpy.

Unfortunately for Veronica, her reflexes were good, and she changed direction in mid-dash to compensate. She ran straight through the center of the chamber and the tiny singularity passed straight through the center of her, translating a cylinder of tissue including part of her heart and spinal column to another tír.

She stopped dead in her tracks and her eyes widened as her brain tried to make sense of the signals it was receiving. She tried to speak then fell forward, dead before she hit the ground.

"Ronnie!" roared McCabe, and he and the rest of the gang ran forward to Veronica's body.

With a blinding flash, the sidh expanded to fill the chamber, and a rushing sound filled Mark's head. He was jerked off his feet and felt like he was being pulled forward by a hook through his navel. The only thing in his experience that felt remotely similar was an insane rollercoaster he'd once been on, but this was orders of magnitude more terrifying and visceral.

A writhing tunnel of space-time opened out before him. He saw McCabe's gang, and Veronica's body accelerate away from him towards a distant point. Ferdia and Niamh, eyes terrified and limbs thrashing in mid-air, flew past him towards the same destination.

Then he felt himself accelerate.

The swirling walls of the sidh, reflecting like liquid amber, flew past him, faster and faster. Every so often, he felt a nexus of space-time, a cluster of alternate realities and possibilities, nudge by as he gathered momentum. Eventually these nexi were so frequent, they felt like rumble-strips on a road.

Onwards he dashed until a light ahead grew brighter and larger. It was like flying into a star. Terrified, his breath got faster and shallower until his vision started to narrow. As he passed out from hyperventilation, he felt himself exit the sidh and fly into bright light.

His brain's last act before insentience was to give up a memory long lost:

He remembered being born.

CHAPTER TWENTY-SEVEN

THE OTHER SIDE

There was something wrong with the air.

That was the first thing that struck Mark as he awoke. It was chill like early spring and after weeks of stifling summer heat, the air scalded his sinuses like ice-water.

That wasn't it, though.

Vision clearing, he found himself on a grassy headland, overlooking a familiar bay. He had no idea whether the sidh had translated him through time or some other dimension, but this was still Wicklow.

And yet it wasn't.

Looking north across the bay, the familiar sickle shape of the coast along the Murrough looked like home, but up close, things told a different story.

The harbor, as he knew it, didn't exist. There were no east or north piers, and the north bank of the Leitrim River where it discharged into the harbor, a towering concrete packet pier at home, was little more than a sandbank with a wooden beacon. The town was smaller too, hardly a town at all, more a collection of steep-roofed wooden buildings flanking the river which, without quay walls to constrain it, took a wider and more natural course to the sea. In this tír the harbor was a natural river bowl protected by the jutting sandbank and there were wooden jetties and longboats all about its perimeter. People milled about near the jetties and several longboats were plying the current.

Mark had been holding his breath as he took all this in. His brain eventually took control and he drew a gasping breath.

Then it struck him. There was no air pollution. The ever-present smell of traffic and industry, so pervasive at home, was absolutely absent. It was like being transported from the kerosene stench of an airport runway to a remote beach, but not even the most unsullied beach at home had air like this. It was ozone fresh, like wind-dried cotton, but orders of magnitude purer and sweeter.

He got to his feet, his rucksack dangling from his hand, and looked around.

Behind him, where the Black Castle should have been, was a circular wooden fort with huge doors. It occupied the whole outcrop and had a drawbridge over the defensive trench. Behind the fort, where the Danes' Steps should be, he could just see the dragon-headed prows of wooden sailing vessels. Interest piqued, he crossed the headland to get a closer look.

It was impressive.

The fort's engineers had built a complex of wooden jetties and buildings on stilts around the entire outcrop. From the sea it must have looked like a small wooden village perched on numerous levels on the cliff. Dozens of longboats were moored along the jetties which extended around the base of the cliffs to Travelahawk beach.

A watchtower with a lighted beacon rose out of the sea on stone foundations midway between the fort and the cliffs to the south of the beach. Two robust rope-bridges joined the tower to the fort on one side, and to the cliffs on the other. Where the bridge was anchored to the cliff-top was another wooden fort containing numerous buildings, and a series of wooden steps and buildings on many levels down the face of the cliff leading to another set of jetties below.

Mark's admiration of the complex was interrupted as the main fort doors creaked and began to open. Not waiting to see who emerged, he ducked behind a nearby hillock. He heard several men's voices as they crossed the drawbridge and passed his bolt-hole in the direction of the village. He waited, his heart hammering, until the voices faded.

At that moment it struck him hard that there was no sign of Niamh and Ferdia, or of McCabe's crew. Fear gnawing at him, he looked about. Maybe they had arrived in a different location. He searched the environs of the fort, going as close as he dared to the walls and defensive trench, but there was no sign of them.

Now he was really scared. He stood alone near the fort, and for the first time in his life experienced absolute isolation. He'd have been grateful to run into Chris McCabe at this stage. He looked at the village, then at the fort, then back at the village, and with a crawling sense of helplessness, realized he had no idea where to go or what to do.

He was completely alone in an alien world.

THE END OF TÍR I – THE MAGUS CONSPIRACY

THE JOURNEY CONTINUES IN
TÍR II – THE LEBOR STARA

ABOUT THE AUTHOR

Michael J Synnott is a writer from Wicklow in Ireland. During his career he has been a software developer, a computer science lecturer, a radio DJ, a rock musician and a writer for computer magazines.

He lives on a quiet farm in Ashford, Co Wicklow, Ireland with his wife Dee and their Bengal cat Mira.

The Magus Conspiracy is his first novel.

He can be reached at
mike@synnott.me
http://www.synnott.me